I0613226

Miss Brightwell

So Great Love!

Sketches of Missionary Life and Labour

Miss Brightwell

So Great Love!
Sketches of Missionary Life and Labour

ISBN/EAN: 9783337118037

Printed in Europe, USA, Canada, Australia, Japan

Cover: Foto ©Andreas Hilbeck / pixelio.de

More available books at **www.hansebooks.com**

BRAHMIN EXPOUNDING THE SACRED BOOKS.

SKETCHES OF

MISSIONARY LIFE AND LABOUR.

BY

MISS BRIGHTWELL,

Author of "Palissy the Potter," "The Romance of Modern Missions," &c.

London:

JOHN SNOW AND CO.,

2, IVY LANE, PATERNOSTER ROW, E.C.

1874.

UNWIN BROTHERS, PRINTERS BY WATER POWER.

CONTENTS.

SO GREAT LOVE

SKETCHES

OF

MISSIONARY LIFE AND LABOUR.

INTRODUCTORY CHAPTER.

Recollections of Missionary anniversaries and Missionary deputations
—John Williams—J. J. Freeman—J. Johns—Dr. Philip—James
Read, senior — Dr. Medhurst — Samuel Dyer — Mr. Helmore —
Robert Moffat—Dr. Lockhart—Dr. Mullens—George Pritchard—
Mr. Heath—Native Converts from the South Seas—A Chieftain's
courtesy—Pictures in " Péron's Voyages"—Pining for home—
The Chieftain's death—*Tantus Amor*.

OME of the happiest recollections of my
early days are connected with Missionaries
and Missionary anniversaries. My beloved
father was Treasurer of the Norfolk and
Norwich Auxiliary of the London Missionary Society,
and yearly entertained some member of the deputation at his house. It was quite an era in our family
when these annual meetings came round, and a goodly

number of Missionaries and friends assembled. How many of these devoted men have we had under our roof! Yes, many of my happiest and best memories are associated with their visits, and their very names awaken pleasant thoughts.

Among the earliest and best remembered was Mr. WILLIAMS, of the South Sea Mission, who was in England in 1836, and who, alas! three short years later, fell by the hands of the natives of Erromanga. Never was there a man whose manner was more fitted to inspire confidence—so simple, kind, and earnest.

After him came Mr. FREEMAN, one of the earliest Missionaries to Madagascar, who, with his devoted fellow-labourer Mr. JOHNS, spent many years of toil in the Island. He was accompanied by one of the Malagasy converts, who, with five others, had escaped, as by a miracle, from a bloody death.

There came also to our house Dr. PHILIP, the Superintendent of the London Missionary Society's stations in South Africa,—a man of noble heart and noble presence, with whom my father was greatly pleased. He brought with him the native chief Tzatzoe. Another year our guest was JAMES READ, sen., whose history was a veritable romance of Christian life. He went in the ship *Duff* on her second voyage to the South Seas, but was taken by a French privateer. Afterwards, in the year 1800, he joined Dr. Vanderkemp in South Africa, and subsequently laboured with great success in Kaffraria and elsewhere for more than five-and-thirty years.

Dr. MEDHURST, the well-known Chinese Missionary,

and his colleague, SAMUEL DYER, also visited us. The latter died shortly after : his manner was that of one who felt himself on the verge of a glorious eternity.

At a later period we received Mr. HELMORE, the circumstances of whose tragical death awakened such a widespread interest throughout the land a few years ago. And at various times we welcomed a host of others, all honoured and beloved for their works' sake, whom I cannot mention here; but I must not omit the name of the venerable ROBERT MOFFAT, the father-in-law of Dr. Livingstone. Then he was in the meridian of his life, full of zeal and energy ; and during more than a quarter of a century which has since elapsed he has been unremittingly engaged at his post, the revered patriarch of the Bechuana Mission.

Among the latest of our Missionary visitants were Dr. LOCKHART, of China; Dr. MULLENS, of Calcutta, now Foreign Secretary of the London Missionary Society; and Mr. PRITCHARD, who was first Missionary and afterwards Consul at Tahiti: the latter was with us in 1863.

One of our Missionary parties will always be kept in remembrance. There were present at the dinner table a large company of friends, and Mr. HEATH, a Missionary from the Navigator's Islands, accompanied by two of the native converts. The latter were, without exception, the most remarkable specimens of our race I ever beheld ; their huge mouths and dazzling teeth appeared to fascinate the gaze, but their manners were gentle, and there was even an air of conscious superiority about one of them, who had been a chief among his countrymen. Our friend, Mr. Borrow, who was among the guests, said, "He is evidently a gentleman," and he proceeded to try the whole polyglot of languages at his command in the effort to converse with him, but in vain.

While the gentlemen were finishing their after-dinner business, the two strangers were introduced by their guardian into the drawing-room, where my mother and I were sitting. The weather was very cold, and these poor natives of the warm sunny South Sea Isles suffered from the chills of our ungenial climate. We retreated from the fire to make room for them ; but the Chief, with natural grace, waved his hand, to intimate that he would by no means displace us. His companion, who was younger, was evidently of an inferior grade. He appeared lively and in health ; while there was an aspect of suffering and reserve about his superior which interested us more in him.

Desirous to amuse them, we brought out Péron's "Voyage aux Terres Australes," and placing it on the table, opened it at the picture of the young chieftain of New Holland, Nourougal-dirri, "s'avançant pour combattre." The moment he cast his eyes upon it the younger native uttered a loud cry in his own tongue, which had the effect of bringing his companion in a moment to his side, and the two began, in their soft, flowing, liquid language, conversing with the utmost vivacity, pointing with their fingers to each of the plates, and showing, by the expressions of their countenances, that they were indeed alive !

"Ah ! you would like to return to your own land,

is it not so?" "Yes! yes!" There was no mistake about it: they were pining for their home and for the sunny skies of the South. Alas! the Chief was not destined again to behold them, for he died, not many weeks after, "a stranger in a strange land." His fellow-countryman was absent from him at the time, as it was not apprehended his end was so near. The Missionary's wife alone was present to soothe the dying pillow and to point the eye of the expiring South Sea Islander to the Heavenly Home, where he is now, it is thankfully believed, numbered with the "great multitude out of all nations and kindreds and people and tongues, who have washed their robes and made them white in the blood of the Lamb."

The following pages contain a series of short memorial sketches of Missionary life. Several of those mentioned therein were personally known to us, and all deserve an honourable record in the annals of modern Missions. The motto or watchword I have chosen for my little book points to the genuine source of all self-denying labour: "So great love,"—*Tantus Amor*,—constraining the heart, could alone prompt to the devotion of the life in a cause so purely Christian and philanthropic.

Love is indeed "stronger than death," and by its Divine power the regeneration of the world shall be eventually accomplished. May the writer and her readers know something of its influence and share in its blessed rewards.

> "They that turn many to righteousness
> Shall shine as the stars for ever and ever."

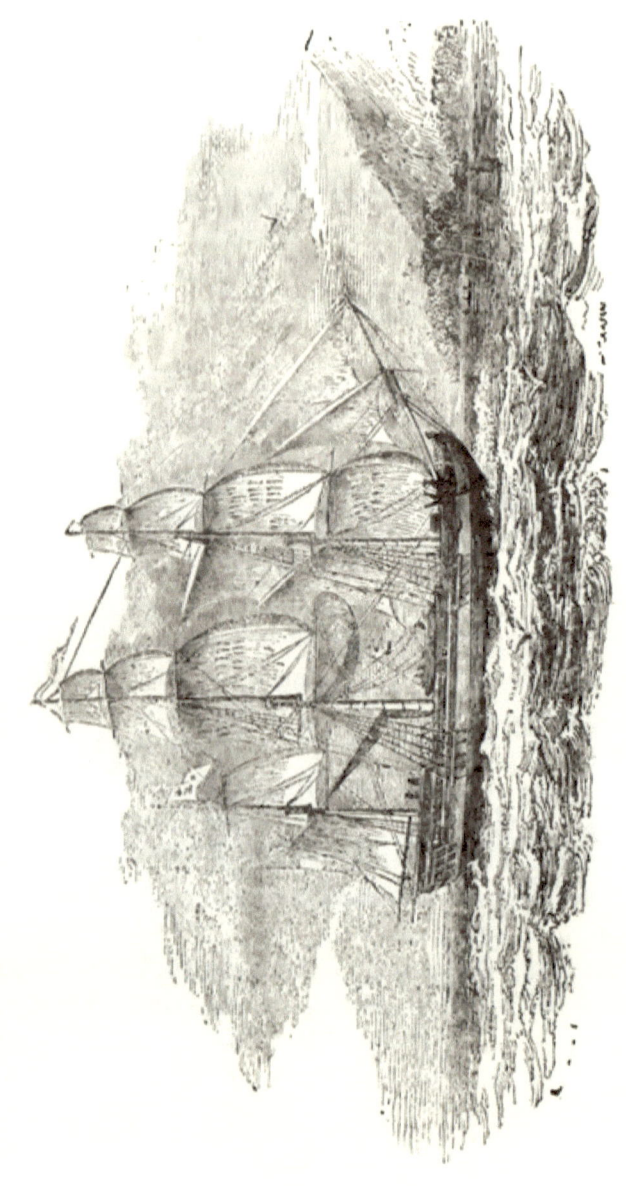

THE MISSIONARY SHIP "JOHN WILLIAMS."

JOHN WILLIAMS:

THE MARTYR OF ERROMANGA.

CHAPTER I.

EARLY DAYS.

My recollections of Mr. Williams—His birth and parentage—Youthful
characteristics—Starting in life—Skill in handicraft—Conversion
—Rev. Matthew Wilks and "The Tabernacle," Moorfields—
Desire to be a Missionary — Loving relationship between Mr.
Wilks and Mr. Williams — Accepted by the London Missionary
Society — Appointed to the South Sea Mission — Marriage and
departure from England.

HAVE said that Mr. Williams was among
the earliest and best-remembered of our Mis-
sionary friends.   He arrived at our house
one summer evening in the year 1836, having
come to attend an anniversary meeting of the London
Missionary Society.   When I shut my eyes and look
through memory's camera, I can see him as he was
then—a plain, simple, earnest-looking man, to whom,
as by an instinct, one felt drawn with a sentiment of
trustful satisfaction.   Here is a man to be depended

upon; he is good, gentle, and true-hearted; not poetical in speech or appearance, yet not prosaic, for in his heart there dwells a divine enthusiasm, a genuine love for souls, so deep, so practical, so intense, that it rules the whole life and prompts him in all his actions.

We were soon excellent friends, and as he came once and again to visit us, there was opportunity for converse and for knowing something of his feelings and character. He interested himself much in us young people, and brought out some of his treasures and keepsakes, by which we should remember him. I have them yet—those pretty egg-like snow-white shells and beautiful branching corallines, and they serve to remind me still of Viliamu, the beloved friend of the poor Samoans. When he was leaving us for the last time I slipped into his hand one of Baxter's little pocket psalters, and he said he would keep it in his waistcoat and read from it. Perhaps it was with him when he died, and he had used it on that fatal morning when he went forth to meet the deadly blow.

I did not then know the incidents of his early life, which I am about in brief to narrate.

John Williams was born on the 29th June, 1796, at Tottenham High Cross. He had a pious mother, whose loving words touched the young heart and awakened a glow of childish tenderness. By nature conscientious, he showed, even from his infancy, a scrupulous regard to truth, and was affectionate and good to the younger children of his family. When at school, he wrote for himself a morning and evening

prayer and hymns. The verses show he was not
devoid of taste and observation. The vision of the
moon riding forth in beauty called forth these lines:—

> " He gave the gentle moon to cheer
> The still and gloomy night;
> Like a large pearl 'mong diamonds clear,
> She looks, and sheds her light."

At the age of fourteen he was apprenticed to a fur-
nishing ironmonger, his master engaging to teach him
the commercial part of the business only, and to ex-
empt him from the more laborious and mechanical
parts. The lad, however, speedily showed a taste for the
practical, and forsook the counter for the workshop,
lingering near the workmen and eagerly watching their
proceedings. Soon he resolved to try his skill at handicraft, and during the time when the men were at
meals he stole into their places and was seen busily
blowing at the forge. In this manner he taught himself in a surprisingly short time to make many of the
common articles belonging to the trade. In process
of time he became a skilful workman, and was able to
finish with greater perfection the more complex and
difficult processes of the manufacture, so that he
" turned out " his work beautifully. Anxious to perfect his self-acquired skill, he volunteered his services
for out-of-door employment, and with his working
apron on, and his basket of tools slung across his
shoulder, would sally forth to execute any order in
which greater delicacy and exactness were required.
Thus, unconsciously, he was preparing himself for
future usefulness in the best possible manner. So

much did his strict integrity and general good conduct commend him to his master, that during the latter years of his apprenticeship, the chief management of the business was entrusted to his care.

But though externally moral and exemplary, he was irreligious. The fair promise of his childhood had not been realised, and he fell into the evil habit of Sabbath-breaking and consorting with those who scoffed at religion, for there was no fear of God before his eyes. He was in his eighteenth year when the Divine Voice arrested him. It happened in this wise : one Sabbath evening, 3rd January, 1814, he had appointed to meet some idle companions at a tea-garden near his master's house, but arriving at the place of rendezvous he found they had not made their appearance. Annoyed at the disappointment, he was sauntering about in the neighbourhood, when Mrs. Tonkin, his master's wife, a good and pious woman, passed by on her way to evening service at the Tabernacle. Her eye caught a glimpse of Williams's face as he approached a lamp, and she asked what he was doing there. He frankly told her the truth, when, with a few earnest, pleading words, she induced him to accompany her. The minister that night was Mr. East, of Birmingham; his text was, "What shall it profit a man if he gain the whole world and lose his own soul ?" As he listened the heart of the youth was solemnly impressed, and "from that hour," he said, "my blind eyes were opened, and I saw wondrous things out of God's law."

No more powerful stimulus can be applied to the

conscience of such a man as John Williams than that which now animated him to every good work. He was indefatigable in all the duties of the Christian life, and having united himself in fellowship with the Church under the care of the venerable Matthew Wilks, gave his aid in all the societies at the Tabernacle for the benefit of the poor and ignorant. At the time the Tabernacle auxiliary to the London Missionary Society was in full operation, and great interest had been recently awakened by tidings of success in the African and South Sea Missions. Mr. Wilks employed every means in his power to multiply the friends and enlarge the resources of the Society, and established a Quarterly Missionary Meeting, which the young were especially encouraged to attend.

It was on one of these occasions, and by the fervent appeal of his beloved pastor, that the sacred fire of Missionary zeal was first kindled in the soul of the youth. "At the time," he said, "I took but little notice of it, but afterwards the desire was occasionally very strong for many months. My heart was frequently with the poor heathen. Finding this to be so, I made it a matter of serious prayer to God that He would totally eradicate and banish the desire, if it were not consistent with His holy mind and will; but that if it were consistent, He would increase my knowledge together with the desire."

Having pondered these thoughts in his mind for several months, he at length opened his heart to Mr Wilks, who received his statements favourably, and after a while, becoming satisfied concerning the mental

2

as well as spiritual fitness of the young candidate, promised him his best counsel and assistance. And he was as good as his word, taking him into a class of youths preparing for the ministry, whom he educated in his own house.

The intimate relationship thus established between them grew into a holy friendship, reminding one of that which subsisted between St. Paul and his son Timothy; and it continued to the end, undiminished by distance or their disparity of years. What manner of love was that entertained for him by the venerable pastor, we may judge from the following lines, written when Mr. Williams was at Raiatea :—

"My DEAR, DEAR WILLIAMS,

"Dear to me as the apple of the eye, I do love you. My heart leaps when I think of you. I do pray for you, that you may never be weary in well-doing. I pray that you may abound in every good word and work. I pray that you may be the living epistle of Christ, known and read of all men. I pray that you may live long and be useful all your life; and when you and I are called to render an account, that we may hear our Master say, 'Enter ye into the joy of your Lord.' Then we will answer, 'Yea, Lord, through Thy infinite mercy.'"

In July, 1816, Mr. Williams offered his services to the Directors of the London Missionary Society, and having successfully passed the usual examination, was unanimously received and appointed Missionary to the South Seas. In the month of September of the same

year, together with several others devoted to similar
service among the heathen, he was solemnly set
apart to this work in a public service held at Surrey
Chapel, and two months later sailed in *The Harriet*
for Sydney. But he did not go alone : he was accompanied by one who showed herself not only a " help-
meet " for her husband, but who in Christian heroism
proved his equal, and was in all respects worthy of
the man to whose happiness and success she largely
contributed.

One parting glimpse we will take at the young couple
before they quit their native home. " As soon as we
had come on board," wrote Mr. Williams, " we set to
work at our cabins, put them in very nice order, made
our beds, hung up our looking-glasses, drove hooks
and nails in various places for our garments, fixed
our cabin-lamps, laid down our little bits of carpet,
and now all looks very comfortable indeed ; so much
so, that Mary was determined to sleep on board.
Having read and prayed together, we retired to rest,
and though it was a boisterous night, we slept as
comfortably and undisturbed as possible."

Bravo ! young beginners : you are evidently not
easily to be discomposed, and will make the best of
everything with cheerful, buoyant hearts.

CHAPTER II.

Arrival at Eimeo—Domestic anxieties—Learning the language after
a new fashion—Removal to Raiatea, the island home—Reception by the natives—Description of the island—Great religious
and political influence of Raiatea on the neighbouring islands—
Providential preparation of the people for the reception of the
Gospel—Selection of the Mission site—House-building and fur-
nishing in European style—Effect on the natives—The Missionary's home life—Regular attendance at the chapel and schools—
Powerful influence for good exercised by the King—His fearful
character when an idolater—Wonderful results of Missionary
labour in the island.

FTER a prosperous voyage, the Missionaries
arrived in the month of November, 1817, at
Tahiti, and exactly twelve months from the
time of their embarkation landed at Eimeo,
"our hearts leaping for joy," said Mr. Williams, " at
sight of the long-wished-for land." There they were
gladdened by intercourse with those who had preceded
them in the field, and who were now reaping in joy
after long years of toil and sorrow.

Several months were passed at Eimeo, during which
time their first child was born, the parents rejoicing
at his birth, but full of anxious thoughts "on account
of the temptations to which the young must be here

exposed, surrounded by wickedness, the customs of the natives being debased and abominable." This is indeed one of the great trials of all Missionaries in heathen lands. Those who knew Mrs. Williams will remember how she would recur to her anxieties for the children, and tell with what eagerness she watched

EIMEO.

them, often snatching them up and running indoors with them when she saw a heathen native approaching their dwelling.

At Eimeo, Mr. Williams made great progress in learning the language of the people, and this he did after a fashion of his own; not poring over books or learning from his senior brethren, but going among the natives, listening to and interrogating them, by which means he soon learned the meaning of words, and, what was of great importance, caught the correct accentuation. To the surprise of all, he made such rapid progress that he was able to preach intelligibly as soon as he reached Raiatea, which was finally fixed upon as the destination of himself and colleague, Mr. Threlkeld.

It was the 11th September, 1818, when they first set foot upon their island home, the place in which they were to pass many long years. Their welcome was warm, and the poor natives testified their regard after a very substantial fashion. "They made a feast for us," says Mr. Williams, "consisting of five large hogs for Mrs. Williams, five for myself, and one for our little Johnny; the same provision was made for Mr. Threlkeld."

While the feast is going on, we will say a few words about Raiatea, which is the largest and most central island of the Society group. It is nearly 50 miles in circumference, and stands within a noble reef, which engirdles both it and Tahaa, a smaller island, about six miles from its northern shore. Through this reef are numerous inlets, deep and wide enough to admit ships of any burthen, and within there is a splendid lagoon, with safe and commodious anchorage.

The island is not only the largest but also the most lofty of the group; a belt of rich cultivable land skirts the shore, and there are some fertile glens and valleys; but the central part consists of huge mountain masses rising abruptly, in some cases to the height of 2,000 feet above the sea.   At a distance it wears a sombre aspect, but as soon as the stranger lands upon its shores he sees verdure and beauty everywhere, and finds himself upon a lovely island, well watered by streams, which, leaping from the rocks and winding through the numerous glens and valleys that intersect the mountains, bathe in their course the roots of in- numerable bread-fruit trees, bananas, plantains, and other precious productions of that fruitful clime.

There were two or three causes which led to the choice of Raiatea.   In the first place, although the number of the population was small, yet its political influence was great.   For ages its chiefs had been lords paramount of both the Society and Georgian groups, and in addition to civil allegiance, they had claimed and received divine honours, Tamatoa, the regnant monarch, having been worshipped as a god.

Beside this, from time immemorial the island had been the focus and source of the abominable idolatries of the surrounding peoples.   There were found the types of the manifold obscene and cruel usages which were the customs of the race ; there were the temple and altar of Oro, the Moloch of the group, and to his shrine hecatombs of human victims had been brought from near and distant shores.   It was a kind of holy isle of heathendom—a citadel where Satan's stronghold was established.

There was yet another and urgent motive for placing the Mission standard in Raiatea.   Two years before Mr. Williams arrived, a small vessel, having on board a Missionary, with Pomare, King of Tahiti, and nine-teen of his people, had been driven by a violent gale to the island, and been kindly received by the people, who entertained them three months. It was a happy event for the Raiateans, who learned from their guests

LIGHTHOUSE AT TAHITI.

the glad tidings of the Gospel, and the hearts of many were touched with a desire to know more. Among the rest, Tamatoa and a few other principal men were so much impressed, as to give up many of their evil practices, and to determine to observe the Sabbath, and to keep in remembrance the things they had

learned. So deep was the impression made upon the
King, that he resolved, if possible, to obtain teachers
for himself and his people, and he went to meet Mr.
Williams, to conduct him to Raiatea.

Thus was the way opened for the reception of the
Missionaries, and hence the cordial welcome they
received. Soon after their arrival it was decided to
form a settlement and gather together the people, who
had been scattered over the island, that they might
thus come within reach of instruction and be under the
observation of their teachers. A suitable place was
chosen on the leeward side of the isle, and in a short
time a temporary chapel and school-house were erected,
and preparations made for laying out and clearing
the ground and commencing their dwelling-houses.

Mr. Williams determined to make for himself a
house in the English style, superior to any building
of which the natives had an idea, and before long the
astonished and admiring eyes of the people saw rising
up a commodious dwelling, with three front and four
back rooms, French sashes, shaded with verandahs
and blinds, the framework being of wood, and the
walls wattled and plastered with lime and neatly
whitewashed. A splendid view of the harbour was
seen from the front, and on either side was a spacious
garden, while behind the house was an enclosed
poultry-yard well stored with feathered fowl, and
beyond this a large kitchen-garden, which furnished
many British roots and vegetables. The furniture of the house showed our Missionary's taste and
skill; tables, chairs, sofas, and bedsteads, quite

in English style, made the dwelling look most inviting.

Time soon discovered the sagacity of thus exciting the native curiosity and interest. The people were eager to imitate what they saw, and learned all manner of handicraft, being thus aroused from their habits of indolence and sluggish unconcern. It is pleasant to take a peep at the home domesticities. Mrs. Williams says : " I wish you could taste some of our bread-fruit and arrowroot cakes. I dare say you often talk of us, and wonder what we have to eat. I'll tell you. There are plenty of fowls here, and we dress them in various ways. Sometimes we have fresh pork, and occasionally kill a sucking-pig, and get it well cooked after this fashion : we run a long stick through it, and let the ends rest on two forked sticks, and a fire being kindled behind, a native sits to turn and baste it until it is well done. I wish only we had a cow, for I should then make butter, but we have plenty of milk for our tea, as we have five goats." Her husband adds in a P.S., " My dear Mary is a famous cook. I know not what a poor man could do by himself in such a place as this."

" In labours more abundant " is an appropriate motto as descriptive of the life henceforth led by our Missionary friends. On Sabbath days the people thronged to the chapel, the congregations sometimes being as many as 1,000 or 1,500, all listening attentively, and behaving with serious decorum. With very few exceptions all came regularly to school, the King and Queen among the rest ; and in the evenings

instruction was given by hearing and answering ques-
tions. One would ask "Who the Scribes were, and
whether they were secretaries to the Missionary
Society?" Another inquired, "How can we get this
true faith you talk of? Were it locked up in your
boxes, they would soon be broken open." Another
complained of temptations to sin when he knelt down
to pray. "I say to myself," he added, "if Satan
would come to me in the form of a man, I would fight
him and stone him to death—now, is that a good or
a bad thought, teacher?"

It was a great blessing to the infant cause of
religion in Raiatea that the King Tamatoa threw his
powerful influence into the right scale. He was truly
an extraordinary man: we have a very graphic picture
of him drawn by Mr. Williams. He says: "He was
a remarkably fine figure, being 6 feet 11 inches in
height; formerly he was worshipped as a god, and to
him the eye of the human victim was presented before
it was offered in sacrifice. When in his heathen state
he was addicted to the use of the intoxicating juice
of the kava-root, and when under its influence was
exceedingly desperate, so that, if irritated by any
means, he would seize a club or spear, and wreak his
vengeance on the first creature he encountered. In
this manner several persons had been sacrificed to his
ferocity. His look and manner at such times must
have been terrific; the flashing fury of his eye, the
curl of his thick lip, the lowering aspect of his brow,
together with the growling tones of his voice and the
violent gestures of his herculean frame, were enough

to inspire the most courageous with dread. Once
when maddened by drink he rushed out of his dwelling,
and chancing to meet an unoffending passenger, struck
him so violent a blow as to knock his eye out, and
so mutilated his own hand that he lost, in consequence, the first and second bones of his forefinger!''

Thus he continued until he heard the Gospel, and
was brought to feel its power and grace. He then
made a solemn vow that he would never again taste
intoxicating drink, and he kept his vow most sacredly.
What must it have been to see this monster in his
right mind, clothed and sitting at the feet of Jesus!
'' From the first of our coming,'' says Mr. Williams,
'' he was constant in his attendance at our school, and
at six o'clock in the morning always took his seat on
my right hand, and read in rotation with the class;
he was evidently pleased when his answers were satisfactory, was present at the prayer-meetings and usual
services at all times, and his place was never vacant.
At a later time he was baptised, and became one of
our Church members. In short, his conduct was
exemplary, and his influence of incalculable benefit
to his subjects and countrymen.''

Before many months had elapsed there was a visible
and truly delightful change in the habits and circumstances of the Raiateans. When first the Missionaries
landed there were only two native dwellings at Vaóaara
(the name of the settlement), and it was difficult to
walk along the beach for the bushes; in twelve months'
time all was changed. The former wilderness was an
open, clear, pleasant place, with a range of houses

extending nearly two miles along the sea-beach, in which resided about a thousand of the natives.

What a reward for all the toil and self-denial they had undergone! No wonder they said, " Our work is our delight ; in it we desire to spend and be spent, and we have no other desire but to win sinners to Christ. Upon the whole our prospects are indeed encouraging, and we doubt not, if blessed with faith, patience, and perseverance, we shall be made very useful."

CHAPTER III.

RAROTONGA AND SAMOA.

Raiatea as a Christian island—Rarotonga, the unknown land—Mr. Williams' yearning towards it—His determination to go in search of the island — Bafflings and perplexities — A momentous half-hour—The burst of sunshine—" Land ho ! "—Discovery of Rarotonga—" Led by a right way "—Marvellous progress of the Gospel—Rarotonga a "garden of the Lord "—Description of the island—Mr. Williams builds *The Messenger of Peace*—Voyage to the Samoas—Superiority of the Samoan race—Difference of their religion to the surrounding idolatries — Willingness to receive Christianity—Second visit to Samoa—The power of kindness—Native mode of showing honour to the Missionary.

SOME years have passed since the events related in the preceding chapter—years of mingled joy and sorrow, in which the Mission work has been gradually progressing, until now Raiatea is a professedly Christian island,

governed by a code of laws human and Christian,
having its hundreds of children taught in the schools,
enjoying its Sabbath services and holy days, holding
its Missionary anniversaries, contributing liberally to
the parent Society, reading the Scriptures translated
into the original tongue, the volumes being the pro-
duct of the native press—and, in a word, presenting a

COOK'S TREE, TAHITI.

truly marvellous and blessed contrast to its former
condition.

All this has been done, and joy and gratitude fill
the hearts of the devoted men who have wrought
the work. There have been also seasons of sorrow
and grief, tears shed over little graves, hearts pierced

with anguish at parting from one of their number,
long and wearisome sicknesses, and "perils among
the heathen," occasioned by the fierce enmity of some
of the natives. The work of the Missionary is one of
" much tribulation," but if great are its trials, glorious
are its rewards !

The discovery of Rarotonga, the principal island of
the Hervey group, is one of the most heart-stirring
episodes in Mr. Williams' "Missionary Enterprises."
His heart had long been yearning toward the unknown land, vague accounts of which had reached
him, and he at length determined to go in search of
it. He took with him Papeika, a worthy member of
the Raiatean Church, a man full of zeal for the cause,
and burning with desire to convey to his countrymen
the knowledge of the Gospel. They picked up at
Aitutaki (an island which had been one of the Missionary out-stations) some natives of Rarotonga,
whom chance had taken thither, and who were anxious
to return to their own people, to tell them of the
wonderful things they had heard.

For a considerable time the voyagers were baffled
in all their efforts to reach the desired land ; they
found several small islands and encountered various
adventures. At length — but let us hear Viliamu's own account: "Many days passed, during
which we were baffled and perplexed by contrary
winds ; our provisions were nearly spent, our patience
all but exhausted, when early one morning the captain came to me and said, 'We must, sir, give up the
search, or we shall all be starved.' I answered, 'We

will continue our course till eight o'clock, and should
we not succeed by that time, we will return home.' This
was a time of great anxiety; hope and fear agitated
my mind; I had sent a native to the top of the mast
four times, and he was now ascending for the fifth, it
being within half-an-hour of the time fixed for relin-
quishing our object. Suddenly the clouds were dis-
persed by the sun, whose rays breaking forth revealed
to view the towering heights of distant mountains.
The man, beholding this sight, shouted, ' There is the
land we have been seeking ! '

" Many years have passed since that day, but I have
never forgotten the sensations I then experienced.
The brightened countenances, the joyous expressions,
and the lively congratulations of all on board, showed
they shared our feelings, nor did we fail to raise our
voices in grateful thanks to Him who had graciously
' led us by a right way.' "

And who will not sympathise with the holy satisfaction with which he stood gazing from the prow of
his little bark upon that new-discovered land ?   Long
had the thought of it filled his heart, and often, when
listening to the tales and traditions of the loquacious
natives when rowing on the sea or reclining in the
shade, had the name of *Rarotonga* (found in many a
legend) awakened his ardent desire to visit its people,
and strengthened in him the purpose, should God give
him opportunity, to go in quest of that interesting isle.
And now his prayers were heard, his hopes realised !
The long-desired land was before him ; his faith and
perseverance were rewarded.

Nor was his rejoicing vain. This was no barren discovery; it resulted in the moral and spiritual renovation of the island, and glory to God. It is well known that this lovely isle—the finest and most populous of the groups—soon became a very " garden of the Lord ; " its inhabitants shortly after embraced Christianity, and from thenceforward its devoted discoverer watched over and provided for it with fatherly care, frequently visiting it, and ever gladdened by the sights and sounds which greeted him there, evincing the favour of God and the progress of the Gospel.*

Let us take one peep at it as described by himself, and with this we must be satisfied. " Beautiful are the rocks, hills, and valleys of Rarotonga, and one valuable peculiarity of the lovely island is the extent of low land. Its soil must be exceedingly rich, and the climate peculiarly adapted to the fruits which grow there, for we were surprised to see the *taro* and *kape*, the *ti* and sugar-cane growing luxuriantly nearly down to the edge of the sea ; the whole island was also in a high state of cultivation, and I do not remember having seen anything more beautiful than

---

* When addressing an assembly at Exeter Hall, Mr. Williams, speaking of Rarotonga, said :—" I found the people all heathens ; I left them all Christians. I found them with idols and maraes; these I left in ruins, but their place was supplied by three large places of Christian worship, in one of which a congregation of 3,000 assembles every Sabbath-day. I found them without a written language; I left them reading in their own tongue the word of God; and the last intelligence I have received informs me that in one of the schools there were 1,034 children present on the morning the letter was written."

the scene I beheld when standing on the side of one of the hills and looking towards the sea-shore. In the first place there are rows of superb chestnut-trees, planted at equal distances, and stretching from the mountain's base to the sea, with a space between each row of about half-a-mile wide. This space is divided into small *taro* beds, which average about half-an-acre each, the embankments round each being thrown up with a slope, leaving a flat surface upon the top, planted with stately bread-fruit trees.

"There is a good road round the island, lined on both sides with bananas and mountain plantains, and these, with the Barringtonia, chestnut, and other trees of spreading foliage, protect you from the rays of the tropical sun, and afford even in midday the luxury of cool shady walks, several miles in length. The houses of the people were situated from ten to thirty yards or more from this pathway, and some of them were exceedingly pretty. The paths leading to the houses were strewed with white and black pebbles, and on either side was planted a tree bearing a beautiful blossom, interspersed alternately with the gigantic taro. Six or eight stone seats were ranged in front of the premises by the side of the principal pathway. These were relics of some antiquity, and were regarded with much veneration by the people, who would point to them and say, 'Here my father, grandfather, or the great Chief so and so sat.' There in the cool of the evening, after the labours of the day, with a wreath of flowers on their brow, anointed with a sweet-scented oil, and wearing a new garment of the shining *pakaku* (a fine native cloth), sat the inmates of the house, to chat with any loquacious passenger about the events of their own little world."

In his "Missionary Enterprises" (Chapter xx.) Mr. Williams relates his first visit to the Samoan group. Long had his heart been set on carrying the Gospel to the people inhabiting those isles, and who were still heathen. At length, in the summer of 1830, he found himself on board his own home-built craft, *The Messenger of Peace*, starting for his far-distant bourn. After visiting on the way several of the out-stations where Missionary labours were being carried on, they sighted Savaii, the most extensive and popu-lous of the Samoan group, whose towering mountains were descried at the distance of from sixty to seventy miles. The size and grandeur of its appearance favourably impressed the visitor, who was filled with surprise and delight. "To our astonishment," he says, "we found two of the islands larger than Tahiti."

Their vessel was quickly surrounded by canoes, which brought intelligence that led Mr. Williams to determine on steering for Sapapalii, the place where dwelt the principal chief, Malietoa. They found him absent, but were favourably received by his brother, and invited to land. The result is thus described in our Missionary's journal: "Wednesday, August 21. This day we have seen the accomplishment of our desires, and obtained a full reward for all our anxiety and toil. In the morning the native teachers whom we had landed over night returned to the vessel,

3 *

accompanied by the chiefs and about fifty canoes.
They gave us the most favourable account of their
reception ; the teachers are highly delighted with their
prospects, and the poor heathen no less so. One
thing affected us much. The two largest islands of
the group, Upolu and Savaii, are only ten miles apart.
Between their inhabitants war was raging when we

SOUTH SEA CHRISTIAN VILLAGE.

arrived, and they were actually fighting on the shores
of Upolu while we were landing the teachers on the
opposite shore of Savaii; indeed, the houses and
plantations were blazing at the very moment!"

On the following day Messrs. Barff and Williams
landed, and were most cordially welcomed. The sun

having set before they reached the shore, the people had kindled a blazing beacon, and conducted their visitors by torchlight. An immense crowd covered the beach, forming a guard of honour to the house of Malietoa, whither the brethren were borne in triumph, " sprawling at full length upon their extended hands and arms." A song in honour of "the two great English chiefs " was improvised and sung, to the accompaniment of all manner of native instruments and dancing, by the people in full chorus.

It was soon apparent to Mr. Williams that the natives of Samoa differed considerably from those he had previously known. They were inferior in height and muscular power, but excelled in grace and agility. Of all the Polynesians he had seen, they were the most symmetric in form and polished in manners. Of this they were themselves fully aware, and neglected nothing to set off or enhance their personal attractions.

Two portraits, drawn by their visitor's hand, will give us some idea of the people among whom he had now arrived :—" Picture to yourself a fine well-grown Indian, with a dark sparkling eye, a smooth skin, glistening from the head to the hips with sweet-scented oil, and tastefully tattooed from the hips to the knees, with a bandage of red leaves, oiled and shining also, a head-dress of the nautilus shell, and a string of small white shells around each arm, and you have a Samoan gentleman in full dress, and thus dressed, he thinks as much of himself as would an English beau fitted out in the highest style of fashion.

A Samoan lady, in full dress for a ball, wears a beautifully white silk-looking mat around her loins, with one corner tucked up, a wreath of sweet-smelling flowers around her head, a row or two of large blue beads about her neck; her skin shining with scented oil, and the upper part of her person deeply tinged with turmeric rouge. The ladies spend a considerable time in preparing themselves for company."

That which interested him more than all beside was the marked religious difference which separated the Samoans from all the other islanders he had met with. They had none of the temples, idols, altars, and priests which abounded elsewhere; and their superstitions, though equally gross, were less cruel and demoralising. But though they did not worship idols of wood and stone, they regarded their gods as incarnate in many of the birds, beasts, fishes, and creeping things by which they were surrounded. It was also evident to him that they held their idolatrous opinions with less tenacious hold than was the case with many of the Polynesians.

After a short stay, the Missionaries quitted Savaii, full of hope for its future. They had been treated with great kindness, and the king, Malietoa, as well as the people generally, showed a hearty willingness to receive the native teachers, and pledged themselves to protect them, and to listen to the message they brought.

In closing his journal of this first voyage to Samoa, Mr. Williams says: "It is impossible to reflect upon it, and not discover the hand of God. At that time

we were quite ignorant of the state of the islands,
the character of the people, and the various points of
moment to the Missionary about to commence a Mission. The result was that, had we possessed all the
knowledge we have since obtained, we could not have
selected a better station than that to which, without
wisdom or foresight of our own, we were directed."

Of the second visit to Samoa, a truly delightful
account is given in the "Missionary Enterprises."
Large numbers of the inhabitants of Savaii and
Upolu had embraced the gospel, and many more were
only awaiting his return to follow their example. With
a heart full of thankfulness, their beloved 'Viliamu'
preached· to them the glad tidings. A vast congregation assembled to listen, and anxiously hung upon
his lips. No wonder he said "it was impossible to
behold them without deep interest, as a people just
emerging from the darkness of ages into the light of
life. In the afternoon I preached again, and felt
much."

All the incidents and the intercourse of the few
days passed at Savaii confirmed his feelings of satisfaction. The people learned to love him. Savage as
they had been, and still were, they saw his goodness,
and felt drawn by it. Love beamed in his eye, made
itself felt in his words and actions, and produced its
invariable result.

Mr. Williams' favourite proverb was, "Kindness is
the key to the human heart," and no man exercised
its captivating power more than he. It opened for
him the hearts of thousands who had previously been

inaccessible to civilised man. "Everywhere the natives clung around him : he seemed to be one of
them," was the testimony of his brethren ; and it is
apparent in every page of his history. By his personal influence, he did much to prepare the way for
the native teachers, and for the future operations of
the Mission in Samoa.

Before he took his departure from Sapapalii, the
tamaitai, or chief women, requested permission to
perform in his honour. Fearing lest the entertain-
ment might not prove to his taste, he respectfully
declined the compliment, but they would take no
denial, and the evening was spent by the *élite* of the
settlement in singing and capering in his praise. I
cannot refrain from giving a few verses of one of
these songs :—

> " Let us talk of Viliamu :
> Let cocoa-nuts grow for him in peace for months ;
> When strong the east wind blows, our thoughts forget him not.
> Let us greatly love the Christian land of the great white chief.

> " The birds are crying for Viliamu ;
>   His ship has sailed another way.
>   Long time is he in coming ;
>   Will he ever come again ?

> " Now our land is sacred made, and evil practices have ceased.
>   How we feel for the *lotu !* Come, let us sleep, and dream of Viliamu.
>   *Pistaulau** has risen ; *Taulau** has also risen ;
>   But the war-star has ceased to rise,
>   And war has become an evil thing."

---

* Names of stars.

CHAPTER IV.

CLOSING SCENES.

Return of Mr. Williams to Rarotonga — Bible translation and Missionary duties—Last visit to the surrounding islands—Departure for England—Cordial reception—Publication of " The Missionary Enterprises "—Appeal to the public for a ship—Return to the South Seas — Once more at Samoa and Rarotonga — Death of Makea, the Rarotongan chief—Determination to visit Erromanga —Presentiments of danger—Devotion of Mr. Williams—Faithful unto death—The Martyr's memorial.

AVING completed his second visit to the Navigator's Islands, Mr. Williams returned to Rarotonga, which he reached in safety in the month of January, 1833.

It had been for some time determined that he should pay a visit to England, and many things rendered it desirable that this purpose should be accomplished without delay. He found, however, so much to detain him, that more than twelve months elapsed before he was able to leave. Some important matters claimed his attention—especially the completion of the Rarotongan New Testament, in the translation of which he was aided by Messrs. Pitman and Buzacott. He also discharged the usual services of the station, and during the months of his delay new and handsome

Mission premises were erected, and various arrangements made for the future management of the newly-formed church and congregations.

It cost him a heart-pang to leave these endeared scenes of his labour. His love for his brethren and for the natives, and for the lovely island whose existence he had been the first to make known to Europeans, all rendered it especially trying to say farewell. He hoped indeed to revisit it again some day; but the future is all uncertain in this world of change and of death, and who can reckon upon it?

There was yet another trial for him to undergo. Anxious as he was to embark for England, he could not resist the desire to pay one last visit to the surrounding islands, whither he had gone so many years preaching the Gospel of the grace of God. In his "Enterprises," he has recorded the incidents of those closing scenes, and to them the reader is referred.

At length he felt free to depart for England, and after an absence of nearly eighteen years, on the 12th of June, 1834, beheld again the white cliffs of his native land. Probably no Missionary ever received a more cordial welcome, on his return home, than did our beloved friend. The volume of "Missionary Enterprises," which he published and circulated very extensively, and the urgent appeals he made in all the principal towns of the kingdom, combined to excite more than ordinary attention, while his personal manners and character secured the esteem and affection of multitudes. He passed through the length and breadth of our British Zion—as he himself said to a Norwich friend — and everywhere hearts and homes were opened to receive him, and hands ready to supply whatever he required.

When the Government declined to provide him with a Missionary ship, he appealed to the liberality of the public, and the result far exceeded his expectations. A beautiful vessel was provided, at a cost of £2,600, and he said, " I might have had much more than I asked."

Two-and-thirty years have passed away since he quitted England for ever, but there are still some who, looking back to their early days, can recall his image, and his memory is endeared to the many thousands of poor islanders whom he lived to serve and bless. The best likeness of him is that in the " Evangelical Magazine;" it is, indeed, an excellent resemblance. The one prefixed to Mr. Prout's Memoir is very unsatisfactory.

There remains not much to tell. He returned to Polynesia, spent a few months with his beloved Samoans, and revisited his own Rarotonga, where he had a touching meeting with its chief, Makea. " They fondly embraced each other, and Mr. W. exclaimed, ' Oh, Makea, how kind are God's dealings to us, in sparing us thus far, and permitting us to see each other again.' "

Little did they think they should so soon meet in a better world. Makea died on the 19th of October— eight months after this interview—and Mr. Williams was cut off on the 20th of November. Referring to his death, Mr. Williams wrote : " The good chief

Makea is gone. He was invaluable while he lived;
his influence and power, great as it was, was given to
God. He died most happy. I never knew a chief I
loved so much, or thought so highly of."

It is too painful to recall the particulars of the end.
Erromanga is a name that thrills one with horror.
Very remarkable and noteworthy is the fact that Mrs.
Williams, the guardian angel of her husband's life,
besought him at parting not to land upon its shores !
The intuitions of loving hearts may seem weak, and
cannot be brought to the test of reason, but they
doubtless have a meaning, and occasionally have
served as useful warnings or intimations of the Divine
will.   If the endeared and lamented Viliamu had
hearkened to the last pleadings of loving affection, he
might have lived to accomplish the project which
filled his heart, the evangelisation of Western Polynesia ; but He who knows the end from the beginning
had otherwise determined.

      *   *   *   *   *

That the devoted missionary had "counted the
cost," and was prepared for the issue, we know from
his own words in his parting address : they are truly
impressive and consoling. "I am fully aware," he
says, "of the dangers to which we shall be exposed.
The people at some of the islands we propose visiting
are particularly savage, but we recollect how we have
been preserved, and thus encouraged, we shall go
forward. Should God, in His providence, so arrange
it that we fall in the conflict, there is sweet consolation to the mind, and we trust that we shall have

NATIONAL PASTIME, ERROMANGA.

grace to bow with submission to His will, knowing that others will be raised up by His providence to carry into effect that work which we have been employed to commence. . . . I have looked at the violent storms we may expect, at the ferocity of the savages among whom we are going, and having viewed it all, I have just placed the object in view in the opposite scale, and fixing the eye of the mind intently upon the greatness and sublimity of that, I trust I can say, in the face of all difficulties and dangers, 'None of these things move me, neither count I my life dear unto myself, so that I may finish my course with joy, and the ministry which I have received of the Lord Jesus, to testify the gospel of the grace of God.'"

Inscription on Mr. Williams's Monument at Apia.

Sacred to the Memory

OF THE

REV. JOHN WILLIAMS,

FATHER OF THE SAMOAN AND OTHER MISSIONS,

AGED 45 YEARS AND 5 MONTHS,

WHO WAS KILLED BY THE CRUEL NATIVES OF ERROMANGA,

NOVEMBER 20TH, 1839,

WHILE ENDEAVOURING TO PLANT ON THEIR SHORES

THE GOSPEL OF PEACE.

MUSSULMAN MOSQUE.

ALPHONSE LACROIX:

THE MISSIONARY EVANGELIST OF BENGAL.

CHAPTER I.

INTRODUCTORY.

Pioneer Missions to India — Interest of Missionary biographies — Dr. Mullens's Memoir of Mr. Lacroix — Early life in Switzerland — Martial ardour — The interposing Voice, " You have been praying for me " — A nobler service — Visit to Holland — Ordained as a Missionary.

HOW instructive and encouraging is it to look back upon the earlier history of Missionary life in India. As we contrast the present time with those older, but yet comparatively recent days, when the devoted Carey and his coadjutors were compelled to take up their residence at the Danish settlement of Serampore, because the shelter of their own country's flag was refused them—days when one of the Directors of the East India Company declared he would rather see a band of devils enter India than a band of Missionaries,—we may well exclaim, " What has God wrought !"

4

It was only by slow degrees, and as the result of patient, self-denying labour, that the foundations were laid upon which so much depended. Many faithful men wrought with apparently little success, yet the aggregate result of their combined efforts has been truly wondrous, as is acknowledged even by those who have no cordial love for the men or their work. One seems to desire a minute and true account of every individual labourer, but unhappily there are few detailed biographies of Missionary life. Would there were more, especially if they were written with the piquant zest of a traveller's story, while possessing all the higher interest of a Missionary's zeal.

Such a book is the Life of Mr. Lacroix, by his son-in-law, Dr. Mullens. As a narrative it is truly charming, and it has the special excellence of placing the reader in the very midst of the work and the workers. You seem, as you read its pages, to go with the man, and to behold the scenes amid which he moved and the people by whom he was surrounded.

It would be a pleasant task to sketch the story of his boyhood and youth, but a few lines only can be given to them here. He was born in the little village of Lignières, in the canton of Neufchatel, Switzerland, on the 10th May, 1799. His childhood was passed amid scenes of natural beauty and magnificence, and his young eyes gazed on the glorious Alpine heights with their snowy crowns. Those were the days of martial ardour on the continent of Europe, and as the boy grew up he longed to serve in the armies of Napoleon, and actually determined to enlist in the ranks. His excellent uncle, under whose care he had been reared, and whose guardian love had been almost paternal, in vain remonstrated with him. Even his mother's entreaties were unheeded. He shouldered his knapsack and set off for the head-quarters of the Swiss recruit dépôts, some thirty miles away. Already he was approaching Berne, and crossing the ravine of the Aar, when he seemed to hear a voice ringing in his ears, saying, in distinct tones, "What doest thou here? — Return!" He paused, obeyed, and at once hastened back, his purpose relinquished for ever, and, flinging himself into his uncle's arms, cried, "Ah! dear uncle! you have been praying for me and calling me back, and here I am!"

When about fifteen years of age, his mind seems to have been deeply impressed by religious convictions. On attaining his seventeenth year, he was induced by some means to visit Holland. This step was the turning point of his history. It led eventually to his entering the Mission College at Rotterdam, and he was shortly after ordained as a Minister and Missionary of the Dutch Reformed Church, to proceed forthwith to the field of labour in India. On his route he visited England, and reached London on the 2nd September, 1820. By a singular coincidence, on that very day, and in that city, his future son-in-law and biographer was born.

4 *

CHAPTER II.

AT CHINSURAH.

THE period at which Mr. Lacroix arrived in India was one of much interest. The old system of exclusiveness had been broken through, and a transition to a much better state of things was in progress. The influence of Englishmen was recognised, private trade open, individuals had access to the country, and capital was beginning to pour in. The improvement was indeed but partial, and there was ample room for further advancement. The vast and rapid changes which have taken place during the last half century are such that it is difficult to realise the position in which our predecessors were placed.

Chinsurah, the station at which our Missionary commenced his Indian life, was a small Dutch town on the west bank of the Hoogly, thirty miles from Calcutta and fifteen from the Danish settlement of Serampore. There were the Dutch and Native por-

tions of the town, the former principally located on
the river, the latter chiefly inland. As in other
Indian towns, large numbers of trees and plants,
especially those of tropical growth—palms, cocoa-nut,
and tamarind trees — grew everywhere about the
streets, roads, and gardens, and, in the rainy season
especially, imparted a delicious greenness to the
settlement.

At that period the Dutch houses were about one
hundred in number, small, quaint buildings, flat-
roofed, and consisting of but one story, painted yellow,
detached, but crowded closely together. The floors,
on a level with the ground, were often saturated with
water six months out of the twelve; there were also
a few better houses, and the church, an antiquated
building, whose tower was originally built to bear the
clock of the settlement—the part adapted for worship
being added five-and-twenty years after—a fact sufficiently indicative of the views of the inhabitants respecting religious ordinances in the middle of last
century! Not the least interesting part of the strange
old town was its burial-ground, with its tall triangular
pillars and monuments of curious forms, with strange
inscriptions marking the graves in which, for two
centuries, the settlers had been laid.

This was the Dutch part of the town; but there
was a Native portion, consisting of three or four
bazaars and streets, with a very active thriving population, who were profiting greatly by the business
they carried on with their Dutch neighbours.

The number of the Dutch inhabitants in 1820 was

greatly reduced. Little genuine piety was to be found among them, but there was a good deal of immorality and much infidelity. There was also something of a higher and better kind, and there were a few whose simple and genuine piety shone brightly amid the surrounding darkness. The manners of the people were quiet, somewhat quaint, and very sociable; there were no newspapers published, few books were to be had, and still fewer were read.

The youthful Missionary was received very kindly by the best families of Chinsurah. His personal manners and appearance must have recommended him; he was tall, somewhat spare, but decidedly handsome, most courteous in address, extremely active and spirited in all his movements, and his genial temper and lively, hearty manner, soon made him a favourite with the whole settlement, especially with the Governor, Mr. Overbeek, who kindly gave him rooms in his own spacious dwelling.

From the three Missionaries of the London Missionary Society, Messrs. Pearson, Townley, and Mundy, he received the most cordial welcome, and their counsel and aid were ever at his command: they were to him, so long as life lasted, faithful brethren and dear friends. He attached himself with special affection to Mr. Townley, by whose conversation, example, and experience he greatly profited.

For some years his principal work was to master the language of the country, to acquaint himself with the habits of the people, and their religious views, doctrines, and precepts; to trace the practical in-

fluence of the Hindu faith upon the native life and
character; and to learn by the experience of his predecessors in Missionary operations. His facility in
acquiring language enabled him quickly to overcome
the difficulties of Bengáli, which he soon spoke with
great correctness and fluency.

Mr. Lacroix was the constant companion of Mr.
Townley when he went to preach in the bazaar-
chapels or to examine the vernacular schools. At
times they witnessed together the horrid rites of
Hindu idolatry in its most appalling and cruel forms.
Those were the days of Suttee, and they were present
at one of these dreadful burnings, which took place on
the bank of the river immediately opposite Chinsurah.
There was a great crowd assembled with the Brahmin
priests, the sons of the family, the dead husband, and
the victim widow. Mr. Townley remonstrated calmly
but earnestly with them, but they paid no attention
to his entreaties : the preparations commenced and
were completed. The pile was formed of long bars
of wood, the dead was laid on it, and the widow placed
herself by his side ; bamboos were fastened over
both. Then the sacred texts were pronounced, and the
son put fire to the pile and set it ablaze ; while to
drown the cries of the unhappy sufferer, the drums
beat their hideous din, and the surrounding multitudes raised their loudest shouts. The memory of
this awful scene, and the horror at the Hindu system
which was its cause, Mr. Lacroix never lost during
his whole lifetime.

Scarcely had the young beginner commenced work

when he was laid aside by a severe attack of inflammation of the liver. He was brought so low that his life seemed in jeopardy, but through God's blessing he recovered, and from that time his constitution seemed able to bear the heat with greater comfort and security. Much of his time was devoted to teaching in the schools, and in this work his services were acceptable and useful. A pleasing proof of this came to his knowledge. Thirty years after he had left Chinsurah he was preaching during a short visit at Agra, when, at the close of the service, Mr. F., a respectable Government employé, came to him, and with tears poured out his thanks for all the kind care bestowed on him in the school so many years ago, at the same time expressing his joy at thus unexpectedly meeting with his beloved teacher. It was a touching meeting for both. It appeared that Mr. F. had been long a decided Christian, and was then an elder of the Presbyterian Church at Agra, and that his daughter was usefully engaged in works of education and philanthropy, all which he attributed, under the Divine blessing, to the instructions of Mr. Lacroix in bygone years.

Preaching in the native language was a prominent feature of Missionary operation, and in about two years Mr. Lacroix was able to join his brethren at the work. Often they taught in the school-houses, and at sunset the chapels were opened, and earnest appeals were made to any listeners whom chance attracted. Sometimes they betook themselves to the open air, when a crowd would gather. It was a great thing to keep the people in good temper and attentive, and a good deal of tact and ready wit was wanted.

An amusing scene took place on one of these occasions. Mr. Mundy had been addressing a large assembly under the branches of a spreading tree, when an old Brahmin, who had not been at all pleased with the people's attention, asked, in a querulous tone, What was the use of merely talking to the people; they were all poor; why did not the pádri do something sensible by relieving their wants? "Very true," said Mr. Mundy, " it is right to assist the destitute ; and as you, Brahmin, have no hat, here, take mine ;" and without giving him time to object, he forthwith put his old hat on the Brahmin's head and pressed it down. The latter, quite discomfited, made off, amid the laughter of the people, who perfectly relished the jest.

One of Mr. Lacroix's natural tastes yielded him much satisfaction during his entire residence in India. He had a great fondness for natural history, and took particular notice of the habits and instincts of the numerous animals, great and small, which fell under his observation. In this manner he gathered a great deal of correct information respecting them, and would often recount anecdotes of what he had seen and heard.

A favourite story, which he told in after days, was related to him, when at Chinsurah, by his future father-in-law, who witnessed the occurrence.

At the country house of a gentleman residing at Chandernagore, there was a little pet elephant, ex-

ceedingly tame.   It was allowed to roam all over the
house, and was accustomed to go into the dining-room
after dinner.   One day, a large party being seated at
dessert, the elephant came round, and putting his
trunk between the guests, begged a little fruit.   One
gentleman refused to give him anything, and as the
animal persisted in his importunity, feeling annoyed,
he took his fork and pricked the elephant's trunk with
the prongs.   The creature went off and finished his
rounds, then disappeared for awhile, but presently
returned with the bough off a tree he had plucked
from the garden, and which he shook smartly over
the gentleman's head.   In a moment he was covered
with large black ants that lay hidden in the leaves.
Their bite is severe, as the unhappy man soon experienced.   They filled his hair, crept down his neck,
crawled up the sleeves, while he roared and stamped
in vain.   There was nothing to be done but to leave the
table, undress and get into a bath, to free himself from
his tormenters.   Of course the other guests laughed,
and the elephant was petted more fondly than before.

Mr. Lacroix remained in Chinsurah until the spring
of 1829, completing there a service of eight years,
characterised by patience, industry, and self-denial.
It was the seed time for him, by which he was well
fitted for subsequent usefulness.   He had learned to
preach readily and powerfully to the heathen in their
own tongue, had carefully studied their customs,
history, and superstitions, and was by these means
the better prepared to meet their wants, and to deal
efficiently with them.

One event which occurred during his residence at Chinsurah must not pass unmentioned. On his arrival from Europe he had been early introduced into the family of Mr. Herklots, a Dutch civilian of high position and honourable standing in the community. This gentleman and his family had been brought to the knowledge of the truth by the teaching of the Missionaries, and amid the irreligion and the infidelity of a dark time had maintained a holy, consistent Christian character. Mr. Lacroix was a frequent and welcome visitor in their household, and became early attached to Hannah, one of the younger daughters. Their marriage took place in the spring of 1825, and the union proved a truly happy one, and lasted throughout his life. But, while thus he drank the cup of purest joy, his tender and affectionate spirit suffered deeply from domestic bereavement. In the third year of his marriage he lost his second child, a boy of six months old, who was suddenly snatched away by one of the fearful epidemics so prevalent and fatal in that sultry clime. This loss he felt acutely, and mourned it long and deeply. Many years after, when in great weakness and suffering he wept, it was remarked that he had not been known to shed a tear " since little Alphonse died."

Alas! these baptisms of tears that follow so often close upon seasons of earth's brightest sunshine! What do they mean, but that this is not our rest, and that our hearts must be set upon that which is unseen and eternal?

CHAPTER III.

THE RICE-FIELDS OF BENGAL.

Removal to Calcutta, and association with the London Mission — Native village of Rammakalchoke—The rice-plains of Bengal— A Sunday with the Missionary—Starting in the palankeen—Halt at the margin of the lake—Waiting for the boat—Punted up the creeks—Arrival at Rammakalchoke—Sabbath services—Relieving the sick—Journeying homeward—The great hurricane of 1833— Fearful distress of the inhabitants—Voyage of relief by Messrs. Lacroix and Gogerly.

MR. LACROIX removed from Chinsurah to Calcutta early in 1829, having in the meanwhile united himself to the London Missionary Society. There a new and interesting field of Missionary labour was recently opened, and many native converts had been made. This movement had taken place in the rice-fields of Bengal, among the numerous villages scattered throughout that singular and unique region.

Mr. Lacroix was desired by the Calcutta District Committee to go and assist for a time the brethren, Messrs. Ray, Piffard, and Gogerly, in their work there. He found that the Christians were scattered in about twenty villages, among which Rammakalchoke and Gungrat were reckoned the principal. About eighty adults, with their children, had been baptized; a few others had decided to join with

CHURCH IN COOLY BAZAAR, CALCUTTA.

them, and large congregations continued to attend the public services of the Sabbath.

Rammakalchoke is about eight miles south of Calcutta ; it was there the movement had originated. A Hindu named Ramjee, with his whole family, which was a large one and of some standing and influence, had renounced Hinduism. He had torn up the sacred *tulsi* tree, had destroyed his family temple and idol, and erected a chapel in its place, with a bungalow on the roof for the Missionary's residence.

Dr. Mullens gives a very graphic picture of the country where these things happened.

The southern part of Bengal, between the Hoogly and Mutlah rivers, consists of an extensive plain scarcely above the level of the ocean. Strong embankments have been raised all round this plain to exclude the sea, extending for some hundreds of miles. The country thus enclosed is a broad, level plain, in the early months of the year, dry and clothed with a thin grass, but during the season when the Ganges is in full flood, covered by its fertilizing stream, it becomes an enormous freshwater lake, some sixty miles long, and as many broad. It is then entirely navigated by boats, the numerous villages of the district being raised a few feet above the level, and consisting of cottages closely packed together, and abounding in plantations of the usual tropical trees, especially the cocoa-nut, palmyra, bétel-nut, and plantain, and in some parts the thorny acacia, tamarind, and bamboo are very common.

The inhabitants are nearly all Hindus of the fisher-man caste, accustomed from their infancy to live an amphibious life, sowing these vast plains with rice, and as the creeks swarm with fish, contriving to make a tolerable living from their double trade.

In this strange country Mr. Lacroix was now to spend much of his time. He who had been born in Switzerland, had passed his youth clambering over the limestone rocks of the Jura, and through its dark woods; who had gazed enraptured upon his native Alps, with all their glorious panorama, now found himself on a wide-spreading, level plain, moving from village to village, amid little islands of varied hue, rising from the watery waste amidst thousands of the tall, lithe cocoa-nuts, or through the profusion of wild water-plants rich in flowers. Through scenes like these he pursued his mission, his canoe, as he passed along, disturbing "flocks of teal, rising on whirring wing from the reedy swamp, or from the light rice-stalk bending gracefully to the breeze, and thrilling the ear with the liquid music that its gentle waving pours upon the air."

Amid those islets the Missionary found scenes en-abling him to realise the New Testament pictures of the Christian Churches in the apostolic age. His rule was to visit his two central stations, which were distant eight and twelve miles from his own house, twice a week — on Sundays and Thursdays. He went and returned the same day, except in the dry season, when he would remain two or three days at a time.

His biographer invites us to accompany him on one of these pastoral journeys, towards the close of the year :—

"He leaves home before eight in the morning, in a palankeen with eight bearers. He traverses Calcutta, and passes through the suburbs of Bhowanipore and Kalighat, whose streets, shops, and bazaars always present a busy scene. In Kalighat bazaar he finds numbers of cheap and simple toys, which, on his return on week-days, he often purchases for his children. They consist of birds or huge frogs of painted mud, pith custard-apples, pictures of crabs, horses, and elephants; or pictures of a young Bengáli gentleman, with well oiled hair,' or native young lady, dressed in the whitest muslin, wearing a profusion of jewels and smoking a silver hookah. Passing over a wretched mud road, lined by gigantic aloes or the thick-branching cactus, he at length reaches the first village on the borders of the rice-plains. Here he quits the palankeen, and finds waiting for him the Mission-boat, in which he will be punted among the fields and villages till he arrives at his destination. The boat is a long canoe of saul-wood, about two feet wide and the same deep. It has a low wooden roof and canvas curtains. An arm-chair with amputated legs is the only furniture. He brings a basket with the necessary provisions, a supply of medicines, and the materials for the Communion Service.

"While his boatmen are busied in making preparations, he walks up and down the bank, smoking a cigar and chatting with the inhabitants, to whom he is well known. He stands among them, a tall, broad-shouldered, massive figure, six feet high, with a firm, active step—a perfect contrast to their short, thin, and supple frames. His dress is of the coolest—white trousers, an easy coat of blue check, or a linen jacket with a narrow black ribbon round his neck. His head and curling white hair are protected by a broad-brimmed pith hat, covered with silk half an inch thick, and very light: he carries also a large double umbrella, with its white cover outside.

"Starting afresh, the canoe is pushed or towed by the boatmen, first up a small stream, then into side creeks for three-quarters of an hour, till he arrives at the bank on which stands the chapel of Rammakal-choke, its white front conspicuous among the trees.

"On landing he is greeted heartily by several of the Christians who have watched the progress of his boat, of whom, not least in his esteem is the good Ramjee. His first visit is to the boys' school, containing about thirty lads who are ready to be examined in Scripture history, catechism, and so on. At noon the congregation gathers for public worship (the people for several years numbered more than a hundred and fifty persons). They all sit on the floor, upon grass mats, the women to the left of the preacher, the men on his right. Then commences the singing, a series of twists and turns, repeated again and again, and screamed and shouted at the very tops of the voices of the men and boys! The reading, prayer, and sermon follow, all bending forward with their faces to the ground, in prayer. Lastly comes the Communion, administered once a month, and received by many with rejoicing faith.

"The service over, dinner followed, the curry portion of it being supplied by Ramjee's excellent wife, who cooked the dish with her own hands. Afterwards the minister would see the catechist, school-master, and other members of the church, inquire into their various circumstances, and administer relief or counsel, as required. Sometimes he would give a simple medicine in a case needing it. His duty completed, he would retrace his steps, reaching home soon after sunset."

This was the Sabbath routine : the Thursday visits were also very important. Then were held the church meetings, the reports of the catechist and school-master heard, and pastoral visitations made to candidates, individuals, and families, with other similar work. His kind sympathy and wise advice were invaluable to these poor people in various cases of daily occurrence, family troubles, persecutions inflicted by the Zemindars, and the like. Occasionally he passed in the boat to the neighbouring villages, gathering the people together, and holding special services for their benefit. At times he would remain two or three days, sleeping in the room over the chapel.

Such was the character of his pastoral life among the converts of these village churches. For more than twelve years, with brief intervals, he continued to fulfil its responsible duties and accomplish its great ends. Not only in pleasant days, when the air was cool, the journeys easy, and the people prospering, but

when the creeks were muddy and the fields were dry,
when the heavens were fiery brass over his head, and
the hard, cracked earth scorched his feet; when outward persecution sought to crush the disciples, and
when apostacy and vice came in like a flood to destroy
their inward vitality and growth—through all he held
on his way, steadfast, unshaken, and abounding in the
work of the Lord.

In the spring of the year 1833, there burst upon the
southern districts of Bengal the most awful hurricane
that had been known for a hundred years. The
description given of it in these memoirs is most striking, and great was the desolation and misery it occasioned among the poor villagers, Christian and Hindu.

"It came on, as usual, from the south-east, the wind
continuing to increase for two or three days, until at
last its fury was indescribable. The most remarkable
and appalling feature of the hurricane appeared in the
height of the storm : a series of terrific rolling waves,
the least of which was ten feet in height, burst upon
the land, broke down the embankments, crossed the
country like mighty walls, with steady march sweep-
ing everything before them, and reaching to a distance
inland of more than fifty miles over the level plains.
The peasants, alarmed by the distant rushing sound,
saw with astonishment the foaming wall marching
across the fields, and clambered for safety on to the
roofs of their frail cottages; but the walls crumbled
in the waters, and the refugees were drowned. Wild
deer, wild boars in hundreds, driven from the neighbouring forests, and with them many tigers, all panic-

stricken, came bounding along the plain, fleeing from the relentless destroyer. And soon the mighty waves came rushing past them with appalling roar, washing whole villages away with all their people. In that hurricane it was reckoned that 20,000 persons lost their lives. The rice-plain, in all its length and breadth, was tainted by the salt water: for two seasons rice would not grow, and the peasantry could scarcely live."

A few months later, when the Ganges flood had covered the whole plain with its rich supplies, it presented a wonderful appearance. The waters were perfectly transparent, and reflected the deep clear blue of the Indian sky. The plain with its numerous villages looked like a vast sea, studded with a thousand green and wooded isles. In after years Mr. Lacroix often spoke of that sight as one of the most beautiful he had ever beheld.

Great was the distress consequent upon this dire calamity. Starving multitudes poured into Calcutta, and lined the roads and suburbs, exhausted and dying. The Christian settlements suffered most deeply, but soon found aid. The Hindu population were wretched in the extreme. Mr. Lacroix was indefatigable in his efforts to succour them, and for many weeks long rows of starving villagers were fed in his garden. Wherever he travelled he carried bags of Indian halfpence, to distribute among the crowds, and when the distress was at its height, accompanied by his friend Mr. Gogerly, he took a journey towards the mouth of the Hoogly in a large pinnace laden with rice, to relieve the famishing multitudes there.

CHAPTER III.

THE PREACHER.

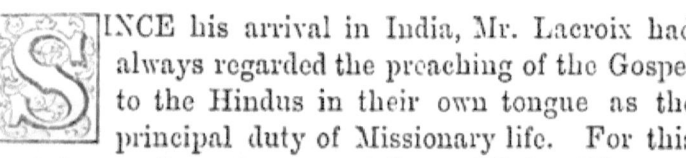

SINCE his arrival in India, Mr. Lacroix had always regarded the preaching of the Gospel to the Hindus in their own tongue as the principal duty of Missionary life. For this work he was by nature especially qualified. His commanding presence and powerful voice alone sufficed to insure him an audience. To these were added a clear, correct pronunciation of the Bengáli, and a most attractive style. He preached well in English, but far better in Bengáli. That language is said to be admirably adapted for narrative. The people to whom he addressed himself were unaccustomed to sustained discourse ; and he broke his addresses with admirable pieces of common-sense comment, impressive applications of truth, and illustrations drawn from history and Hindu legend. A servant once remarked that whenever Mr. Lacroix preached, every Bengáli's heart trembled! In fact, he was acknowledged to be the most eloquent preacher of the language the country contained. The Hindus are accustomed to the moving tales of their own professional orators, who produce great impression by the striking stories they derive from Hindu books; but they had never listened to such heart-stirring and eloquent words as fell from his lips, and the effect was great.

In Calcutta, with a view to provide the best opportunities for vernacular preaching, the Mission had erected several small buildings called bazaar-chapels. These primitive structures were only a superior kind of huts; but they afforded convenient space, comfortable seats, and a roof to shelter the hearers. With a slight effort of the imagination, we may see the Missionary at work in one of these so-called chapels. Fancy a large building, with tiled floor and brick pillars bearing up the roof; no windows, neither glass nor frames, whether for window or door; the doors, large frames of bamboo and mat fitted to the openings between the pillars, which can be entirely removed, leaving two sides of the place completely open; a small railed platform a foot high, with a book-board in front, some benches for the accommodation of hearers, and altogether it looks something like a respectable ragged-school.

Let us visit the place at sunset, the time most favourable for getting a native congregation. The streets are then full of people, and they pass along the great thoroughfares, an endless stream—artisans, clerks, coolies, etc. The chapel is lighted with numerous lanterns. The Missionary arrives alone, or with a young colleague or native teacher. No audience waits his arrival, there is no one in the place. The junior begins to read some narrative from the New Testament; then, when a few have gathered in the building, the preacher stands up. He announces no text, but selecting some story from the sacred Word, he lingers over every particular of it, and then expounds, illustrates by parables and incidents, argues, explains, and enforces. Sometimes interruptions take place, the congregation will change many times during the hour's service, and the Missionary will adroitly repeat himself, varying the manner, but still dwelling on the main lesson to be enforced. The sermon concluded, a short prayer is offered, and then the people gather round the preacher to receive his tracts and Gospels.

The great suburb of Bhowanipore, on the south side of Calcutta, seemed to Mr. Lacroix to present a very desirable post in which to establish himself permanently, and in January, 1837, he resolved to rent a house there in an excellent situation, and to make it a settled sphere of labour. The district itself is thus described:—" In size it is a mile square, and the great road which runs down the centre of Calcutta divides it in half. A short distance beyond it are the temple and bazaar of Kalighat. The town of Bhowanipore consists of a compact mass of houses, interspersed, like all Indian towns, with small gardens containing lofty trees, with numerous spaces for ponds of water, called tanks, many of which are exceedingly shallow.

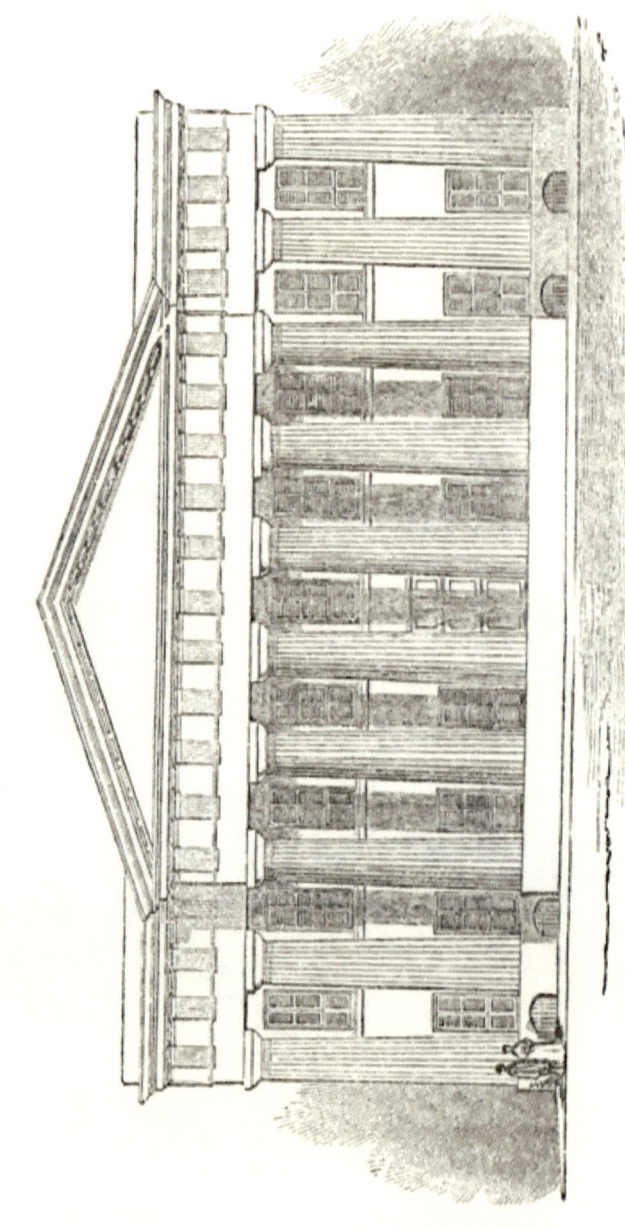

BHOWANIPORE MISSIONARY INSTITUTION, CALCUTTA.

The population numbers at least 20,000 persons, and within a radius of two miles, not including the Calcutta side, it must amount to 40,000. By far the largest proportion are Hindus, among whom are numerous families of wealth and respectability. The smaller streets and lanes which lead from the central road are crowded with brick houses; in other parts are seen dense masses of thatched and tiled cottages, such as form the staple habitations of the Bengal villages and towns.

" A small stream runs from the Hoogly ; and being considered a branch of the true Ganges, is daily bathed in by the inhabitants. In several places there are ghauts, or landing-places, where the sick may lie in sight of its sacred waters, and where the bodies of the dead may be burned."

For several years the Missionaries had preached and taught in this vast suburb, and there Mr. Lacroix now took up his permanent abode. A chapel and boarding-school were established; and so successful did the effort prove, that the London Missionary Society decided after a time to make Bhowanipore their head-quarters in Calcutta. Our Missionary's life at this period was exceedingly happy : his years passed steadily away in pursuits which, while indeed they caused anxiety, yet afforded him the purest satisfaction, in the enjoyment of excellent health, and surrounded by his family and numerous friends. Amongst his brethren his friendships were close and endearing, and he was bound to them by many ties of sympathy ; they were all, indeed, men of true excellence, " able for the work of the service of the house of God," and they all loved and esteemed him.

The systematic maintenance of these preaching efforts during a series of years could not but produce a variety of results. The orthodox Hindus generally avoid all collision with Missionaries. They remain concealed in sacred retirement, and rarely hear or read a word respecting Christianity, except from the unfavourable reports of relatives and friends. While they see Hindu society around them changing its views, and dread the consequences, they nevertheless rarely exert themselves to stem the rising tide. In the meantime the minds of the people have been gradually prepared for greater changes, and the frequent encounters with an idolatrous system, so indefensible at a thousand points as that of Hinduism, have done much to shake the confidence of its supporters; but the terrible domination of caste gives the system immense strength, and its influence must—humanly speaking—long maintain its hold. It tells well for the courtesy and general kindly feeling of the Hindus of Bengal, that although Mr. Lacroix was in constant intercourse with them for many years, arguing against the religion of their fathers, and urging the claims of an alien and despised faith, he was always treated with respect. Though frequently alone with them while travelling and visiting places in the interior, when he was completely at their mercy, he scarcely ever experienced the slightest rudeness.

On one occasion only was he threatened with

serious injury. He was preaching in a chapel in Calcutta one evening, when, without apparent cause or offence from him, a Hindu fanatic stole noiselessly behind him, and with a big stick aimed a blow at his head, endeavouring to knock him down. Providentially he turned at the moment, and the blow fell on his shoulder. The people immediately seized the man and called for the police. He stopped them. And then placing the man in front of the crowd, quietly said : "You have endeavoured to injure me severely, and I might justly have you punished; but the religion I preach teaches us to forgive our enemies. I therefore forgive you, and let you go away." Struck with the magnanimity of this action, the audience, Hindus as they were, at once shouted aloud, " Victory, victory to Jesus Christ ! "

Another branch of labour to which Mr. Lacroix attached great importance, was that of Missionary journeys undertaken for evangelising purposes. These he accomplished, together with other brethren, and kept journals full of interest and instruction, detailing in lively and graphic narrative the incidents that fell under his observation. Two of these journeys were made by land in the district of Burdwan, about sixty miles from Calcutta. A third, by land also, was made in the district of Moorshedabad, a hundred miles away. In two others he went by boat to Saugor Island, and in the sixth, also by boat, he visited the much-neglected districts of north-east Bengal, on the banks of the Berhampooter.

A few extracts from his journals will suffice to show

the kind of life he led at such times, and the singular sights he witnessed. When visiting Saugor, he says : " As we were talking with a knot of pilgrims who had gathered around us, a respectable-looking man exclaimed, 'What, are you here also ? When I am in the north of Calcutta I am sure to meet you ; and here you talk about Jesus Christ. When business takes me to the south of the city, there you are, again telling us about the same Jesus Christ. If I go to a distant village, I am sure to hear the same story ; and here, in the midst of the very jungles, I hear the name of Christ resounding in the solitude. You really seem to be everywhere.' "

Again he writes :—" After preaching, we tried to distribute tracts and Scriptures to those who could read ; but the pressure of the crowd made this no easy work. One man, more determined than the rest, pushed his way through, and coming on me from behind, seized me round the waist and lifted me in his arms. 'I want a book,' he cried. 'Let me down this moment; don't you see the stick in my hand, with which I can strike you?' 'You may strike me as much as you please,' he said ; 'but until I get one of your books, I will not put you on the ground.' Thereupon I promised him a book, upon which I was placed on *terra firma ;* and having given him two or three, he made a low salaam and departed, greatly pleased."

In several places the Missionaries, during these tours, had the satisfaction to meet with young men who, having received their education in the Calcutta institutions, had returned to their respective homes, and by their decidedly improved views and feelings, and by the knowledge they imparted to their idolatrous countrymen, were indirectly but effectually preparing the way for the Gospel. Such educated youths are now scattered all over the country, and are widely different beings from the generality of Hindus around them.

The natives of India are greatly given to superstitious observances, and pay much regard to omens. For instance, they consider it a very bad sign when they are leaving a place, or about to commence any undertaking, if the well-known Indian house-lizard utters its shrill cry, or when a person from whom they have just taken leave calls them back. These notions exert a complete thraldom over them. Mr. Lacroix relates that he once knew a Brahmin pundit give up a situation he had procured for him as Bengáli teacher to a young gentleman, merely because, having something further to say, he called him back after having taken leave.

An affecting illustration of the nature and influence of Hindu ideas was witnessed by him at the Saugor fair in January, 1846. "In the evening, after the labours of the day," he writes, "we took a walk through the whole mela, and conversed with many of the people. Having reached the extremity of the fair, near the sacred bathing-places, we observed a few solitary beings surrounding a funeral pile in full blaze. It was the funeral of an aged woman, a hundred and ten years old, we were told. The last duties were being performed by her son, grandson, and great grandson. None of them wept nor appeared to grieve; on the contrary, their faces looked joyful. We asked the reason for this, to which they replied that the present event was a most fortunate one; that their relative had reached a good old age; that she had died at the most auspicious time, viz., the time of the full moon, and on the most auspicious day, *i.e.*, the principal day of the mela, and at the most sacred spot in all Bengal, Gunga Saugor! What more could they desire? Her happiness was assured, and they would be regarded by all as a highly-favoured family."

Another incident related by Mr. Lacroix shows in a very practical way the notions current among the Hindus concerning transmigration. " Passing along the shore, we observed at the bathing-place a man with a couple of parrots. After completing his own ablutions he took the parrots, and one by one plunged them also into the salt water, much to their dissatisfaction. I asked why he did this. He replied, ' When I was leaving home I thought if bathing in the holy place will give me merit, why will it not benefit my birds, who, for some sins in a previous birth, have been condemned to their present condition? The merit of bathing here will advance them to a higher state of existence than their present one.' "

When journeying with Mr. Gogerly in 1833, he met with a striking proof of the perils to which Hindus at times expose themselves in the cause of their religion.

It refers to the salt-makers near the sea. " In order
to be preserved from beasts of prey, they present a
daily offering at the shrine of some deity, whose altar
is generally erected in the midst of the jungle. This
evening, having come to anchor in a place so exceedingly wild that we imagined no human being in his
right senses would attempt to put on shore, we were
astonished at perceiving two men running with all
their might along the beach, occasionally entering
the jungles for a few minutes, then emerging again
and pursuing their course with the greatest possible
speed. We were afterwards told that they were the
salt-makers going to present the evening sacrifice of
their party; and in order to prevent their being seized
by a tiger they kept constantly on the run ; the habits
of that animal, as they suppose, not allowing him to
seize on his prey whilst it continues in rapid motion.
There is no doubt, however, that many of these poor
infatuated beings are destroyed."

Occasionally the ministrations of these devoted men
met with a favourable reception, and a blessing evidently attended them. When Mr. Lacroix and Mr.
Weitbrecht were visiting the town of Chondrokona,
" the townspeople kept their word. From early in the
morning flocks of people came to our tents for books.
In the afternoon, so dense a crowd surrounded us that
we requested the people to proceed to a short distance,
where about 600 seated themselves in rows upon the
grass. These I addressed on the all-important subjects of eternity and salvation. It was a solemn
occasion the attention was intense. When I had

concluded the people would not stir, and were again
addressed by Mr. Weitbrecht and the catechist."

Again, when itinerating with Mr. M. Hill, in 1844,
he records a pleasing instance of earnest inquiry
after truth :—" When we had retired to our tent
about nine o'clock, we heard the steps of several
persons approaching, and found them to be those
of twelve men who had heard us preach in the
afternoon, and who were coming by night, like
Nicodemus of old, to inquire further concerning the
way of salvation. After conversing with them, Mr.
Hill gave them an account of his own conversion, and
told them of the dying expressions and happy de-
partures of several Christians which he had witnessed.
I concluded with prayer for the Divine blessing upon
them.   This was a most pleasing meeting, these poor
people evincing an evident hunger and thirst after
righteousness, and an earnest desire to know what
they should do to be saved.   The following morning
I was delighted to hear that one of our visitors, who is
a poet, had immediately composed a piece of poetry,
wherein he introduced the most important truths he
had heard.   This reminds me that at Doulta bazaar
also, one of the inquirers had put into verse the whole
of the thirteenth chapter of the 1st Corinthians, with
which he had been much struck, besides several of
the sermons I had preached there."

Many more interesting details of these Missionary
journeys are given in the Memoir, but these will suffice
to give our readers an idea of the work and of the
labourers.

CHAPTER IV.

CLOSING YEARS.

Visit to Europe —Lectures in Geneva—Return to Bengal—Journey to
the car festival of Jogonnath — Liberty of Conscience Act —
sorrows and sicknesses — The Missionary's sick-chamber —
"Tantus amor"—Mr. Lacroix's domestic life—Its charm over
his children and friends—Abiding in the Divine presence—The
life of faith and love — The Missionary's death-bed — "Perfect
peace."

IN 1842 Mr. Lacroix visited Europe. It was a
pleasant time of rest and recreation to him,
though the rest was only an exchange of one
kind of effort and labour for another. While
in England he revived old friendships and formed new
intimacies. His voice was heard in Exeter Hall and
elsewhere, but his principal work was among his native
cantons. After visiting the hallowed scenes of his
youth, he went to Basle, preaching there in German and
in French. In Geneva he gave a course of lectures on
Missions, which created an intense sensation. The
like of them had never been heard in those regions,
and multitudes thronged to listen to the eloquent and
impassioned orator. The concluding lecture was given
in the church of the Madeline, filled often, in years
of old, to hear the burning words of Farel, and no
such audience had been seen within those walls

since his day. These lectures were repeated in various continental towns, and in London. His visit to Europe was timely, and productive of much good.

The closing years of our Missionary were spent in India, the land of his adoption, from which he could not be induced again to depart when failing health seemed to make it desirable. He returned to his

HINDOO DEVOTEES.

beloved charge in Calcutta, to his preaching in the villages amid the waste of waters and in the rice-fields, and among the crowded bazaars and chapels in the cities. Occasionally, also, he undertook distant journeys. One of peculiar interest was made in 1849, at the invitation of the Orissa Missionaries, the especial object being to preach to the crowds of pilgrims gathered at Puri, on the sea-shore of the Bay of Bengal, on occasion of the annual Car Festival, and to arrange measures for laying the question of the public payments to Jogonnath before the Government, with a view to bring them to an end. On returning to Calcutta Mr. Lacroix gave a most impressive account of what he had witnessed. He described the sacred localities of Puri ; the broad way along which the idol-cars were drawn ; the filthy lanes and lines of shops ; the stone convents and lodging-houses for pilgrims, of which the town largely consists ; the sacred tanks where they bathe and the heavenly turtle feed ; the awful burning places, with their 300 bodies lying exposed to view, and beside them countless skulls and innumerable birds of prey ; the holy temple, with its tall tower, its massive walls, its jewel throne, on which the image stands, and the lion gate, by which the enclosure is entered ; and gave a complete picture of that world-celebrated place of pilgrimage. He described also the establishments of priests, their many offices, their oppressive tyranny, and enormous gains. He pictured the painful scene when, after many hours of weary waiting, in an awful storm of wind and rain, the 100,000 pilgrims at that time gathered in Puri, packed together in a dense mass, and crowding every point of view, at last beheld the long-desired face of the great idol, and saw him seated on his car. He exposed the gigantic evils attendant on these oft-repeated pilgrimages to the honoured shrine, and especially the fearful sacrifice of human life from fatigue and disease. Finally, he showed the evil of the connection between the Government and the temple, and its injurious influence as an encouragement to idolatry.

The Missionaries lost no time in urging this subject upon the attention of Government, and the last act of Lord Dalhousie's distinguished career in India was a final settlement of the question; the hateful and obnoxious payment was withdrawn, and this great stumbling-block to usefulness removed.

Many and varied were the affairs which absorbed the time and filled the heart of Mr. Lacroix during the remaining two years of his life. He passed through the terrible season of the Great Mutiny, and drank of the cup of trembling which fell to the portion of all our countrymen during those awful months of suspense. Many also were the sorrows that pierced his heart through the deaths of friends and beloved brethren. They passed away to their rest and reward, while he still continued at his post; but, alas! with greatly diminished powers. Sickness again and again brought him low, and he suffered from disease, while his days were weariness and his nights pain. How different from the sicknesses of Europe are the fierce maladies of the East, and what comforts surround the patient at home as compared with the lot of the poor Indian exile! The temperature stands above eighty degrees during eight months of the year. Behold a picture of the sick-chamber:—

"A lofty room, in which the venetians are partly and the glass windows wholly closed, to keep out the blinding glare and fiery heat; a light bedstead with cotton mattress for the bed, posts, tester, and curtains all removed; the broad punkah swinging to and fro overhead, and fanning the patient with mild movements of air already warm; bare white walls around, the beams and rafters of the flat roof all exposed; these are the externals of the sick-room. There he lies, in his white linen and wide Turkish drawers, upon the surface of the bed, not in it, watching the movements of the punkah as it swings; counting the folds of its deep frill, counting the rafters of the roof and following the movements of a lizard as, with sprawling feet, he creeps to the mosquitoes on the walls, and swallows them by dozens; or interested in that delightful cobweb in the corner, where a clever old spider, who has learned many 'dodges' in his long experience, draws into his cruel wiles the strongest flies. No cooling breezes, laden with fragrance, blow to him; dust streams in at every aperture, by day the air is fire, it is still hot by night. No pleasant sound of birds, no sound of the surf–roar fall on his ear; no trim maidens wait upon his comfort, speaking the tongue of his childhood, but grown men are his attendants, impassive though they be gentle, who speak a language every word of which reminds him that he is a stranger in a strange land."

" Tantus amor!" How great must be the love that constrains the faithful Missionary to abide, while life endures, subject to privations and distresses such as these, described with such pathos and life-like fidelity by one who has himself witnessed and endured them!

It is impossible to read these memorials without

feeling how brave and noble-hearted a man is here portrayed. His devotion to his work, his truly catholic and exalted spirit, his gentle bearing to the weak, and his chivalrous feeling for women, make us love and admire him. A truly charming sketch of his domestic life is given by his daughter, Mrs. Mullens.

"The sweetnesses of love," she says, "circled me in my early years. To these, and to the teachings of my beloved father, to his example, and more than all, to a silent influence he was wont everywhere to exert, do I owe much of the development of after years. . . . For an eminently practical man, as he was, his character was strangely tinged with a romantic mysticism, which, while his children were young, showed itself in the histories he chose for their amusement, and the lessons he inculcated. He loved to tell them of personal adventures in his own life, when God had marvellously interposed on his behalf. Once he had well-nigh been precipitated from a window, had not an invisible hand drawn him back. Once he had been saved from drowning in a 'most remarkable manner. Once he had fought with a boa-constrictor, and at another time had slept with snakes crawling about his room. Then again he had witnessed in broad daylight a terrible encounter in the jungle between a tiger and an alligator. There was not much personal danger, but it was an exciting story, full of thrilling romance, in which we were made to sympathise, as well by his spirited description as by a series of eight pencil sketches illustrative of the different stages of the fight, which he drew with his own hand, and sent to my mother from the scene of the adventure. He would tell us of the wonderful instincts of animals, and how they at times were instrumental in saving men from destruction; of the sufferings of the primitive Christians, how very near God was to them in their afflictions; and of the grand old myths of the ancient Greek mythology; so that from a very early age his children learned to believe that temporal things are strangely linked with those that are spiritually discerned; and these teachings prepared them in after life to receive his speculations on the world to come (ever in accordance with Holy Writ) almost in the light of a revelation. . . . [He hardly looked upon heaven as wholly beyond this life, but in some part essentially in it, as the root of the flower is within the mould. He saw that the tiniest wheel in the loud whirring machinery of time is some way indispensable to the final consummation of the soul's destiny in heaven, and to him this faith was no cold, intellectual creed, but something far more real. Not content with believing it in a general way, he used often to speculate on what would be the particular bearing in the next world of any event, sad or joyous, that might befal him here. The most trivial circumstances were chords to render complete the eternal harmony, which he was wont to say would constitute the happiness of heaven. Truly it was precious faith, for—

'It linked all perplexed meanings
Into one perfect peace.' "

We must not linger over the last scenes in this long and useful life; long—not in years, for he was but sixty years old—but in labours. During nearly forty years he lived in India, and there he died, in Calcutta, on the 8th of July, 1859. His end was perfect peace. When told it was approaching, he replied, "So much the better." He gently murmured, "All well;" "No doubt, no fear;" "Perfect peace;" "Jesus is near;" and so at last the silver cord was gently loosed, and the noble spirit took its flight.

All united to mourn his loss. His funeral was attended by almost every Missionary in the city, the Bishop and Archdeacon Pratt being present, with many of the Government chaplains. The native converts, members of his churches, students whom he had trained, and others to whom his ministry had been a blessing, followed in the train, and "made great lamentation over him."

Truly, he was a worthy member of that noble band of Missionaries who sleep in the soil of India. Who will not unite in the prayer that their faith may find many followers, that though dead they may still speak by the glorious story of their lives, and may the Church delight to hold their names in the everlasting remembrance promised by their Master!

WORSHIP OF ANCESTRAL TABLETS IN CHINA.

ROBERT MORRISON:

FIRST PROTESTANT MISSIONARY TO CHINA.

CHAPTER I.

PREPARING FOR THE WORK.

Dr. Morrison's account of his youth — Change of heart and life —
Diligent improvement of time—Concern for the sick and irre-
ligious—Systematic course of study—Joins Hoxton Academy—
Accepted by the London Missionary Society—Appointed to China
—Study of medicine and of the Chinese language—Dependence
upon God—Departure for China, *vid* America—Sojourn in New
York—Voyage to China—Arrival at Canton.

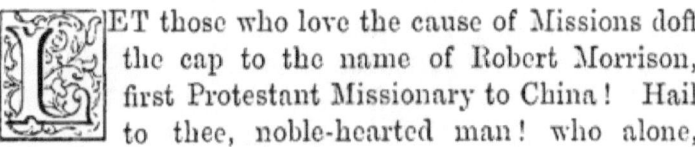

ET those who love the cause of Missions doff
the cap to the name of Robert Morrison,
first Protestant Missionary to China! Hail
to thee, noble-hearted man! who alone,
single-handed, didst enter on that giant task. Hail
to thee, man of commanding presence, and of gentle,
loving heart! Thou didst ever maintain the erect
air and confident step of one walking at liberty, yet
all the while trusting, not in thyself, but in God.

It will be well for us to look at the story of the life

of such a man as this. Perhaps some youth, conscious of Heaven-imparted power, and feeling the love
Divine within, may be animated to worthy deeds by
its perusal. The tale shall be told as much as
possible in his own words :—

"In the early part of my life," he says, "having
enjoyed the inestimable benefit of godly parents, I
was habituated to a constant and regular attendance
on the preached Gospel. My father was ever careful
to keep up the worship of God in his family, and
educated me in the principles of the Christian religion.
When somewhat older I attended the public catechizing of the Rev. J. Hutton, from whose instructions
I received much advantage. By these means my
conscience was somewhat enlightened and informed,
though as yet I lived without God in the world. It
was perhaps about 1798 (at the age of fifteen) that
I was awakened to a sense of sin, though I cannot
recollect any particular circumstance which led to it,
unless it were that I grew somewhat loose and pro-
fane, and more than once, being drawn aside by
wicked company, I became intoxicated. Reflection
upon my conduct occasioned me great uneasiness,
and I was brought to a serious concern about my
soul. The fear of eternal death compassed me
about, and I was led to cry mightily to God that
He would pardon my sins. It was then that I experienced a change of life and, I trust, a change of
heart also. I broke off from my former companions,
and gave myself to reading, to meditation, and to
prayer. Soon after this I joined in communion

with the church under the care of Mr. Hutton, and
also became a member of a praying society. Since
that time the Lord has been pleased to humble and
to prove me ; I have gradually discovered more of the
holiness and spirituality of the Divine law, and more
of my own unworthiness in the sight of God and of the
freeness and richness of sovereign grace. I have sinned
as I could; it is by the grace of God I am what I am."

From this period he seems to have commenced
a diligent improvement of his time. He learned a
system of short-hand writing, and kept a diary, in
which he recorded the incidents of his daily life and
the workings of his mind. This manual was carefully
preserved, and showed his early habits of piety and
vigilance. He had to labour from twelve to fourteen
hours a day at his father's business, so that his time
for study was not much, but he carefully turned to
account every opportunity. Early in the year 1800,
in order to secure a larger portion of quiet retirement,
he had his bed removed to his workshop, where he
would often carry on his studies till one or two o'clock
in the morning. He had also a little garden, in
which he spent his spare time in prayer and meditation, and when at work, his Bible or some other
book was placed open before him, that his thoughts
might be profitably engaged while his hands were
busily employed.

Even at that early age he often conducted the
domestic worship of his father's house, and was
actively engaged in visiting the poor and the sick,
with whom he read the Scriptures and prayed, and to

whose relief he every week assigned a portion of his
scanty earnings. In speaking of him at this period,
his sister narrated the following fact:—One of the
young people of the family was given to wicked ways,
to the great sorrow of Robert, who earnestly remonstrated with him. At length he made this
solemn appeal to the youth:—" Can you dwell with
eternal fire? Can you endure everlasting burnings?"
The young man was a sailor. He afterwards acknowledged that these awful words seemed constantly in
his ears, and ultimately were the means of his conversion. "Thus," said his sister, "did my beloved
brother go about doing good, and dispensing happiness to all around him from his youth upwards."

The year 1801 was an important era in his history,
as he then entered on a more regular course of study.
He thus mentions the fact in his journal:—"Friday,
June 19th. This day I entered with Mr. Laidler to
learn Latin; I paid 10s. 6d. the entrance money, and
am to pay a guinea per quarter. I know not what
may be the end; God only knows. It is my desire,
if He pleases to spare me, to serve the Gospel of
Christ as He shall give me opportunity. O Lord my
God, my whole hope is in Thee, and in Thee alone.
Lord, be merciful to me a sinner, and grant Thy
blessing with this attempt, if it please Thee."

This entry is very significant if taken in connection
with the statement made in his letter of application
to the London Missionary Society: in it he gives
the following particulars concerning the days of his
youth:—

" Some years ago, after alarming convictions of sin
and dread of the wrath to come, I was brought to
look to Christ Jesus for eternal salvation. Some time
later I experienced an earnest desire to serve the
Saviour, and to promote the spiritual interests of my
fellow-men in any way, however humble. It was then
I formed the design of engaging as a Missionary. It
was hardly a design—it was only a wish, an ardent
desire. I indulged it, though I saw no probability of
its ever being fulfilled. I was then in an obscure
situation, nearly 300 miles from town, and had no
one to encourage or second me. For a long time
I thought about it ; the crying necessity for Missionaries dwelt upon my mind. I conceived that
nothing was to be done without learning ; I therefore
saved a little money from what my father gave me, to
pay a teacher of Latin. Continuing in this manner
about fourteen months, my mother died, whereby one
hindrance to my leaving home was removed. Yet
my affectionate friends pressed me to stay with them ;
my father wept and prayed over me, but at last
consented. I endeavoured to weigh every side of the
case, sought direction of the Lord, and finally, in
His strength, determined to give myself up to His
service."

After his entrance at Hoxton Academy, his preference for Missionary service increased, and at
length, early in 1804, he applied to the Directors of
the London Missionary Society, in the letter from
which the above extract is taken. The result was
perfectly satisfactory to him ; he was accepted with-

out delay, and ordered to proceed to the Missionary
Academy at Gosport; "where," he says, "I was well
received by the students and Mr. Bogue; and this
commences a new period of my life."

After some deliberation it was determined that Mr.
Morrison should be appointed to China, as the scene
of his future labours, and his attention was at once
directed to the acquisition of the language. He believed that his destination to China was in answer
to prayer, for his expressed desire was that he might
be sent where the difficulties were the greatest, and to
all appearance the most insurmountable. He therefore cordially acquiesced in the decision, and from
that time had but one ruling object — the conversion
of China to the faith of Christ.

It was no easy matter to gain even a rudimentary
acquaintance with the Chinese tongue. In London
he was introduced to a young native of the Celestial
Empire named Yong-Sam-Tak, from whom he obtained his first insight into the language, and in
whom he found a specimen of the proud and domi-
neering temper for which his nation is so proverbial.
Having acquired the mode of writing Chinese, and
some degree of familiarity with the characters, the
young student commenced the transcription of a
MS. Latin and Chinese Dictionary, lent him by the
Royal Society; and of a Chinese MS. in the British
Museum, which was said to be a version of the New
Testament. It contained a harmony of the Gospels,
the Acts, and all the Pauline epistles excepting that
to the Hebrews. "These were," says Dr. Milne,

"originally the work of some of the Romish Missionaries in China : by whom or when they were com-
piled, has not been ascertained. Doubtless the just
merit of their authors will one day be reckoned to
them."

By indefatigable diligence the task of transcribing
both these MSS. was accomplished in a few months.
Mr. Morrison continued thus laboriously engaged in
various studies which it was thought would be of use
to him in his Mission, until the time of his departure
in January, 1807 ; and in addition to them all, he
found opportunity for preaching and for other efforts
to do good.

A very interesting and instructive account is given
of his habits and engagements during this time by the
excellent woman in whose house he lodged :—" His
strict economy of time was remarkable. He rose
very early, and improved every moment. A servant
girl in the family was by his instruction brought to
the knowledge of the Saviour, and shortly after died,
rejoicing in hope. Frequently he walked several
miles to visit the poor and afflicted, and to teach
children to repeat hymns and portions of Scripture.
. . . At noon it was his habit to retire for private
prayer, and as it was his practice to pray aloud,
it occasionally happened that he was overheard.
Mrs. Smith (his landlady) discovered this habit, and
frequently used to kneel at his chamber door to listen
to his fervent supplications. He continued thus to
pray aloud during his whole life, and many persons
in the more worldly circles of society, with whom he

was more or less called to associate in later years, have thereby had their attention arrested and their minds impressed with the reality and vital importance of religion."

In his diary of this period, under date October 25th, he thus writes:—"After my arrival in London I was exceedingly busy, running from one place to another, and attending to medicine and the Chinese language. The Lord, in much mercy, granted me health and strength for the good work. I mourn that I have not felt sufficiently my dependence upon God, and the absolute necessity of His blessing to give effect to my labours. O Lord! in mercy forgive me, and grant me that which I have not been solicitous enough to obtain."

At length the time for departure from England approached. His journal for 1807 begins with an entry to this effect, to which is added a solemn prayer for the Divine blessing and guidance. On the 31st January he embarked in company with two fellow-missionaries appointed to India, their route being *viâ* America. Their ship was detained for some time in the Downs, awaiting a favourable wind. On the night of Tuesday, February the 17th, a violent gale sprang up, which occasioned immense devastation among the shipping, so that a number of vessels went ashore, and some sank. Serious apprehensions were entertained respecting the safety of the Missionaries, but they were signally preserved. Out of a large fleet anchored in the Downs at the time, their ship—the *Remittance* — was the only one which was able to

pursue her voyage. The passage was a very pro-
tracted, and in some respects painful and disastrous
one, as through the prevalence of contrary winds they
did not arrive at New York till the 20th of April,
having been at sea one hundred and nine days.

The few weeks spent by Mr. Morrison in America
were always remembered by him with pleasure, and
proved the commencement of many a holy friendship
which death alone terminated. The gentleman at
whose house he stayed in New York afterwards drew
up an account of his visit, from which the following
extracts are taken :—

" Dr. Morrison visited this country in 1807, on his
way to China, and brought letters of introduction
to the lamented Dr. Mason of this city. He was
accompanied by Messrs. Gordon and Lee, who, with
their wives, were sent out to Hindostan. I shall
never forget the evening on which the whole company
were brought to my house. The appearance of a
Missionary was then a rare thing, and still more so
that of a company of Missionaries. The countenance
of Morrison bore the impress of the effect of grace on
a mind and temperament naturally firm and somewhat haughty. His manner was serious and thought-
ful, breathing a devoted piety. The interview was
solemn but pleasant, and when at the close we bowed
our knees in prayer, the tears which fell on every
side evinced the reality of that Christian communion
which unites all who love the Lord Jesus Christ.

" In a day or two after, Mr. Morrison was seized with
sudden indisposition. As I sat beside his bed he took

my hand, and in language which told of a mind at ease and prepared for every event, expressed his resignation to the Divine will. After urging me to greater devotedness in the cause of the Saviour, he closed with these words, which I afterwards found were ever on his lips : ' Dear brother, look up—look on.'

"As the notice had been very short, he was placed for the first night in our own chamber. Beside his bed stood a little crib, in which slept my little child. On awaking in the morning she turned, as usual, to talk to her mother. Seeing a stranger where she expected to find her parents, she roused herself with a look of alarm; but, fixing her eyes steadily on his face, inquired, ' Man, do you pray to God ? ' ' Oh, yes, my dear,' was the reply, ' every day : God is my best friend.' At once reassured, the little girl contentedly laid her head on her pillow and fell fast asleep. She was ever after a great favourite with him.

"Having unpacked his books, he showed me two folio volumes in MS., written with his own hand. On inquiring how he learned to write the character, he related his introduction to Yong-Sam-Tak, and the circumstances of his tuition by him. . . .

"There was nothing of pretence about Mr. Morrison. His manners were plain, simple, and unceremonious; his fellow-missionaries looked up to him as a father, resorted to his room for prayer, and took his advice on all matters. He showed less tenderness of spirit than they did. His piety had the bark on ; theirs was still in the green shoot. His mind stood firm, erect, self-

sustained; theirs clung to it for support, and gathered
under its shadow for safety. He was deeply anxious to
render himself without charge to the Christian public,
and this desire was in a remarkable manner gratified.
So eminent were his attainments soon found to be in the
Chinese language, that shortly after he reached China
he received an appointment under the East India
Company, as their translator of official documents,
with a salary of £500 a year. I will only add a brief
account of the parting scene as he left us for his
destination. On the morning he sailed, his Missionary companions assembled in his room, and had a
most solemn interview—their last in this world. We
then set out together to the counting-house of the ship-
owner. When all business matters were arranged, this
person, who evidently regarded Morrison as a deluded
enthusiast, said to him, with a grin of suppressed
ridicule, "And so you really expect, sir, to make an
impression on the idolatry of the great Chinese empire?' 'No, sir,' said Morrison, with unwonted stern-
ness; 'I expect that God will.'

"Descending to the wharf, we took our last farewell
as he stepped into the boat that was to carry him to
the ship. He said little, he moved less; his imposing
figure and solemn countenance were motionless as
a statue; his mind was evidently full—too full for
speech; his thoughts were with God, and he seemed
regardless of all around him."

What were his secret feelings at this sad hour of
parting, we are permitted to see in the following entry
of his journal: "At sea, on board the *Trident*,

May 22.—On the 12th inst. I parted with my dear brethren and sisters. It was more painful than anything that preceded it. The Lord in mercy be with them to the end! In America the affectionate regard shown us for our Master's sake was truly pleasing. Oh, how unworthy I felt myself! I now feel myself to be so; I am less than the least of all saints. I abhor myself, and repent in dust and ashes."

Again, under date May 21, being Lord's day, he writes: "More fully than at any former period I now perceive the force of that exclamation, 'How amiable are thy tabernacles, O Lord of hosts, my King and my God!' Happy should I be in joining with you in a song of praise to Jesus our Redeemer. I do not, however, keep my harp perpetually hung upon the willows. Though I have none to join their voice with mine, I sing with those who join me in spirit on earth, and with the ransomed around the throne in glory. . . . May the Lord be in an especial manner with every isolated Missionary! Comforting is the promise, 'I am with you alway;' and He is faithful who has promised."

During the voyage he laboured incessantly at his studies. Thus he writes: "From morning to midnight I am engaged. I take great pleasure in learning the Chinese, for which purpose the books I obtained in London are highly serviceable, and I by no means exclude poor Sam's assistance. I feel my heart much knit to him, despite all his obstinacy and contempt of me."

On the 29th of August the voyagers entered the

Chinese Sea; and on the 8th September, writing from the American Factory, Canton, our Missionary says : "By the good hand of God I am brought at length to the place of my appointed labour. Last evening I arrived here. The noise and bustle amidst the working of ships, and the rowing of hundreds of boats, in which were thousands of Chinese shouting and calling to each other, were extreme. About eight o'clock, as I passed among their boats, I saw thousands of little splinters of wood, similar to matches, lighted up in honour of their imaginary divinities. I said to myself, 'Oh, whatever can be done with these ignorant yet shrewd and imposing people?' But what were our fathers in Britain, what were Hottentots?" . . .

TEMPLE IN THE ROCK, CHINA.

CHAPTER II.

Under American protection—The Sabbath and the Chinese—Visit to a heathen temple—Removal to Macao—Marriage—Appointed translator to the Hon. East India Company—A settled home—Sedulous study of the Chinese dialect—Afflictions and bereavement—Arrival of Rev. W. Milne—His expulsion by Government, and removal to protection of the American flag at Canton.

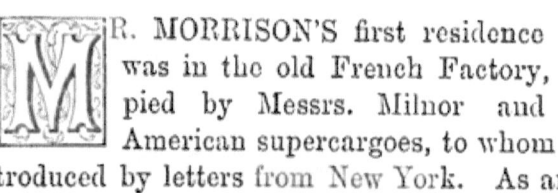

R. MORRISON'S first residence at Canton was in the old French Factory, then occupied by Messrs. Milnor and Bull, the American supercargoes, to whom he was introduced by letters from New York. As an Englishman he dared not be known, and it was as an American that he remained. A few weeks after his arrival he wrote to his brother, and thus speaks of his studies and his circumstances: "I am now fully engaged in the study of the Chinese language. A professed Christian of the Romish Church is my chief instructor. He is connected with the Missionaries of Peking. You know the Romish clergy have been in China betwixt two and three hundred years. Since I came here the American gentlemen have treated me with great kindness, and I have lived in the family of one of their number. The Chinese government does not allow foreigners to live with its own people. Sir

George Staunton, to whom I was introduced by letter from Sir Joseph Banks, has behaved in a most friendly manner.* My health, since I left my native land, has been pretty good. The thermometer often stands here at 90°, 92°, and even 94°, which renders a person exceedingly uncomfortable." . . .

We learn from other letters that, after a short time, he provided himself with two small rooms in the basement story of the factory, where he studied, ate, and slept, adopting the habits and even the dress of the natives, with whom, for the sake of his great object, he almost exclusively associated. So great was his labour and so sparing his diet, that in the course of a very few months he had seriously injured his health and well-nigh endangered his life. Anxious to gain the attention of his Chinese domestics and assistants to the claims of the Sabbath-day, he set them the example by abstaining from all his usual studies, and devoting its hours more immediately to the worship of God. He gathered them together and engaged them in reading the MS. Harmony of the Gospels which he had transcribed, and, as well as he could, instructing them and getting them to join him in singing and prayer. This practice he continued to the close of his life, giving to his services as near a resemblance as he could to those of the British churches, and the effort was blessed to himself and to others.

In his diary there are constant references to this subject, and touchingly do these entries evince his holy

* This kindness laid the foundation of a close intimacy, which was maintained through life.

faith and love. Only by perpetual communion with Heaven could his soul be kept in peace. On the 13th of January (1808) he writes: "I had a particularly comfortable manifestation of the Divine presence in prayer accompanied by perusal of the forty-eighth Psalm, 'God is known in Zion's palaces for a refuge ;'" and, comfortable truth, 'He is known for a refuge to the ends of the earth.' His greatness, goodness, purity, and grace impressed my mind more strongly than for a long time before, and, said I, 'This God shall be my God, even to death.' He is now to me instead of father and mother, brother, sister, and friend. In the midst of disappointments, sickness, imprisonment, or death, I am persuaded He can make me happy. Whence, O Lord, this manifestation? I rejoice with trembling. . . .

"January 27th.—I walked out to the temple of Pih-te-Poosa, 'the great northern deity,' where was a large concourse of worshippers, and which was filled with the smoke of their offerings. They brought in small baskets of fowls, pork, vegetables, and fish, which, after the prostrations were over, they took away with them. They had, moreover, candles, fragrant matches, and gilt paper. These were consumed, and wine poured into a trough before the altar, or thrown on the ground. Several of the worshippers muttered a prayer on their knees, and others, while standing, took up a crooked piece of wood, like a cow's horn divided lengthwise, threw it down again and again, till it fell in a posture they wished, or thought ominous of good. There is nothing social in their worship, nor any respect shown by those who are not engaged. One is praying, another talking or laughing, a third washing utensils, &c. As in every idolatrous country, there appear to be favourite deities, as well as particular times for the worship of one in preference to another. Hence many of the temples are quite deserted, while this was crowded, smoked, and smutted ! "

A change being judged necessary for his health, Mr. Morrison went, in the month of June, to Macao: from whence he wrote to his father as follows :—

" Macao, where I now am, is eighty or one hundred miles from Canton. It is a small island under the Portuguese. I came hither by invitation of Mr. Roberts, the chief of the English Factory. He and other gentlemen have offered to assist me in the prosecution of one part of my object, viz., the compilation of a dictionary of the Chinese language, preparatory to attempting a translation of the Scriptures. They offer me a house here and at Canton. The rent of houses in which Europeans live is extremely high. The English here are the most wealthy, and have great influence. The place belongs to the Roman Catholics, and were it not for the countenance of the English, I should not be permitted to continue."

At the end of three months, his health having improved, he returned to Canton ; but on account of some political circumstances, all Englishmen were ordered to leave that city suddenly, in the month of November, and he forthwith returned to Macao, to the house which he had previously occupied. This second visit was connected with events of the greatest interest in his personal history. These were his marriage, and his official relation to the Honourable Company's Factory as Chinese translator and secretary. His journal and letters show him indefatigably engaged in his studies. " My time," he says, " so far from hanging heavy on my hands, seems to fly faster than ever it did. Morning, noon, and night, I have laboured at the Chinese language. . . . . I must here, once for all, say that Yong-Sam-Tak has behaved thus far extremely well, and has helped me to the utmost of his power. I have mentioned going to Macao: I purpose, if the Lord will, to live there in preference to Canton. House rent is not so high, and there is more liberty to go out for the benefit of health, as well as to receive Chinese and to pursue my studies."

Accordingly, we find him commencing the year 1809 at Macao. There he enjoyed Christian society in the family of Dr. Morton, a gentleman from Ireland, to whose daughter, Mary, he was married on the 20th of February. On the very day of their marriage, the proposal of the East India Company's Factory to appoint him their translator was made. Without hesitation he thankfully accepted the offer, which he looked upon as a plain indication of the path of duty. By this appointment his continuance at his post was rendered secure. So great had been the difficulty of retaining his residence at Macao, that he was on the point of removing to Penang, and the preparations were actually made for his departure.

Upon this circumstance the great usefulness of Dr. Morrison's life turned, nor can we, looking upon the matter from a Christian point of view, fail to recognise and acknowledge the hand of God in this timely and unexpected interposition of His Providence.

Thus, for the first time since leaving England, there seemed for our Missionary a prospect of home and its joys. Cheerfully and with glad heart he betook himself, with even greater diligence—if that were possible —to his work. Writing some months after his marriage, he says: " The Portuguese Roman Catholics at Macao do not do anything violent against us. Mrs. Morrison speaks Portuguese, but has no neighbourly intercourse with any except one family. Her father and mother have left China for England. We cannot take part in the gay amusements of our countrymen, or join much in their society; a distant civility is all that subsists. We have a lonely, solitary house. My Mary longs much for Christian companions and the ordinances of the Lord's house. We greatly desire to have a few from amongst the heathen to have fellowship with us. Be thankful; great are your privileges — great are ours, too, though bereaved of much that you enjoy." . . .

Respecting his studies, he says: "My application to the language has been unremitted. I have now in the house a regular schoolmaster, who has conducted me through part of the classical books of the Chinese. I have now read to the middle of the third of the celebrated four books of the great oracle of this empire, Kung-foo-tze (Confucius). These have much that is excellent, and some things erroneous. Taken altogether, they are, of necessity, miserably defective. He appears to have been an able and upright man; rejected for the most part the superstitions of the times, but had nothing that could be called religion to supply their place. On the relative duties between man and man, he found himself able to reason and decide; respecting the gods he was unable to judge, and thought it insulting to them to agitate the question, and therefore declined it."

During the following two or three years Mr. Morrison pursued his laborious occupations, happy in these and in the affection of his wife, who, he says, "laboured much with me in the study of the Chinese." One trial there was connected with his engagement to the British Factory; it necessitated his absence from his family every year for nearly six months, during which his presence was required at Canton. Often there were stormy scenes to be encountered there. The alleged murder of a Chinaman at one time brought on a discussion with the Government. "I obtained great *éclat*," he writes to a friend, "by the examination of the witnesses; every one being astonished that I could so soon write the language and converse in the Mandarin and vulgar dialects. . . . Through the summer I had frequent conferences with the Mandarins. They are extremely haughty, overbearing, and clamorous; sometimes three or four of them will speak at the same time, and as loud as if they were scolding. A want of truth is the prevailing feature in the Chinese character; hence mutual distrust, low cunning, and deceit. . . . . I want some humble, persevering fellow-labourer." . . .

No wonder he felt this want. In addition to all that came to him "from without," he was called to endure domestic grief and anxiety. His gentle Mary pined away under a mysterious malady affecting the nervous system, and oppressing both mind and body. Her life was despaired of, and the infant son to whom she gave birth breathed but a few hours. "Great is my grief," said the sad husband, "on account of the sufferings of my poor helpless Mary."

There was at that time no proper burying-place for the English. It was necessary to find a spot to be set apart for this sad use. In China there are no enclosed cemeteries, the sides of hills being the favourite sites. Accordingly, the grave was dug on the top of a hill at the northern extremity of Macao. The Chinese at first opposed the interment of the child, but afterwards yielded.

The life of the mother was spared, but her health was never fully restored. Her husband's heart, so susceptible of joy and sorrow, was often pierced with anguish on her account, but in holy resignation he said, "It is the Lord; let Him do as seemeth Him good." His diary shows how indefatigably he sought to instruct his pagan domestics, and others to whom he had access, in the knowledge of salvation. He yearned after the happiness of seeing them converted and brought to the Saviour. Very touching is the following entry, dated April 26, 1812 : "On the 23rd we left the house in which we had resided the last

8

three years, and entered on that in which we now are. I implore the Divine blessing. O my God, make Thy handmaid and me entirely devoted to Thy holy pleasure. Help us to serve Thee with humble, penitent, and cheerful hearts. O let us not turn aside to vanity. Help me to be a good Missionary of Jesus Christ. I would be wholly devoted to Thy service, and make all subservient to Thy glory. O God, have mercy on me, and forgive all my sin. Prepare us both for death. My God, in mercy hear!"

The desire expressed by Mr. Morrison for a companion and helper was now fulfilled, and a truly devoted and excellent man was he, whose name will ever be associated with that of his senior colleague. Mr. Milne, accompanied by his wife, reached Macao on the 4th July, 1813.—"The event was announced just as we (Mrs. Morrison and I) were about to sit down at the Lord's table, it being the first Sabbath-day in the month. Of course we were much agitated. The mingled feelings of hope, joy, and fear which were felt, cannot be described. A companion in labour, whose arrival for six long years I had been wishing, had actually set foot on shore in this remote land. My Mary, who had longed for a companion, was overjoyed at receiving Mrs. Milne—but, would they be allowed to remain, or be driven away?" Ah! that was the question; and it was soon answered in the peremptory order for Mr. Milne's departure. "In vain I entreated the Governor, *on one knee*, not to persist in this order: his answer was conclusive— 'My own court, the senate, and the bishop, require

that he be sent away; no Europeans but those connected with the Companies can remain here.' "   Accordingly the poor ejected Missionary—leaving his
wife with Mrs. Morrison—proceeded to Canton, there
to pursue the same course as his predecessor had
done, to fag away, in solitary estate, at the terribly
difficult language.   Thus he expressed his opinion
respecting it : " To acquire the Chinese is a work for
men with *bodies* of brass, *lungs* of steel, *heads* of oak,
hands of spring-steel, *eyes* of eagles, *hearts* of apostles,
memories of angels, and *lives* of Methuselah ! "

CHAPTER III.

THE BURDEN AND HEAT OF THE DAY.

Translation of the New Testament—Missionary journey of Mr. Milne
to Java, Malacca, and Penang—Determination to establish a
Mission in Malacca—Removal thence of Mr. Milne, and founding
of the Ultra-Ganges Mission — Result of ten years' Missionary
labour — " Brother, faint not ! "—Mrs. Morrison's illness and
return to Europe — Alone again in China—Created Doctor of
Divinity—The Missionary's watchword—Death of Mrs. Morrison
and of Dr. and Mrs. Milne — The Mission College at Malacca —
Its beneficent influence—Ignorance of the Chinese priests and
debasing character of pagan worship.

R. MORRISON had now, by his own unas-
sisted labour, completed the translation of
the New Testament, and at the commencement of 1814 he had the satisfaction of
sending a copy of the work to the Bible Society.   In

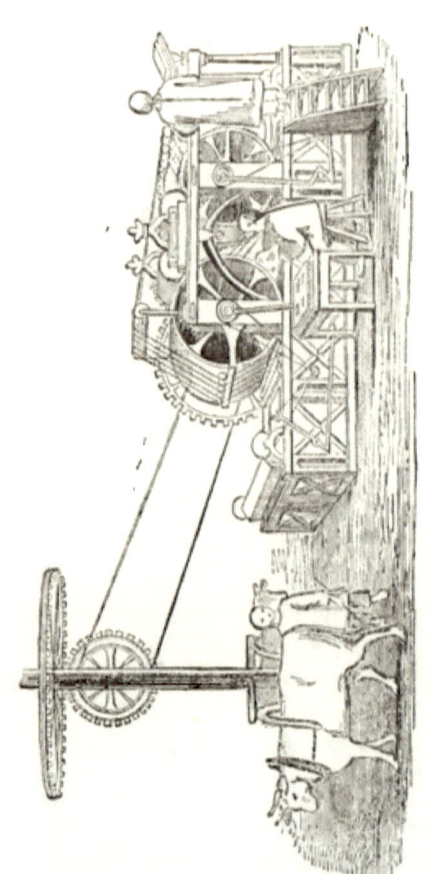

PRINTING THE CHINESE SCRIPTURES.

his official letter he says :—" Allow me to notice that
I give this translation to the world not as a perfect
one.   That some sentences are obscure, that some
might be better rendered, I suppose is a matter of
course in every translation made by a foreigner.   All
who know me will believe in the honesty of my inten-
tions, and I have done my best. . . . The Gospels,
the closing Epistles, and the Book of Revelation are
entirely my own ; the middle part of the volume is
founded on the work of some unknown individual,
whose pious labours were deposited in the British
Museum, and I feel great pleasure in recording the
benefit I first derived from the labours of my unknown predecessor. The Chinese are a docile, reason-
able people.   They receive advice, instruction, and
books, generally with apparent thankfulness, scarcely
ever with rudeness."   Great was the satisfaction felt
by the friends of the London Missionary Society at
the completion of this work, about which their indefatigable Missionary had been so long engaged, and
they "thanked God, and took courage."

In the preceding chapter we have seen how Mr.
Milne was ordered away from Macao and had gone to
Canton, where his colleague soon joined him, and
during some months assisted him in the acquisition
of the language.   They then consulted together on
the best means for carrying on the objects of the
Mission in future, and the result of their deliberation,
as Mr. Morrison relates it, was that "Mr. Milne should
make a Missionary tour to Java, Malacca, and Penang,
to distribute the New Testament amongst the Chinese

settlers in those places, and to endeavour to obtain a
residence for the whole or a part of this Mission. He
will also endeavour to ascertain the facility of printing at Java. . . . The expense of the journey will
be considerable, but the object is important—indeed,
unavoidable; we seem necessitated to act thus." The
spirit of the Missionary was at this time specially
depressed by the incessant troubles occasioned by the
jealousy of the Government. "It was hinted," he
says, "that my Missionary duties ought to give way,
and that, in fact, my serving the Company and being
a Missionary are not compatible with each other. If
this be pushed much further a separation must take
place. The end I have at heart would perhaps be
better answered by my removing to Malacca or Java.
I have advised Mr. Milne to go down there and
prepare a settlement."

The issue of these plans was that the junior Missionary, with his family, went to Malacca to establish
a branch of the Mission there; this was selected as
the most desirable place on account of its nearness to
China, and because of the ready intercourse it commanded with the Chinese Archipelago, as well as with
India, ships to both places frequently touching there.
The climate was healthy and the authorities favourably disposed. It was accordingly chosen for the
purpose of a central station, for Missionaries of different countries, and the seat of a seminary where the
Chinese, Malay, and other Ultra-Ganges languages
might be cultivated.

Mr. Milne was successful in carrying out this project, having obtained a grant of land from the Dutch Government, and from this time until the period of his death the two colleagues mutually co-operated in the formation and management of the " *Ultra-Ganges Mission.*"

In a letter from Canton, dated September 4, 1817, Mr. Morrison thus reviewed the progress of the Mission : "Ten years have this day elapsed since I first landed on these shores. God has been gracious, and has borne with our infirmities, and has, in part, granted us the wish of our hearts, and blessed be His holy name. . . . Our progress may seem small, but we should remember the obstacles which stood in our way : our knowledge of China was very limited, our hopes of a residence small, our interest nothing. . . . Your Mission to this country now possesses considerable knowledge of the land, its people, and its language. The New Testament is rendered into Chinese, and has been, in part, circulated, and will we trust produce salutary results. An important and promising branch of the Mission has been established at Malacca, and from thence, by means of the press, Divine truth has been diffused among many of the Chinese. Two persons have renounced idolatry and professed faith in our Lord Jesus. . . . Let us not be ungrateful ; brethren, faint not ! "

A few extracts from his private letters show how weighty were his public duties, and how grievous his domestic trials. His wife and family had been sent to England on account of the increasing illness of Mrs. Morrison, and he thus was left solitary to labour at his most laborious task, the compilation of the Chinese dictionary, together with his other numerous engagements. Writing to his mother-in-law, under date January 18, 1818, after speaking of his health, he says: "I wish to commit all my ways and the concerns of my family to a gracious Providence. I am very solitary here, and being so very much occupied in writing, I am often very weary of it. Writing the dictionary is such very dry work, and translating it is not much better; one's mind is kept so much applied to mere words. The deprivation, however, is all in a good cause. I have become much of a recluse. I very rarely go to the Company's or anywhere else to dine. I have the same dish week after week — *Irish stew and dried roots*—which I eat with Chinese chopsticks. I am writing from seven in the morning till nine or ten at night. . . . Would that I always felt duly grateful to our gracious Saviour for His great mercy toward me and mine. We are going to erect a college at Malacca for the study of Chinese literature. I hope it will tend to the furtherance of the Gospel."

Mr. Morrison's labours had by this time made his name one of note on the continent of Europe as well as in England, and his correspondence was sought by the most distinguished literary characters of the day. The University of Glasgow unanimously created him Doctor in Divinity, and the London Missionary Society, desirous to conduce to his comfort, proposed his return home for a time; but "*One thing I do*," was the motto and the watchword of the Missionary. "I should like much to visit Europe," he said; "but wishes and the lesser duties must give way to the greater."

The translation of the Old Testament was completed in 1819. Dr. Milne's part in it was comparatively small, but his noble-hearted associate called the whole work "Morrison and Milne's Bible." Between the two there subsisted the most unreserved confidence; they united their energies in promoting the one great object of their lives; they were true "brothers in heart." Alas! the union was of short duration. Dr. Milne died in the month of June, 1822, in the thirty-seventh year of his age. He was at Malacca, and the tidings of his death reached Dr. Morrison a month later, while engaged in his solitary labours at Macao. He thus announced the event in his official letters: "Canton, October 24th, 1822.— On the 2nd June last it pleased Almighty God to remove from our lower world my lamented friend and colleague, Dr. Milne. He died of pulmonary consumption. A more zealous evangelist never existed. Few ever excelled him in piety and devotedness. By the grace of God he was what he was. He still lives in the numerous tracts which he was enabled to print and to distribute."

Beloved and devoted man! His zeal was indeed great and his labours "more abundant," despite the depressing influence of bodily weakness and infirmity. One passage from a letter he wrote shortly after his arrival in China is so striking and characteristic that I give it here: "This is a vast benighted country;

we stand on the borders of it like men on the banks of the vast sea; we see only a little, and dare not venture in but an inch or two. The city of Canton is like the New Jerusalem only in one thing; that *strangers* are not permitted to enter. I have once peeped in at the gate, and I hope yet to enter. A few days ago I went to the top of a little hill, to view this land. I trust it is a land of promise! My thoughts were, 'O that God would give this land to the Churches, that we, their messengers, might walk through the length and breadth of it, to publish the glory of His salvation!' The Chinese are a civilised and industrious people, but their land is full of idols."

Dr. Morrison's private reflections on the loss of his friend are very touching: "Yesterday (July 4th) nine years ago William and his wife were received by me and my Mary at Macao. Three of the four—all under forty—have been called hence, and have left me alone and disconsolate! But good is the will of the Lord. They all died in the faith and hope of the Gospel; all died at their post. They have left their bodies in the field of battle. They were faithful unto death in their Saviour's cause. Happy am I that none of them deserted it. Even my poor afflicted Mary came back to die in China." This is indeed the true-hearted spirit of the Missionary. All honour to these brave warriors of Christ. *Tantus amor!* How great their love.

The two friends had lost their wives under very similar circumstances, and about the same time. They shared in one another's labours, joys, and sorrows. Together they wept over their dead, and when Milne left his orphan children with scant provision, Morrison adopted his eldest boy and educated him with his own.

There is something truly pathetic in the expression of his feelings when thus bereft of lover and friend—alone in the land of pagan darkness. He writes to his mother-in-law: "To the death of my beloved Mary is now added that of dear William. I do not repine, but I have wept much on being left alone and desolate, and I have wept over my sinfulness. I would my heart were more set on heavenly things. I desire to be found actively engaged in my proper duties, waiting the coming of my Lord. In consequence of Milne's death I am going down to visit Malacca, and have deferred my intended visit to England. I have now been fifteen years in this country, and one-half of those years quite alone."

The College at Malacca, which engaged so much of the attention of Dr. Morrison, and was the scene of his colleague's labours, was visited about 1829 by a gentleman, who wrote an account of it, a few extracts from which will interest the reader.

After stating that the religious instructions of Dr. Milne, for many years principal of the College, had been blessed to the conversion of several of the printers and students, among whom should be especially noticed the faithful evangelist Leang-Afa, whose sincerity stood the test of persecution, and who continued faithful to the truth, the writer goes on to say: "The object of the institution is the instruction of Chinese boys, who would otherwise receive no teaching at all : they are taught their own and the English language, and the elements of useful science. No compulsory means are used with a view to conversion. Such of them as evince any disposition to become Christians receive every encouragement ; if otherwise, they still acquire a useful and moral education. When I visited the College it contained upwards of thirty students. Nearly every one of the boys read with fluency the Bible in Chinese and English, many of them wrote elegantly in both languages, and several were proficients in arithmetic, geography, and general history. . . . Many Chinese, educated here, have entered into various pursuits in life, and been employed by merchants, and as clerks in public offices; and their superior education, in addition to their good conduct, has specially qualified them for such situations. I went into the shop of a Chinese retail merchant at Malacca, which was conspicuous for its well-ordered neatness. He said to me, in the most correct idiom, 'I have had the good fortune to be educated at the College, under Dr. Milne, for whose memory I have the greatest respect, and I assure you I have derived great advantage from his instruction.' On my asking if he followed up his studies, he said he was very fond of English reading, and that he generally wrote down passages which pleased him. He then, from a drawer in his Chinese cabinet, took out a thick MS. volume. Amidst receipts for various chemical mixtures, as well for cookery as medicine, were extracts from Confucius and English standard writers. Among others, I saw Cowper's well-known

CHINESE SCHOOL.

lines to his mother's picture, which he had got by
heart, thinking them so beautiful. This was a
Chinese retail shopkeeper, a dealer in tea, tobacco,
and snuff. I afterwards learned that he was frugal,
industrious, and prosperous. He said he did not
mean to go to China. 'I dislike,' he added, 'its
arbitrary government.' How much must ideas and
feelings such as these, diffusing themselves however
gradually through the public mind, tend to dispel the
prejudice of ignorance, and to break down the great
wall of Chinese jealousy and restriction."

Before closing this chapter, I will give a striking
passage from a letter of Dr. Morrison's, describing
the religious services of the Chinese. It was written
during a journey taken by him through six of the
provinces of China, in the suite of the British Embassy. "I am now writing," he says, "from a temple
at Tien-tsin, in which are upwards of one hundred
priests, and as many idols. About fifty priests
worship, with morning and evening prayers which
occupy nearly forty minutes, images of Buddah.
There are three images placed on a line; before
these the priests burn papers, offer incense, and
recite prayers; sometimes kneeling and repeating
over and over again the same invocation, and sometimes putting the forehead to the ground in token of
adoration, submission, and supplication. Day after
day and year after year this is gone through; but
they never associate the people of every rank and
age, to deliver instructions to them. They never
preach or teach orally; occasionally they inculcate

piety to the gods, and the practice of morality, through the press. They are generally illiterate and un-instructed themselves, and are mere performers of ceremonies. The multitudes of people in this country are truly, in a moral and religious view, as sheep without a shepherd. The general principles of our religion give a tone of elevation and dignity to the human mind which is not felt here. The idea often suggested, when associating for worship, that all earthly distinctions are comparatively nothing, raises to a manly feeling the hearts of the poorest and most abject. How different the system of paganism which prevails here. The contrast struck me very forcibly during Divine service in this very temple, as performed by the chaplain of the embassy. We have heard much here about sitting or not sitting in the presence of great men. The Chinese carry their objections to a ridiculous extent, to persons sitting in the presence of persons inferior in rank to themselves, and on no occasions do superiors dispense with this usage. Hence, when looking round the congregation during the sermon, and seeing English noblemen, gentlemen, officers, merchants, soldiers, and servants, all sitting in the same room, and listening to the same instruction, the idea mentioned above occurred with the greater force."*

* The above was written in one of the temples, and Dr. Morrison thus explains the fact. "Temples in China, like religious houses on the continent of Europe, are often employed as temporary inns by travellers; Government also turns them to this purpose. Hence it is that the temple from which I address you is made the residence of the British Ambassador."

CHAPTER IV.

CLOSING YEARS.

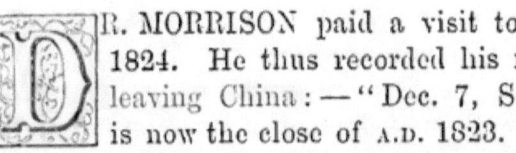R. MORRISON paid a visit to England in 1824. He thus recorded his reflections on leaving China: — "Dec. 7, Sunday.—This is now the close of A.D. 1823. I arrived in China in 1807. Sixteen years have I lived in that land; a country full of idols; a land in which the Creator is forgotten and unknown, as much as in any part of the earth. Satan here keeps his throne, but the duties of the second table of the law are still discerned with considerable precision. Justice and equity between equals are understood, but superiors, as fathers, elders, and magistrates, tyrannize much over the inferior relations of life. My public life in China has been a period of great industry: my domestic life has been a chequered scene of pleasure and of pain, but even the painful circumstances are very dear to my recollection. I have some misgivings or apprehensions that I may not live to return and be buried in China, but, all circumstances con-

9

sidered, I hope the voyage will be for my own good, for that of my children (Mary and John), and for the good of the heathen. Oh, may the Lord grant it for Jesus' sake!"

God was better to His servant than his apprehensions, and after a prosperous sojourn in the land of his birth, permitted him to return to the home of his adoption, and prolonged his life for some eight years of useful and honoured service. In England, the high reputation he had acquired for scholarship secured him a welcome from men of learning and high standing in society, and cordial indeed was his reception from the Directors and friends of the London Missionary Society. Honours were conferred on him, multiplicity of engagements crowded every hour of the day, and when he journeyed to France, he received the most flattering attention from Baron Humboldt, who presented him to the National Institute, at whose annual meeting he was present. He was also introduced to the Asiatic Society, and to the Bible Society of Paris, where he saw Baron de Stäel, Professors Remusat and Kœfer, and many other notabilities. On his return, he travelled to Scotland and Ireland, and was everywhere listened to with lively interest.

"I have," he writes, "in private as well as in public intercourse with pious people, been pleading the cause of China and the surrounding countries, and I hope some impression favourable thereto will remain. I have much reason to be grateful to God, whose good providence has kept me, and I am humbled at the kindness of many Christian friends."

The time flew rapidly by: many matters of importance delayed him beyond the period he at first
proposed for his stay; among others, his marriage—
an event which was productive of great happiness to
him through the remainder of his life. At length,
breaking away from the ten thousand attractions of
"Home, sweet home," he resolutely prepared for
departure. Alluding to the subject of separation
from the endeared objects of affection, he says:—
"There is in my character a mixture of the softest
affection, and of stern severity, when duty calls. In
the day of battle I cannot be the coward that would
stay at home. Heaven help me!"

Before his departure, the Directors of the London
Missionary Society held a farewell service, at which
Dr. Morrison delivered a very impressive address.
Its concluding paragraphs were as follows:—

"A voyage to China is one of the most distant
that is performed. The variety of climate through
which we shall have to pass is very great. From
a place where the leaves are scarcely on the trees,
we shall, within a month, reach a part where
nature is always green. In another month we shall
pass the Cape of Good Hope, but which some very
properly call the Land of Storms. In July, we expect
to be in a part which is cold and frigid, where the
sea runs, almost literally, mountains high. As we
approach China, we expect to encounter a sort of
hurricane, in a part where the wind blows from every
point of the compass almost at once, chopping round
continually. Here some of the very best ships are

9 *

dismasted, and sometimes destroyed. An immense
number of vessels, of various descriptions, are
wrecked in the river of Canton, and the Chinese
endeavour in a variety of ways to propitiate the god
who presides, they pretend, in these tempests. In
September we hope to arrive at Canton. This is our
hope, but God only knows whether it will be realised.
Europeans are allowed to live only on the frontiers
of China—at Canton and Macao. . . . Canton is
wholly given up to idolatry, to gain, to dissipation :
Sunday and Saturday are alike. The sound of mer-
chandise, the packing and unpacking of goods, the
chinking of dollars, the firing of maroons to salute
vessels going out and coming in, the ringing of bells
to awaken sleepy gods, &c. &c., are heard every day
alike. There is no such thing as rest to a Chinaman;
all is bustle and fatigue, except for a few days at the
beginning of the year, when rich and poor, old and
young, men, women, and children, all purchase some
new garment, repair to the temples for worship, &c.;
and then eating and drinking, debauchery and drunk-
enness ensue, till the wants of the poor, and the
fatigue of the rich, call them to engage again in their
various pursuits. . . .

"And now, friends, I know not on what topic to
address you last—whether on the trials of time or
the prospects of eternity. Both have their interest.
The trials of families are great, especially in a foreign
land. But, ah! let us ever be silent as to our afflictions. Let us call to remembrance the sufferings
Christ endured, and then our trials will appear light.

Let us look to Him in all His love, and mercy, and mediatorial work. Let these ever dwell in our hearts: so shall we be cheered in every bereavement, and find ourselves at home in every clime. Farewell."

Thus was he permitted to return to the land of his adoption, and again to resume his post, and fill up the measure of the work given him to do. A few years passed speedily by, occupied in the diligent discharge of his pressing engagements. They seemed as numerous and as urgent as in former time, and he hailed with joy the arrival of fellow-labourers, who came to his help. It is truly interesting to recall the names of these pioneers of the Chinese Mission. Two years before his decease, Dr. Morrison drew up a sketch of the first twenty-five years of its history, addressed to Christians " in Europe, America, and elsewhere," — to which the following list was appended : — 1. Robert Morrison, D.D.; 2. W. H. Medhurst (Java); 3. Samuel Kidd ; 4. Jacob Tomlin (Malacca); 5. Samuel Dyer (Penang): these five of the London Missionary Society. 6. Charles Gutzlaff (of the Netherlands Missionary Society). 7. E. C. Bridgman (of the American Board at Canton). 8. David Abeel (of the American Board in Siam). 9. 10, 11. Leang-Afa, Kew-Agang, Le-Asin, native teacher and assistants. The three last named were among the little Church of baptized Christians, ten in number.

Looking back on the past, as he thus recorded events, Dr. Morrison says: " There is now in Canton a state of society in respect of Chinese totally different from what I found it in 1807. Chinese scholars, missionary students, English presses, and Chinese Scriptures, with public worship of God, have all sprung up since that period. I have served my generation, and must — the Lord knows when — fall asleep. . . . It is a matter of great consolation now, when (in consequence of impaired health) I can do so little, that my former labours on the Holy Scriptures are being multiplied by *thousands*. By the Chinese Bible, when dead, I shall yet speak. Great is the honour God has conferred on me, in employing me to put into Chinese the inspired writings of Moses and David, the prophets and apostles of God; but I humbly hope, unworthy though I be, a greater still — that my name is written in heaven. Oh, to find mercy in that day!"

A happy entry in the diary, under date Sept., 1830, relates that his son Robert was with him, and, although only sixteen years of age, he had already been appointed Chinese translator to the British merchants in Canton. " Should his life be spared," said the proud father, " he will, I hope, at some future day revise Morrison and Milne's version of the Holy Scriptures."

In his family circle Dr. Morrison found the joy and solace of these latter years. A sweet group of younger children grew up around him, and pleasing are the pictures drawn of the good man by his loving wife. The Sabbaths were especially days of domestic happiness. The public services of the day were held morning and evening, and in the intervals of worship

he was occupied either in reading, or hearing his
children repeat their hymns, &c. On such occasions,
his usual resort was a retired terrace in front of his
residence, beyond which lay the Bay of Macao, en-
circled by barren hills: the terrace was shaded by
beautiful flowering shrubs, and bordered with European plants and flowers. Here, generally accompanied
by the whole of his family, the little ones on his knees,
or, according to Asiatic custom, sitting on mats spread
upon the ground, with their attendants of various
nations, Chinese, Portuguese, and Caffres, and a
favourite Newfoundland dog, invariably making one
of the group, might be seen the beloved Master and
Head, whose presence caused a general feeling of
happiness throughout the circle. The juveniles gladly
looked forward to these bright hours, and the loving
father, while his heart was filled with thankfulness,
spoke with joy of the tender mercies of his God,
whose hand had thus been filled with blessing. His
wife, knowing how laboriously he had spent the day,
would sometimes ask if he did not feel very tired.
His general reply was, "Yes, love, tired *in* my work,
but not *of* it. I delight in my work."

Public service often kept him long absent at Canton,
and whenever he returned to his home his appearance
was hailed with the liveliest demonstrations of delight
—even by Cæsar, the Newfoundland, whose loud bark
announced the master's approach, of whose caresses
he sought to obtain a share with the children.

The day after these periodical returns was one of
unusual excitement. Books and packages were

unpacked — presents distributed — toys eagerly examined and admired ; while the dispenser of these
valuables, happiest of all, went about the house,
carrying the youngest child in his arms, the next
holding by his hand, and the rest trotting at his
heels, while he gave his orders and superintended the
unpacking and rearrangement of books, MSS., &c.

These were joyous scenes, but they came to a close
all too soon, it being found necessary, on account of
health, that his family should return to England.
This separation was a source of poignant grief to the
tender-hearted man, and in addition to this trial he
had to struggle against increasing debility and sickness. The return of the hot season brought with it
an access of suffering, and it became evident that his
strength was failing. He strove manfully to bear up
against all, but was obliged to confess : "I am weary
and weak, and have the distressing sensations I felt
last summer, but I will bear patiently the will of the
Lord and the course of nature. These bodies must
return to the dust from whence they were taken."

On the 19th June he made the following entry in
his diary :—"I have just finished a sermon on our
Lord's words, ' In my Father's house are many man-
sions.' I trust we are of the family of God, and so
have a rich *inheritance* and a *home* to look to after our
pilgrimage is ended and our warfare accomplished.
Jesus will come and take us to Himself, so shall we
be ever with the Lord." This was the last sermon Dr.
Morrison wrote — just forty days before his decease.
He proposed to preach it the following Sunday, but

the intense heat of the weather, and his increasing debility, compelled him to relinquish his purpose.

On Sunday, the 27th of July, only five days before the end, he gathered around him for the last time his little Chinese congregation, and they joined together in prayer and praise, among them being "old Le, very frail, and thinking he must die soon." None thought he was himself standing on the threshold of the unseen world; but so it was; he fell suddenly out of their sight — "turned a corner and was gone." They came to take him to Macao for change of air, but he died in the night, and only the forsaken body remained to be carried and laid in the tomb, beside his first wife, the gentle, suffering Mary. There they rest together, waiting the day of resurrection, that glorious day of promise, when "many of them that sleep in the dust of the earth shall awake—some to everlasting life, and some to shame and everlasting contempt. Then they that be wise shall shine as the brightness of the firmament, and they that turn many to righteousness, as the stars for ever and ever."

Dr. Morrison was born at Morpeth, January 5th, 1782; and died at Canton, August 1st, 1834.

ISAROTRAFOHY, MADAGASCAR.—THE MARTYR'S HOME.

EARLY DAYS IN MADAGASCAR:

LEAVES FROM A LADY'S JOURNAL.

CHAPTER I.

PRELIMINARY LABOURS.

First Mission to Madagascar—Its disastrous termination—Return
Mr. Jones to the work—Favourable reception by Radama—Mrs.
Jeffreys' "Journal"—Appointment of Rev. J. Jeffreys to the
Madagascar Mission—His departure from England with Mrs.
Jeffreys—First lines from the "Journal."

"THER men laboured, and ye are entered
into their labours." These words of our
blessed Saviour have constantly recurred
to my mind when reading the joyful
tidings which have been recently brought us from
Madagascar. Truly the seed which was sown there
nearly half a century ago by the agents of the London
Missionary Society has yielded a wondrous harvest,
and we have had only to go in and reap it.

All honour to those early labourers whose toil and
suffering laid the foundation of this mission! Messrs.

Bevan and Jones were the first Protestant Missionaries to Madagascar. They landed at Tamatave on August 18th, 1818, taking with them their wives and children. Within a few weeks the little party, attacked by the fell disease of the country, had all perished, with the sole exception of Mr. Jones. His wife and her infant ; his colleague, with his wife and child—all had passed away, and left him alone. Thus solitary and forsaken, the noble-hearted man retired for a season to recover strength, and then, undaunted by all he had endured, sought again the deadly shore, and arrived on the 4th October, 1820, at the capital of the island. In company with him went Mr. James Hastic, the British agent, who had been appointed by Sir R. Farquhar to renew the treaty with Radama I. for the abolition of the slave trade. This object was happily carried to a successful issue, and the king made a proclamation in which he announced to his subjects the total abandonment of the horrid traffic. At the same time, under date October 29th, 1820, he addressed a letter to the Directors of the London Missionary Society, in which he said: " The Missionary, Mr. D. Jones, arrived at the capital of my kingdom to pay me a visit, and to solicit from me leave to settle, with other Missionaries, in my dominions. Having informed myself of his profession and mission, I acquiesced with much pleasure in his request, . . . and now request you, gentlemen, to send me as many Missionaries, with their families, as you may deem proper, provided you send also skilful artisans to make my people workmen, as well as good Christians. I promise them all the protection, safety, respect, and tranquillity which they may require from my subjects, &c. &c.

(Signed) " RADAMA, King."

It was in consequence of this letter, sent to England by Prince Ratafi, the brother-in-law of Radama, that, in the following May, the Society sent out the Rev. J. Jeffreys, accompanied by a number of artisans skilled in various useful arts. In the meantime Mr. Jones was not left without assistance, being joined by Mr. and Mrs. Griffiths in 1821.

In his " Life and Letters of Oliver Cromwell," Mr. Carlyle has availed himself of what he calls "the ancient flute voice" of one of the great Protector's daughters. Her record of passing events has found a place in the chronicles of that age, and those sweet low tones come in to complete the full diapason of historic song: they come in, and we welcome them. Such a soft, flute-like voice resounds from the shores of Madagascar, and it tells a touching story of Missionary adventure nearly half a century agone. It is the wife of Mr. Jeffreys who narrates what befel her and those dear to her while working in the sacred cause of Christian benevolence.

From her memorials we learn that the Rev. John Jeffreys was born at Ellesmere, in Shropshire. His pious mother took him with her to hear the Rev. J. Thomas of that town, under whose ministry he was early brought to choose the better part, insomuch that his companions often saluted him by the name of "Methodist." Soon after his admission into Church-fellowship he felt desirous to enter the Christian ministry, and was received at the Blackburn Academy, then under the care of the well-known and revered Joseph Fletcher. He was admitted student there in 1817, and his attention being especially directed to the subject of foreign missions, his wish to engage in that field of Christian labour was made known to the Directors of the London Missionary Society, who appointed him to Madagascar; and on the 4th August in that year he embarked for Gravesend with his wife and young daughter; the Rev. J. Arundel, secretary of the Society, taking leave of them at the quay, with loving encouragement and fervent prayer for the Divine blessing. The following day they went on board the *Columba*, having for fellow-passengers Prince Ratafi and his secretary and suite, together with their company of four artisans. The young wife of the Missionary must have been a well-educated woman, and a person of considerable courage, true piety, and with an ardent zeal for the cause in which she endured so much. It is a remarkable proof of her perseverance and indomitable strength of will that she kept a journal amid all the discomforts and difficulties of her voyage and subsequent journeyings.

Oh, these forlorn hopes of our Missionary enterprises, these young, ardent spirits that hasten to the van, crying, "Here are we; send us!" No marvel the men of this world and of this life esteem them fools. *They are fools,*—but it is for Christ's sake; and the great Apostle of the Gentiles was their exemplar. There is always something affecting and instructive in looking back at the first beginnings. "Our hearts were crowded with anxieties," says the sweet young wife, "more easily conceived than described, as we felt that we were leaving our beloved country, and withdrawing from the fond ties of natural affection and endeared friendships. We said, 'Who is sufficient for these things?' and here is the answer: In obedience to the voice of Him who said, 'Go ye into all the world and preach the Gospel to every creature,' we can leave all and go to distant climes. And as my lingering looks hovered over the receding shores, in my heart I said:—

'Should Heav'n command me to the farthest verge
Of the green earth, to distant barbarous climes,
Rivers unknown to song, ... 'tis nought to me,
Since God is ever present, ever felt,
In the void waste, as in the city full;
And where He vital breathes there must be joy.' "

TRAVELLING IN MADAGASCAR.

The voyage—The Cape of Storms—Arrival at Mauritius—The Abbé Flageolet—Visit to the old priest's dwelling—His catholicity of spirit — Departure of Mr. and Mrs. Jeffreys for Madagascar — Arrival at Tamatave—The Missionaries' grave—A lady's impressions of the Malagasy.

ND so they sailed, and for nearly four months were on the seas, beholding wondrous sights and also terrible ones, for when rounding the Cape a strong north-west wind arose. "The storm increased, and at times it appeared as though we must become a prey to the fury of the elements; the wind, lifting up the waves, passed over us in sudden gusts, like mighty torrents, which, united with the noise of the thunder and the roaring of the waters, made it truly terrific. Now the sea opened in great gulphs, and we sank into the deep, as though no more to rise, and then suddenly we mounted aloft; the sea began to break upon the deck in torrents; the heavens gathered blackness that for a moment hid all from our view, yet there immediately succeeded such vivid flashes of lightning as served again to discover and to heighten the horrors of the scene. The voice of the Almighty was heard in the heavens, and His power was seen in the mighty deep. At this moment my mind was comforted by hearing the voice of my husband repeating those lines of Dr. Watts—

> 'The God that reigns on high,
> And thunders when He please,
> That rides upon the stormy sky,
> And manages the seas,' &c.

Shortly after the sky became more serene ; the lightning's vivid flash ceased, and the roar of the thunder died away into a distant murmur."

No further incident worthy of record occurred, and on the 28th November the voyagers arrived in safety at Port Louis, where they received a kindly welcome from Mr. Le Brun, the Missionary of the station, and thus the sweet "fellowship of saints" cheered them alike at their going out and at their entering in. Mrs. Jeffreys' journal commences on the first of the new year. "January 1st, 1822.—This must be a day of gratitude and praise to the God of our mercies. We have been brought through innumerable dangers, trials, and sorrows in the past year, and it is probable we shall, in the course of this new season, have to pass through many more if spared to see its close. . . . O for grace to enable me at all times to wait for the Lord as well as to wait on Him. . . . .

" This place presents many painful proofs that the slave trade is not yet abandoned. This inhuman and brutalising traffic is carried on here to a considerable extent. As we sat at breakfast the morning after our arrival, we saw a heavy carriage of manure pass by, drawn by human beings, very partially clothed, and

10

guarded and urged forward by a guide who carried a lash in his hand, and who often used it very smartly ; and this is a common sight. These poor creatures are generally yoked together in pairs of six or eight, according to the weight of the carriage given them to draw. Any persons possessing slaves have power to send them to the bazaar to be publicly whipped if they have been guilty of theft or of running away. Here the treatment is sometimes very inhuman."

A few weeks later we have a very pleasing account given by Mr. Jeffreys of his visit to a Catholic priest, residing at Port Louis. He says : " Mr. Le Brun accompanied me, and the road was pleasant as it lay through many fertile and well-cultivated lands. The abbey is situated near a branch of La Grande Rivière, which, in a serpentine direction, sometimes winds over a bed of craggy rocks, so that its surface is greatly agitated, and then softly glides through fertile valleys till it pours its tributary stream into the main river. Mango and other fruit-trees nearly concealed the abbey and the grange until we came within a few yards of them. The abode of the Abbé Flageolet was built after the cottage form, and was near the place of worship. The entrance was much decayed by time ; a small lobby conducted us to the foot of an old staircase, considerably inferior to an English step-ladder. Seeing no person, we ascended, and at the top were met by an old black domestic, who introduced us to his master. We were much interested in his appearance ; he was truly venerable both by age and profession. When we entered he was eating his breakfast, which consisted of rice and potatoes, dressed as a salad, and he appeared to eat it with great relish.

"We inquired after his age : he replied, in French, seventy-eight. All his countenance appeared marked by age and close study, but his eyes still retained uncommon animation, especially in conversation. His manner was perfectly devoid of all that harshness and severity which too generally mark the Catholic priest-hood. The cheerful smile which beamed upon his countenance bespoke the natural amiableness of his temper. His clothes were of a very inferior descrip-tion ; he had no coat, but wore a loose old robe which he told us had been his covering for twelve years. The size of his room appeared to be about 15 feet by 10. The spider's web was its only ceiling ; the roof tapered to a point in the centre ; the furniture con-sisted of two old tables, on one of which were kept different articles for domestic use and a few books, and the other bare the provision which its owner was eating. These, with a few broken chairs, were the whole of his furniture ; and one servant, two turtle-doves, a cat and a dog, were, I believe, all the inmates of his dwelling.

"When he had finished his repast we began a con-versation with him, from which we found that he left Europe with the design of going to Madagascar as a Missionary, but various circumstances had con-spired to prevent his accomplishing this purpose. He appeared much delighted when he found I was going to the island, and seemed very anxious that all the earth should be brought to the knowledge of

10 *

the truth. When speaking of the goodness of God in supplying all our constantly returning wants, he said that His kindness ought to make us fall down in grateful homage before Him. He spoke of the errors of the Catholic Church, and said that it was his opinion Popery would ultimately be abolished. He told us that he regularly performed Divine service in the adjoining abbey, and was constant in visiting among his flock.

"On parting, he very cordially shook hands, and wished me much success in the great and good work of proclaiming the Gospel of Christ. Surely we may hope that the period is approaching when Christians of every denomination shall cordially unite in aiding the triumphs of pure and undefiled religion."

So might it be! The Lord hasten it in His time.

Our Missionaries were delayed five months at St. Louis by the unfavourableness of the season, a disappointment very trying to their spirits. At length, on the 1st of May, they sailed, hoping to reach their destination in a few days. Accordingly, on the 6th instant, the journal records: "As soon as Mr. J. went on deck this morning he was told that land was in sight, and hastened to my cabin with the good news. I was dressing my babe, then three months old, but without delay accompanied him to take a look at the long-desired object. . . . About 10 o'clock a.m. we came to anchor in the roads of Tamatave. On entering the harbour, Prince Island is seen to the north-east, a short distance from the main land. The front ground is chiefly low, and covered with

immense quantities of wood. In the background
rise, in somewhat rapid succession, mountains, the
real face of which we were too distant to distinguish.
Mr. J. said that in many parts it reminded him of
the English coast around Lancashire.

"The harbour of Tamatave is situated in lat. 18° 12',
and is by no means contemptible. Ships of a mode-
rate burden may lie at anchor here in perfect safety.
A reef of coral extends for a considerable distance
from the shore, and shelters it from the great surf
which comes in from the eastern seas. The following day we went on shore about ten o'clock, and were
immediately conducted to one of the best houses in
the little town, where we found the mechanics who
had come with us, and had landed the preceding
evening."

Of the town itself her account is very unpre-
possessing; it lies very low, and is surrounded by
woods and much marshy land; the houses in
general miserably put together, and many of them
inferior to our English barns. They consist of a
few poles fastened together at a little distance from
each other, which form the frame of the building.
A few more poles are added to bear up the roof,
which is generally of a conical form; the sides
are also enclosed with poles, and covered with the
leaves of trees sewed together. Such materials must
naturally soon fall into decay, and the more so on
account of the frequent rains, succeeded by the fierce
rays of the sun. The vegetable matter is constantly
decomposing, and, together with the fall of the foliage

from the numerous trees, gives out a most unwholesome miasma. This, combined with the want of
cleanliness among the people, and the extensive
marshy and undrained lands in the neighbourhood,
is sufficient to account for the unhealthiness of the
place.

A few days' delay was necessary before proceeding
inland, until the maroumita (or bearers) should have
arrived. In the meantime they gazed about them
with deep interest, paid a sorrowful visit to the quiet
resting-place of their predecessors, Mr. Bevan and
his wife and child, and Mrs. Jones and her infant;
dined one day at Mr. Hastie's, with the chief of
Tamatave, the French consul, and Captain Morsby;
held a quiet Sabbath service, and observed the
manners and appearance of the people. As to the
latter point, Mrs. Jeffreys says : "They are rather
above the common stature, and have generally fine
open countenances, the natural indication of a tolerable share of intellectual capacity; the men are
robust as well as tall, and the women mostly good-
looking, their colour varying according to the in-
termixture of the different tribes, some being dingy
white and others quite dark."

The Malagasy, it is evident, have many excellent
qualities. They are industrious in their habits and
peaceable in their dispositions, hospitable to strangers,
and friendly and kind to each other. Did they enjoy
the blessings of an enlightened and liberal government, they would rapidly rise in intelligence and
power, and their country would speedily advance in

fertility and comfort. From time immemorial they seem to have acquired many of the arts and habits of civilised life. They possess large flocks of cattle, cultivate and irrigate extensive tracts of land, are familiar with the value of property, and live in large communities, with considerable regularity of municipal government. The only native metal worked is iron. The people have long known the manufacture of various articles in that metal, as well as in horn, wood, silk, and cotton. They also excel in the manufacture of silver chain from dollars procured by the sale of their produce.

CHAPTER III.

ESTABLISHMENT OF THE MISSION.

Start for the capital — Native soldiers and native smiths — At the mouth of the river—Picturesque views—The maritime lakes of Madagascar — Stormy passage — First night in a native village — Social customs of the Malagasy — Perilous travelling — Arrival at Antananarivo—Cordial reception—A native Kabara—A peep at the Mission schools—Death of Mr. Brooks.

TO return to the journal of Mrs. Jeffreys, whom we left awaiting the arrival of the bearers who were to transport her party from the coast up to the capital—a tedious and dangerous journey of about two hundred miles.

The day before they started, she writes: "During a walk with my husband we observed a company of soldiers, belonging to one of the chiefs, who went through the different manœuvres with wonderful exactness in the European manner. We were also gratified by calling upon a blacksmith, whose shop and manner of work carried us back in imagination to Old England. The workers in iron and steel in this country are very clever. We saw also a native woman weaving cloth. The process was tedious, being carried on upon the ground: each thread was carefully drawn with the hand along the woof, which was fixed to a wooden frame. The material with which she was working was prepared chiefly, she told us, from a species of grass called *Roujia*, but the workmanship was surprisingly neat and simple."

The next morning (May 21st) "we left Tamatave, and about 4 p.m. arrived at Yvoundrou. Our route lay over the sands, close to the sea; the scenery, at times, was quite picturesque. This small but beautifully situated village lies at the mouth of the river from which it takes its name. It would be impossible to describe my feelings as I stood upon its banks. Everywhere the eye rested on some object most worthy of admiration — whether the majestic ocean, beating with its impetuous waves the huge banks of surf, which separated the mighty bed of waters from the gently flowing stream; or the beautifully sloping banks of wood rising in quick succession, losing, as it were, their topmost foliage in the distant horizon. Yet, as I gazed on this enchanting prospect, a painful feeling was awakened by the recollection that this lovely spot is the land of disease and death, owing to its rude and uncultivated state. At the same time I looked forward, hoping that the time may not be very distant when, by the hand of cultivation, these marshes shall become fruitful plains, and the people, occupied in agriculture or commerce, shall be united in mutual compact, and through the instrumentality of Christian Missionaries be brought to love each other and to devote themselves to the service of the true God and our Saviour Jesus Christ. Then shall the country, now waste and desolate, be beauteous as the garden of the Lord."

The beauty of the scenery in this part of the country has been described by subsequent writers. In proceeding from Tamatave to Antananarivo the road follows the coast for nearly seventy miles southward. When leaving the shore, the traveller strikes directly westward, into the heart of the island, ascending many miles before crossing the mountain chain and the great forests of the interior. One remarkable peculiarity of the eastern coast in Madagascar, probably found in no other country, is the existence of numerous lakes, which run parallel with the sea-shore for some hundreds of miles. Mr. Sibree says: "The coast-scenery is in many parts exquisitely beautiful, and the combinations of wood and water present a series of pictures which constantly reminded me of some of the loveliest landscapes that English river and lake scenery can present. Our route lay, most of the way, between the lakes and the sea. Occasionally a great part of this journey is performed in canoes; but, as the lakes are not perfectly continuous, there is a frequent change to the palanquin."

It is scarcely to be wondered at that our traveller should have been timid in venturing upon the untried perils of such a navigation. She thus describes her experience: "May 22.—We now proceeded by water in small canoes formed from the trunk of a tree, which, being round-bottomed, are very dangerous, as the least unequal balance would upset them. I scarcely knew how to hope for safety, but recollected that I had set out on the path of danger and could not retire; and my affectionate partner, seeing my uneasiness, said : 'Remember our rounding the Cape; we have the same God in the canoe as we had in the ship.' . . . The following day we could not proceed for storms, but the next morning ventured on the large lake we had next to cross. Two of the canoes were quickly upset by the agitation of the waters, and when all attempts to go forward proved fruitless, we landed and encamped on the plain, where we erected a temporary shelter of boughs, and made a roof with broad leaves which we gathered, and our bearers hung up their scarfs or robes to shelter us from the burning rays of the sun. At sunset we again set off, the wind having sunk, and after a pleasant row of some hours by moonlight, reached a village, at which we halted. . . . How shall I describe my feelings on being carried into one of its wretched huts, in which was a large fire burning on the ground, whilst the almost naked people were dancing and singing, to the dreadfully discordant sounds of the tum-tum. This, together with the wretchedness of the house, and the horrid gestures of the people, and the howls, or (as they call it) *mitiry*, which they all set up for a few moments, so frightened me that I ran out of the house. It was some public festival they were commemorating."

Occasionally the picture is a bright and joyous one:—"Our route still continues to be delightful; the lands are well watered by rivers and streams that intersect the country in different directions, and cover the whole with a beauty and fertility that cannot be surpassed, perhaps, in any part of the world. Perpetual verdure covers the plains. . . . On the 28th instant we came to Maroumandca, a place, in comparison with many we have passed, deserving the name of a town, and formerly very flourishing. Here, for the first time since we left Tamatave, we saw a herd of cattle, with flocks of goats and sheep.

" The people received us after their usual custom. Strangers, on their arrival at a town or village, are visited by the chief and his attendants, bringing presents of poultry, rice, fish, &c. They seat themselves upon a mat spread on the floor, and, after a pause, the chief generally makes a speech, to which the stranger replies, if a foreigner, through an interpreter. They request to know whence he comes, and his intention in coming to their country, and so on. In return, with much frankness, they relate to him all that is going on among themselves. It is common for them to eat a few grains of the rice in presence of the stranger, doubtless to remove any distrust. We, however, felt little fear, as the people manifested a feeling of kindliness scarcely to have been expected from those who were unaccustomed to foreigners."

After some days' journeying by canoes, there was a change, and the bearers and their cots came into requisition. A new kind of peril had now to be encountered: much of the route consisted in ascending and descending lofty hills, passing through thick woods, crossing rivers, ditches, brooks, &c. At one point, after passing over lofty heights, they came to a spot where the sea was distinctly visible at a great distance. The sight greatly moved the feelings of our travellers, as they thought it probable they might never see it again, or, at all events, not for many years. As they proceeded, the difficulties of the way increased, the weather being also very unfavourable. Mr. Jeffreys was at one time greatly disheartened. He thus wrote: "Being terrified at the appearance of the road, I resolved to walk, and did so till completely fatigued and drenched by the pelting rain. Quite exhausted, I got into my cot, but soon repented doing so, not only because of the danger, but on account of my poor bearers, who could scarcely keep on their feet. My anxiety and alarm were also much excited on account of my dear wife and her infant, as I knew she would suffer from fear, and from difficulty in keeping herself in her cot. At one time we ascended steeps, or rather precipices ; at another we descended as into deep caverns ; sometimes we were thrown suddenly on our feet, and then tossed again nearly upon our heads. I left my cot as soon as it was possible, but found myself unable to stand, unless one of the bearers assisted me up and down the steeps, and carried me across the water we had in several places to pass through. I was perfectly astonished to see the bearers travel so easily along places where I could scarcely stand, at the same time carrying burdens of fifty pounds each."

A pleasing entry, under date the 6th of June, mentions their arrival at a place where Mr. Hastie related having witnessed a heartrending scene some months before, when, with Mr. Jones, he was on his way to the capital, to negotiate the abolition of the slave trade. At this place they met more than a thousand slaves, fettered and chained together, going to the coast, there to be sold to dealers who were awaiting their arrival. It was heart-cheering to learn that these were the last poor victims of that vile traffic, and to be told of the success which crowned the embassy, and rejoiced the hearts of thousands assembled at the capital when the treaty was signed ; and also how, when the proclamation reached the coast, the unsold slaves were sent back to their own country, and assurance given them that they were henceforth safe.

As they advanced nearer the close of their journey, the travellers found the lands through which they passed exhibiting greater marks of cultivation. Small enclosures surrounded most of the houses, in which were plantations of rice and barley, while herds of cattle grazed in the meadows, the whole scene bringing to mind some parts of England and Wales.

The last place they reached was Ambatonamanga. "This town is full in view for three miles before entering it. It stands on a lofty hill, and around there is an extensive plain, which yields large crops of rice. Near at hand stands an immense rock, on the top of which three houses are placed; they have the appearance of a fortification commanding the town. This, together with the buildings standing one above another, and scattered on the sides of the hill, afford a picture of no small interest. We passed here a quiet night, in a house belonging to the King, which was so completely enclosed that the crowds of natives could not come to annoy us by looking into the dwelling, as they had done at every other place where we rested."

At length the longed-for moment arrived. From the top of a hill, about five miles distant, Antananarivo appeared full in view, a sight greeted by "a sudden and amazing shout," followed by mutual rejoicings and congratulations. It is unnecessary here to give a description of the capital, which is well known to all readers of our "Missionary Chronicle." As soon as the company had reached the foot of the hill on which it is built, they were met by Messrs. Jones and Griffiths, and after a short halt and refreshment, made their public entrance into the town, which was thronged with gazing multitudes, who showed great curiosity but preserved the utmost decorum.

They were most graciously received by the King
in person, who conducted them to his palace and
entertained them at dinner, which was served up in
excellent style, the various dishes being well cooked.
The company present were the King, the two princes,
two generals, General Brady, Mr. Hastie, and the
Missionaries, with their families.   At the conclusion

VIEW OF ANTANANARIVO.

of the repast the newly-arrived guests were conducted
to a house appointed for their use, and on the following day they received a handsome present from
the palace, of a sheep, some fowls, and fifty eggs,
accompanied by two servants, a boy and girl, each
about eleven years old.

Not long after their arrival, the strangers witnessed

a remarkable sight, of which we have the following animated description :—" The King has returned from the war in which he had engaged, having brought it to a happy termination by a marriage with the daughter of his adversary ; and we have been to the *Kabara*, at a place in which the people assemble, and which is so formed by nature as to make a large amphitheatre, covering an extent of about six acres. The number present on this occasion, including the soldiers, was not less than fifty thousand. The scene was overwhelming, and the order and silence were such, during the whole *Kabara*, that the least discordant noise might have been heard. The approach of the King was announced by the firing of cannon and musketry ; he sat in a gig, accompanied by his new wife; his dress was rich and splendid. The King ascended a platform erected for the occasion, and was saluted by his people. The chiefs of the surrounding villages presented a kind of tribute usual on these occasions. A principal chief then arose, and, in the name of the people, made a congratulatory speech, expressing their joy at his victory and success. He was followed by an officer of distinction, who, in the name of the soldiers, thanked the monarch for the valour and heroism he had displayed, and for his protection. His Majesty then arose and addressed the multitude. He congratulated his people, and informed them of the great extent of territory added to his dominions by the late victory. He expressed his warmest approbation of the courage and conduct of his soldiers, and concluded by assuring all present of his sincere desire for their prosperity and well-being. He was again heartily cheered, and the meeting broke up. The Missionaries and the British agent afterwards waited on the King, in the court-yard, and welcomed him back to his capital."

The first peep we have at the Missionaries and their charge is a very pleasing one. "June 16th. Sabbath-day.—We attended the school under the direction of our friends, as early as seven o'clock. The appearance of the children was so cleanly and respectable that we were delighted; the boys dressed in white jackets and trousers, and the girls in white frocks. They preserved admirable order, and sang in concert; after which they were catechised in their own language, the catechism having been drawn up by Mr. Jones, and being very much like that of Dr. Watts.

"At ten o'clock we had service at the house of Mr. Griffiths, and in the afternoon the children again met, and much pleased us by the correctness with which they repeated their various lessons.

"At three o'clock the King, in his state dress, accompanied by the British agent and Prince Ratafi, attended a public examination of the schools. They first went to that under Mr. Jones's care. The first class showed their writing, read the seventh chapter of the Acts in English, and translated some words into their own language; the second followed, and the third, fourth, and fifth classes were also examined. The number of children was about forty-eight.

11

"Afterwards a similar visit was paid to Mr. Griffiths's school, the number of pupils being thirty-seven. The girls showed some work, which did them much credit ; indeed, the progress made by all was highly gratifying, and we departed full of hope that we beheld the dawn of happy times in Madagascar."

A melancholy and unexpected event is the next record in Mrs. Jeffreys' journal. Mr. Brooks, one of the artisans who had accompanied the Missionaries, died, after a few days' illness. He was a young man, full of activity and promise, and much endeared to his fellow-travellers. The fatal epidemic of the country seized upon him, and he had but a few hours of suffering, after which, having expressed himself perfectly resigned and happy to depart and be with the Saviour, he slept in death. As it was the first death of a European that had occurred at the capital, it was necessary to secure a place suitable for a burying-ground. This was granted, and set apart for a place of sepulchre for Missionaries.

CHAPTER IV.

THE DAY OF TOIL AND THE NIGHT OF DEATH.

Learning the language—Opening a new Mission School—Forming the
Malagasy alphabet—Success of the schools—Ardent attachment
of the scholars — Despising the idols — Intrepidity of a native
youth—Great influence of the heathen priests—Removal of Mr.
and Mrs. Jeffreys to Ambatonamanga—The Missionary at his
work — "Streams in the desert" — Notes from the Missionary's
diary—Sowing the good seed—Failure of Mrs. Jeffreys' health —
Journey to the coast—Departure for Mauritius—Death of Mr.
Jeffreys at sea—" The patience and faith of the saints."

MR. JEFFREYS was, for a few months,
stationed at Antananarivo, where he commenced the task of acquiring the native
language, in which he seems to have made
rapid progress, so as to be able to converse with the
people ; and for some time before he left the country
he delivered regular discourses on Sundays, either at
home or in the surrounding villages.   From their
first arrival, the Missionaries commenced teaching
a school of children, and in this work they found
much interest and satisfaction.   The journal gives
some details of their proceedings : the first entry is
as follows :—" We opened our school on the 25th of
June, with nine boys and three girls, and soon found
the children possessed excellent abilities.   Our instructions were received with eagerness and gratitude,

and their progress astonished as well as delighted us. Two boys, in the short space of five months, proceeded as far in arithmetic as the Rule of Three, and some others were not far behind them. These children are quite as capable generally of receiving instruction as any in our own country, and their application is unwearied. Often, at a very early hour, we were disturbed by their standing outside our dwelling, and repeating aloud the multiplication table, or any other lesson of the day. When it is remembered that they were taught in a foreign language, their perseverance must appear very surprising and admirable.

" It was soon found impracticable to continue this method of teaching, and it was accordingly abandoned, and an alphabet of the Malagasy was formed. It was made to consist of twenty-two of our letters ; the vowels take the French sound ; the diphthongs are *ao*, as in *laolao*, play ; *eo*, as in *babeo*, to carry ; *ai*, as in *derain*, praised. They have only one double consonant, which is *ts*, as in *tsara*, good."

The great advance of the pupils under the new system was soon manifest, and the results were such as amply to compensate for the toil and trouble of the work. That these children were naturally shrewd, and in the habit of reflecting on what they learned, was proved by their answers to the queries of their teachers. An instance is given by Mrs. Jeffreys : " As I stood one day by my husband, while he was catechising the boys," she says, " I asked them which of the Commandments they thought most difficult to keep. One, after a pause, mentioned one, another a different precept, till at last a boy about twelve years old said, ' *Ny farana mafty indrinda*,' ' The last is the hardest.' Mr. Jeffreys said, ' Why is it so, my boy?' He replied, ' Because for one who is poor to see another possessing a great deal of money, many clothes, and much cattle and rice, without wishing for some of them, is very hard. I think no person can keep this Commandment.' "

Before long the little ones seem to have completely won the hearts of their instructors. Their strong and generous attachment to each other and to their friends was a distinguishing trait in their characters, and it was impossible not to become interested in creatures so lively, tractable, and affectionate. " One proof of their regard much touched me," Mrs. Jeffreys says. " The first time my husband went away from home, three of the younger boys came to me and said, ' We will sleep in your house till he returns. No rogue shall come to you, and we will do all we can to keep you from being sorrowful.' They did as they said they would; they came every evening, and slept on the mat in the sitting-room."

A still more striking instance of attachment was shown by a lad named Ratsaraube. Mr. Jeffreys having heard that in a neighbouring village there were some of the native idols, regarded by them as gods, went, accompanied by several of the boys, to examine into the matter. When ascending the hill leading to the village, the boys all took off their hats, and desired their master to do the same, saying,

"This village is sacred, and the people will be angry if you do not put off your hat and shoes." He refused, saying that he did not believe in their gods, and that it would be wrong for him to countenance their superstition. The boys were evidently uneasy, but still proceeded, until, on entering the village, some of the natives approached, upon which they threw their hats down the hill, and requested him to take off his hat and shoes; and on his refusing to do so the people became very angry, and their dogs surrounded them. Upon this all the boys, excepting Ratsaraube, ran off. He firmly stood by his friend and teacher, and, although alarmed, assured the exasperated people that Mr. Jeffreys was a very good man—that he was the friend of the King, and that, if they injured him, the King would be angry. In this way he appeased them, and they were permitted to leave the place without further trouble.

"In this poor, untaught heathen youth," says our Missionary's wife, "we found an example of faithful attachment such as is rarely to be met with. He was willing to face danger with his friend, and declared his resolution never to forsake Mr. Jeffreys in any similar case of peril. Of course this very much endeared the lad to us, and he continued his regard ever afterwards. When, at length, we were leaving the country, he hung about us and wept, discovering great unwillingness to leave us, and saying, 'I shall see you no more! You will die before you reach the coast; I shall see you no more!' His words were mournfully prophetic; he saw our faces no more in the body.   May the God of salvation give us to meet him in the better world."

The danger incurred by offending the superstitious prejudices of the natives was by no means slight, and several instances of it are given in the pages of Mrs. Jeffreys' volume.   The priests possessed a strong hold upon the minds of the people, and soon discovered that their craft was in danger.   When told that God alone could preserve them amid the dangers of the terrific storms which so frequently injure and alarm them, they said : " We do not know as to that ; we believe that the mischief done by the storms, since you came, is all owing to your speaking against our gods, and making your servants work on Friday." (Friday is their sacred day, when they abstain from labour.)   When he saw a storm approaching, the priest of the village went out with a pole, to which was attached a bit of sacred wood, which he shook at the clouds, and in case the danger were averted he claimed a sacrifice from the inhabitants.   Very commonly he required that a black sheep should be slain, and the blood poured over a particular stone, while the best part of the flesh was kept for his own use.

So terrible was the power of these men, and so great their ascendency, that having discovered that three of the natives had laboured in the grounds belonging to the Missionaries on their *fading*, or day of rest, it was determined to put the culprits to death ; and this doom was only averted by their humble expressions of contrition, publicly asking pardon of the god, and promising that if they ever committed the offence again they would consent to be sacrificed.

After remaining some months at the capital, Mr. Jeffreys and his family removed to Ambatonamanga, to which station he was appointed by command of Radama. This place has been already described, and it became the permanent home of our Missionaries until their departure from the island. Here they settled to their work with diligence, finding much to encourage and cheer them, together with not a few drawbacks and trials. "We had, at this our new station," says Mrs. Jeffreys, "a considerable school, which was solely under our own superintendence. It was formed on the Lancastrian system, and we found the children thus disciplined were very soon prepared to assist in teaching others, and much pleased to be so employed. We had about twenty girls and as many boys. They were taught reading, writing, and arithmetic, and the girls also learned to do needlework. They were punctual in attendance, eager to obtain instruction, and, before separating every day, united together in singing a song of praise to the God of our salvation. Beside school engagements, Mr. Jeffreys, when the weather and his strength permitted, daily went among the people in our neighbourhood, for the purpose of conversing with them."

The heart of this good man was indeed filled with holy love and zeal. "Often," his wife says, "the tears would trickle down his cheek as he indulged the hope that some one of his beloved pupils, or an adult native, was manifesting earnestness in inquiry after

the great salvation. With mournful pleasure I recall
to mind the spots where, with affection and energy, I
have heard him urge his dusky hearers to come to the
Lord Jesus Christ. Often, too, I remember those domestic services when the servants were all present, and,
in their native language, we united in prayer and praise.
How delightful and refreshing were those occasions!
Then, indeed, God opened to us streams in the desert,
without which our souls would have fainted."

It may not be uninteresting to give a few extracts
from his own notes, which show how he carried on his
labours among the people. " June 13th, 1823.—It
was with much delight I found myself this morning
surrounded by about forty adults, besides the school,
who had met to hear the Word of Life. They listened
with great attention as I discoursed, and some seemed
much impressed, and said that all I said was just and
good. . . August 1st.—After catechising the children
I preached. At the close of the service I walked to a
village about two miles distant, and collected a few
people, to whom I addressed the words of eternal life.
Afterwards I questioned the children, and then sang
and prayed : the poor ignorant people were astonished
and pleased, and asked me to come again. . . Lord's
day, September 29th.—I left home after the morning
service, intending to visit a village nearly five miles
distant, but met a number of men who were going to
the forest to fetch wood for the King. Whilst talking
with them it struck my mind that an opportunity
presented itself for preaching the Gospel. I asked
them if they could remain a short time to hear me

speak of God.   'Yes, and they should be very glad to hear what I had got to say.'   Accordingly I spoke to them of God and His goodness, and of the Saviour and His willingness to save all who desire His salvation. They listened attentively, and with apparent pleasure. October 12th.—This afternoon I preached at a neighbouring village, and was cheered by the willingness with which the people came to hear.   They were so pleased, that before the service could close, some of them went out and brought two ducks to present to me, and would have interrupted me to offer their gift, but I begged them to wait a short time, so they sat down again.   Having finished the sermon, I requested them to kneel down whilst we prayed ; some laughed ; but an elderly man bade them be quiet or leave the house, upon which they all kneeled down.   It was a pleasing — may it prove to have been a useful — season ! "

    *   *   *   *   *

The last chapter of this memorial is one of sorrow, disappointment, and death.   Early in the year 1825 Mrs. Jeffreys' health failed, and the only hope for prolonging her life seemed to be a visit of some months to the Mauritius.   Accordingly, on the 4th June, the little household set out from their peaceful and loved home, and travelled to the coast, saying to their servants and neighbours that they hoped to see them again before long.   After a journey of about thirteen days they arrived at Tamatave, and embarked on board a trading vessel, which proved a miserable craft, and afforded them wretched accommodation.   For the first

few days all seemed well, but on the tenth morning
the eldest girl and Mr. Jeffreys complained of head-
ache, and soon the worst symptoms of the dreaded
fever showed themselves. Elizabeth, the poor little
daughter, sank rapidly and died, and her father soon
followed her to her watery grave. On the night before
his departure he fell asleep, and about 11 o'clock, as
his poor suffering wife was attempting to snatch a
little rest, she was aroused by his beginning to sing to
the tune of the 100th Psalm the well-known doxology,
" Praise God, from whom all blessings flow." He went
through the whole verse with great feeling and
emphasis, though with evident difficulty, on account
of his extreme weakness. It was the last expiring
effort. The next day (the 4th of July) he peacefully
expired.

It is difficult to imagine a more distressing condition
than that in which the bereaved widow now found
herself ; her husband gone, and three infant children
left to her sole charge. But she did not yield to
despondency. Like one of old, this noble-hearted
woman "encouraged herself in the Lord her God," and
she thus writes : " In my solitary condition, under
feelings of indescribable anguish, I was able to have
recourse to prayer, and can attest to the praise of His
glory that I found Him faithful who has said, ' Call
upon Me in the day of trouble, and I will answer
thee.' "

Surely for such devoted, self-denying labourers in
the cause of the Redeemer, the record of the Spirit is :
" Here is the patience and the faith of the saints."

CHAPTER V.

REAPING AFTER MANY DAYS.

Death of Radama and banishment of the Missionaries—Messrs. Freeman and Johns—Results of fifteen years' Missionary labour—Favouring circumstances attending the introduction of Christianity into Madagascar — Twenty-five years of persecution—Steadfastness of the Malagasy Church — Rasalama, the first martyr—Martyrdom of eighteen confessors—Burning of the four nobles—Rain-storm, and triple rainbow—The expelled Missionaries: Mr. Jones, Mr. Freeman, Mr. Johns.

IT was in the month of August, 1841, that Mr. Freeman, Missionary from Madagascar, visited Norwich, accompanied by two of the natives of that island, who, together with four others, had escaped, "as by miracle," from threatened death. A terrible reverse had befallen the good cause. Radama was dead, and his successor, Queen Ranavalona, had determined to eradicate Christianity. Such were the sorrowful tidings to which we listened with deep concern.

Mr. Freeman visited at our house, and we had an opportunity of conversing with him, and of seeing his interesting charge. He had been, in conjunction with his colleague Mr. Johns, for many years engaged in carrying on the Missionary work in Madagascar, and the two friends and co-workers had recently published a "Narrative of the Persecutions of the Christians"

THE ORDEAL OF TANGENA, OR, TRIAL BY POISON.

in that island. From the first commencement of the Mission fifteen years had elapsed. During this comparatively short period much had been accomplished. A written language had been formed, and the Scriptures translated into it and printed, as well as a dictionary of the Malagasy. Large numbers of tracts and elementary books had been circulated, and the number of schools increased to nearly a hundred, in which some thousands of children had been taught. Two large congregations were formed at the capital, and nearly two hundred persons, on a profession of their faith, had been received into Church fellowship. Constant intercourse was kept up with the people, and with many among them habits of intimacy and friendship were formed; and, as the result of these and many other similar means, the minds of multitudes had been in some degree enlightened in the truths of Christianity, and so far affected by what they knew, as to renounce many of the superstitious customs of the country.

Such was the account given by Messrs. Freeman and Johns in their "Narrative;" and they added that much credit was due to the labours of the Missionary artisans, whose instructions had been of the utmost value to the people. Some hundreds of intelligent youths were placed under their tuition by the Government, and had been taught their various trades, as smiths, carpenters, curriers, boot and shoemakers, weavers, &c. &c. They were thus brought under the daily influence and example of men who had at heart the interests of the Mission, and who esteemed it their privilege to impart, as far as in their power, religious knowledge to their pupils.

Doubtless the great moving power was that exerted by the Missionaries themselves—men of indomitable perseverance, zeal, and love. Several of them were permitted to continue for many years at their posts, and from the various letters written by the natives, and from the devoted attachment they manifested to their teachers in the season of trial, it is evident they had grown into the hearts of their people, and had exerted a wonderful influence for good.

After alluding to the ambitious projects of Radama, who by his talents had given a new physical aspect to the country, disciplining his people, and forming a standing army of twenty or thirty thousand men, who were taught European tactics, and thus brought into extensive intercourse with foreigners,—the Missionaries add :—

" All these various circumstances, it must also be remembered, were acting, not upon a dull and sluggish, but on an enterprising, ambitious, and partially civilised people—prepared, therefore, to take advantage of such a fortunate concurrence of affairs, and to advance rapidly in the career of social improvement. Their natural habits of inquisitiveness and familiar intercourse, not to say loquacity and impertinent curiosity, were likewise favourable to the rapid development of the elements of improvement. In such a case, each one is anxious to exhibit his superiority, and therefore communicates his newly acquired and often imperfectly formed ideas to others: mind is thus exercised, invention put to the stretch, and knowledge extended. It is a deeply interesting crisis in the advancement of society when men begin to become conscious of the superiority and dignity which knowledge imparts, and learn to look back on their own former state of credulity and ignorance with wonder and regret.

Such is the deeply interesting view, given us by Messrs. Freeman and Johns, of the state of affairs at the time when they were compelled to withdraw from their field of labour. Never had that field seemed more ripening for the harvest than at this crisis. Only three months before the suppression of Christianity (February, 1835), the Missionaries addressed a letter to the Directors of the London Missionary Society, from Antananarivo, in which they say: " We have been exceedingly gratified with the conduct of many; there is a seriousness, and steadiness, and perseverance, and diligence about them, upon which we look with wonder and surprise, and are often prompted to exclaim: 'This is the finger of God!' We have reason to believe that many are savingly converted to God, and that great numbers are awakened to think and inquire. . . . It is not, moreover, exclusively in connection with those stations that fall under our own personal observation, that a spirit of inquiry is awakened. God appears to manifest His purposes of mercy to this people, in raising up an agency of His own from among themselves : to carry on His own work, He is forming for Himself His own instruments, giving them zeal and knowledge, imbuing

12

them with love to the truth, and compassion for their
countrymen, and thus supplying the exigencies of the
cause by their unexpected instrumentality, and so
compensating for our lack of service."

These statements are very remarkable when looked
at in connection with what so shortly after followed.

The history of the long weary years of persecution
is probably known to all who read these pages.
They know that for a period of five-and-twenty years
the dark cloud hung over poor Madagascar, and that
" during all that time no one could — except at the
risk of losing life, liberty, and property — meet for
worship, pray to the true God, or read the Scriptures.
Yet religious ordinances were, to some extent, observed
in secret : in secluded villages, in recesses of the forest,
in caves, even in rice-holes, worship was occasionally
offered, the emblems of Christ's death were partaken
of, and those who joined the community received
baptism on confession of faith. Leaves and small
portions of the Scriptures were carefully treasured,
something of a very simple yet scriptural system of
Church order and discipline was maintained, and
those among them who were apt to teach and ex-
hort were gradually recognised as pastors or elders.
It is a remarkable testimony to the power and purity
of the life and belief of the persecuted Church, that
during this long period no serious error either in
doctrine or practice sprang up in their midst."*

Of the cruel sufferings and deaths inflicted upon
multitudes of the Christians, we have also read and

* Sibree's "Madagascar and its People."

heard. Our hearts have thrilled with pity and admiration as we accompanied, in imagination, the first martyr to her doom—Rasalama, dear and honoured name! It will ever be held in loving remembrance by her countrymen, and by the whole of the Church of Christ.

Active persecution was not, of course, maintained with equal virulence throughout the whole twenty-five years. There were occasional intervals of rest, but ever and anon the storm burst forth with fierceness of cruelty.

The 28th of March, 1849, is a day specially to be remembered as a terrible yet glorious epoch in the religious history of Madagascar. Eighteen Christians were condemned to death, and in the presence of a great multitude witnessed a good confession with heroic fortitude, and even with joy. Of this number, fourteen perished by being hurled from a precipice which forms part of the bold cliffs by which the western side of the city of Antananarivo descends to the plain. The remaining four were destined to a still more terrible fate. Being nobles, it was deemed unlawful to shed their blood, and they were accordingly sentenced to be burned alive, a sentence which was carried into execution at the summit of the northern ridge of the city hill. They walked to this place singing a hymn, and when they had reached the fatal spot, they calmly gazed on the preparations made for their death, and surrendered themselves into the hands of their executioners. An eye-witness gave the following account of the scene:—"At the

12 *

moment when they were brought to the stakes, a re-markable phenomenon occurred. A huge rainbow, forming a triple arch, stretched across the heavens. One end appeared to rest on the posts to which the martyrs were tied. The rain in the mean time fell in torrents, and the multitudes who were present were so struck with amazement and alarm, that many of them took to flight. The pile was kindled, and amidst the crackling and roaring of the flames were heard the voices of the sufferers, who sang together a hymn of praise. They were also heard committing their spirits into the hands of their Redeemer, and praying, ' Lay not this sin to their charge.'

" Thus," wrote the witness of the memorable scene, " they prayed as long as they had any life; then they died—but softly, gently. Indeed, gentle was the going forth of their life, and astonished were all the people around, that beheld the burning of them there."*

What a subject for the painter's art does the scene so touchingly described present! The multitudes thronging the rugged brow of the mountain, and on its summit the burning pyre, with the four meek suf-ferers raising their hands and eyes upward, while on the dark scowling thunder-cloud shines forth, brilliant with heavenly radiance, the triple arch—

> " Sign of the covenanted grace,
>   Confirmed to all the ransomed race."

Surely it were a subject worthy the piety and genius of a Michael Angelo.

Before closing this short notice of the early opera-

* Ellis's "Martyr Church of Madagascar."

MARTYRDOM OF FOUR MALAGASY NOBLES.

tions of the London Missionary Society in Madagascar, I will add a few particulars respecting the Missionaries, who, thus cruelly banished from their beloved flocks, had never the satisfaction of returning to the home of their adoption, and the people for whom they had so long laboured.

Mr. Jones—the first of their number—did not long survive his expulsion from Madagascar. He went to the Mauritius shortly before his death, which occurred on the 1st May, 1840. A letter from the excellent Mr. Le Brun says: " Since his return from Madagascar in September last (whither he had gone for the purpose of endeavouring to help the persecuted Christians), Mr. Jones was never well, but constantly suffering from pain. On the 26th April he was seized with paralysis, and continued speechless until the end." He is buried near the tomb of the devoted missionary, Harriet Newell. There, near the seashore, in the burying-place of Port Louis, rest the remains of several of the Mission family, awaiting the coming of the resurrection morn.

Mr. Griffiths returned to England, and, I believe, took the pastoral charge over a congregation in this country.

Mr. Freeman was appointed Home Secretary of the London Missionary Society, and died in 1851, having very recently returned from an extended visitation of the Society's stations in South Africa.

Mr. Johns died in the island of Nosibé, on the north-west coast of Madagascar, on the 6th August, 1843, aged 55. Two years previous he had ventured, at some risk, to go up to Antananarivo, after assisting in the escape of the six native Christians: he found, to his grief, that several whom he knew and loved had been condemned to death. In vain were all efforts to assist them in escaping, so strict a watch was kept. Still lingering near the land he loved to the death, he fell a victim to a relapse of the fatal fever from which he had suffered on his former voyage. His illness was long and distressing. The French authorities were kind to him, and followed his remains to the grave. None of his countrymen were near, but his two Christian Malagasy servants never left him, and faithfully ministered to their beloved friend and teacher to the last.

Through the kindness and generosity of Sir John Marshall, Commander of H.M.S. *Ibis*, a suitable monument was erected over the place of his sepulchre, which the French officers and residents had already enclosed with a strong palisade fence. He died at Tasandra, a military post on the island of Nosibé, opposite to the mainland, and his grave is on an eminence close to the French barracks.

> "He sleeps sweetly there, in yon isle of the ocean,
>   Far, far, from the home of his youth;
> But near to the land where, with heartfelt devotion,
>   He preached the Glad Tidings of Truth."

DR. VANDERKEMP:

THE FRIEND OF THE HOTTENTOT.

CHAPTER I.

THE PLIGHTED FRIEND.

The South African Mission—Dr. Philip and the slave trade—George
Schmidt, the Moravian Missionary—His labours among the
Hottentots — Dr. Vanderkemp — Previous history — Joins the
London Mission—Appointed to Kaffraria—Gaika, the Kafir chief
—Hottentots more teachable than Kafirs—Dr. Vanderkemp's
influence over the natives.

> " See Vanderkemp to natives kneeling round,
>   Proclaims the blessed Word of glorious sound ;
>   Or, on some Christian Mission bravely bent,
>   Comes Philip, with his apostolic tent ;
>   Or, much-loved Moffat, labouring all the day,
>   Something for Africa to do or say."

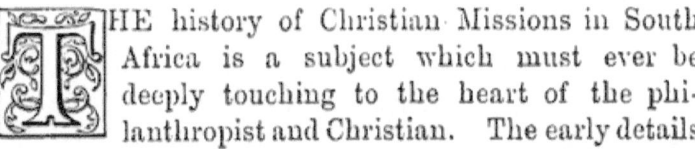

HE history of Christian Missions in South
Africa is a subject which must ever be
deeply touching to the heart of the philanthropist and Christian.   The early details
relative to the work are fraught with much of uncommon interest from the time when the Moravian

Schmidt first pitched his tent at Genadendal and Vanderkemp began his noble course.

I have mentioned in the introductory remarks to these pages that Dr. Philip, of the London Missionary Society, paid a visit in 1836 to Norwich, and was a guest under my father's roof, and that at a subsequent period Mr. Moffat visited us. Deep was the interest awakened by the thrilling accounts they gave of all they had seen and done in the land

"Where Afric's sunny fountains
Roll down her golden strand,"

and the remembrance is still treasured by those who listened to that tale of bitter wrongs and heroic self-consecration. Dr. Philip has been happily called the Las Casas of Southern Africa,—and happier than Las Casas, inasmuch as, while promoting the spiritual and political redemption of the native race, he also aided in breaking the bonds of the negro, and prepared the way for the moral elevation of Africa. His indomitable determination and indefatigable perseverance in standing up on behalf of the oppressed Hottentots, drew down upon him the persecution of the prejudiced provincial functionaries and white colonists generally; but he did not wage the conflict in vain.

In 1819, when Dr. Philip arrived at the Cape, having been appointed Superintendent of the London Missionary Society's Missions in South Africa, he found matters in a languishing and unsatisfactory state. This was mainly owing to the continual discouragements and intolerable oppressions to which the

Missionaries and their Hottentot disciples were subjected by the Colonial Government and its local
agents. For seven years longer the Doctor had to
struggle for free toleration — it might be almost
said, for absolute existence; and whoever wishes to
form a just idea of the obstacles he overcame and the
triumphs he achieved, ought to read his " Researches

PHILIPTOWN, SOUTH AFRICA.

in South Africa," a work which presents a faithful
narrative of the early history of the Society's efforts
in that country.

But it is not to Dr. Philip and the record of his
worthy deeds that this chapter is devoted, but to a
fellow-labourer who preceded him in the same field.
Before, however, I write of Dr. Vanderkemp, I think
it will be well to speak of the first Christian effort
made on behalf of the poor Hottentots, and to give

a short account of the early work of the Moravians in this dark land.

Some pious persons living at Amsterdam being concerned for the poor heathen of Africa, applied to the Church of the United Brethren to send a Missionary to the Cape of Good Hope, for the purpose of instructing the people in the knowledge of the true God. George Schmidt, a man of great zeal and courage, offered himself for this service, and in the month of July, 1737, he reached the Cape, and retiring into a desert place, built for himself a hut and cleared a piece of ground, near Sergeant's River. Finding it impossible to learn the native language, he set resolutely to work to teach the people his own, and speedily succeeded in winning the affections of the poor rude heathen. Assembling a number of them, he opened a school, which soon had nearly fifty children in it, and the blessing of God so rested on his labours, that some of his hearers were brought to a saving knowledge of the Gospel. During seven years he pursued his way with unshaken perseverance, but at the end of that time, owing to certain difficulties which arose, he returned to Europe, hoping to obtain assistance, and to secure the sanction of the Dutch Government for the pursuance of his object. These, alas! were denied him, and he was never permitted to return to Africa. The enemies of religion successfully exerted themselves to crush every philanthropic and Christian effort in the cause of the people; and the Church of Holland, untrue to the principles of Christ's religion, put herself into an attitude of resistance to the Missionary cause. The heart of Schmidt was sorely grieved, but his affections clung, with steadfast ardour, to his poor Hottentot converts, to the hour of his death. He is said to have devoted a part of every day to secret intercession with Heaven on their behalf, and, at length, death overtook him while thus engaged.

After his departure, his little flock, anxiously awaiting his return, met together to read the Bible and pray, and for a while thus kept in communion, but eventually mingled with, and were lost among their countrymen. Nearly half-a-century elapsed, and it seemed as though the prayers of the evangelist were to remain unanswered. But at the end of that period the Brethren were permitted by the Dutch Government to send three Missionaries to the colony. They arrived at the close of November, 1792, and went to the very spot where Schmidt had resided. The ruins of his dwelling were still visible, and a part of the wall of his garden, which had run quite to waste; and the whole valley had become such a haunt of wild animals, that it was called by the name of the Baboons' Glen. The new visitors took possession of the place, gathered together the Hottentots to hear the Word of God, and taught the children to read it, holding their meetings under the shadow of a wide-spreading pear-tree, which had been planted by their predecessor, and was still vigorous and fruitful. Among the inhabitants who came to visit them was a woman named Helena, who had been baptised by Schmidt, and who showed them a Dutch New Testament, which he had given to her. She spent her latter years in peace at the Moravian station, and, amidst many bodily sufferings, maintained the character of a true child of God. She declared to all who conversed with her that she trusted only in the Saviour, and ardently desired to depart and be with Him. She died in January, 1800, and was thought to have attained nearly the age of a hundred years.

Shortly after their settlement, the Brethren opened a school, in which both children and adults were taught. They attended very regularly, and showed great eagerness to learn. After a while, seven Hottentots received baptism, who, it was lamented, had to endure much unreasonable opposition from the Dutch colonists, and even from some of the officials at Cape Town. One of them, finding that his master wished to prevent his going to the Mission, thus addressed him : " If you will answer for my soul, then I will stay away." The conscience of the master was touched, and he replied, " I cannot answer for my own soul, much less for that of another," and then granted full permission.

Before long, troubles arose to try the faith and patience of the Brethren. In June, 1795, receiving intelligence that a band of rebels, called Nationals, were coming to attack the station, they deemed it necessary to retire to Cape Town, greatly to the distress of their poor helpless charge. Some time elapsed before tranquillity was restored by the taking of the colony by the British, when the Missionaries were sent back to their station, and the opposition offered to them gradually subsided. In the year 1799 they built themselves a commodious church, capable of holding a numerous congregation. At that time the station numbered some 1234 inhabitants, of whom 304 were members of the Moravian congregation, whose temporal condition was greatly improved. Profiting by the example of the Brethren, they left off their habits of idleness and sloth, and diligently cultivated their fields and gardens; and when, in the year 1800, a body of Missionaries arrived to join their fellow-labourers, their hearts were gladdened by the welcome they received when, about a mile from the village, a number of the people met them, singing hymns of praise to God, who had thus graciously supplied their spiritual wants.

It was at this precise period that the attention of the London Missionary Society was directed to Africa, and they received with much satisfaction a letter from Dr. Vanderkemp, a physician at Dort, who having seen some of the Mission's publications in Holland, wrote to offer himself for the self-denying and arduous service of labour among the heathen. The circumstances, talents, and character of this remarkable man were so unusual, that Dr. Philip does not hesitate to say he was certainly one of the most extraordinary personages of his age. His reputation for literary attainments stood high. He had studied at the Universities of Leyden and Edinburgh, and having, in his youth, chosen the profession of arms, he attained the rank of captain of horse. Such was his skill in mathematics, that

he was regarded, when in the army, as a man likely
to improve the art of fortification and the military
tactics of his country. After having been sixteen
years in the service of the Prince of Orange, with
the highest promotion within his reach, a personal
misunderstanding with the Prince, with whom he
was intimate, caused him to resign his commission,
and to make choice of another profession. Having
taken the degree of M.D. at the University of
Edinburgh, he returned to his native country, and
established himself as a physician, his abilities and
high repute securing him an extensive practice. He
was subsequently made a colonel of militia, and
afterwards appointed surgeon-general of the forces,
at the breaking out of the French revolution.
During his stay at Edinburgh, his extraordinary
gifts secured to him the notice and friendship of
Drs. Monro and Gregory; and his thesis, when he
stood for his diploma, was spoken of with high
approbation by several of the medical professors,
and recalled to memory when his offering himself as
a Missionary made him the subject of general conversation.

Nor was he less a proficient in literature than in
science. Among scholars he held an eminent rank.
He could read and write in sixteen different languages, and his knowledge of natural history, comparative anatomy, and chemistry, would have
entitled him to a professorship in either of these
sciences in any of the Universities of Europe.

At the time when Dr. Vanderkemp was in the

vigour of his powers, infidel opinions prevailed to a fearful extent on the Continent, and having a taste for the German school, he imbibed all the fatal errors of that philosophy; and (we have the assurance under his own hand) while he was blaspheming the name of the Saviour, and writing against the Divine authority of the Scriptures, he fully believed that he was pleasing God.

From this state of hardened scepticism — these fatal delusions into which he had been drawn by a "false philosophy"—he was suddenly awakened by an overwhelming calamity. By the upsetting of a boat, his own life was placed in the utmost jeopardy, and his wife and child were drowned. So entire a change was wrought in his mind by this terrible event, that he became another man. Bereft of all that made life dear, he found how utterly unavailing were the theories of his philosophy to sustain his spirit; and, by the grace of God, he was enabled to see the Truth and to embrace the Gospel, which alone could impart peace to his distracted soul. From that time forward, a desire to be useful to his fellow-creatures became the motive principle of all his actions, and with the characteristic ardour of the man, he dedicated himself to the work of Missionary labour.

In the month of December, 1798, Dr. Vanderkemp, under the auspices of the London Missionary Society, sailed for the Cape, accompanied by Messrs. Kicherer, Edwards, and Edmonds. They took passage on board a convict ship, and during the

voyage, their zeal and benevolence were exerted on
behalf of the unhappy criminals who accompanied
them. Their efforts were attended with the Divine
blessing: several persons were brought under conviction of sin; little companies were formed for
prayer and Christian converse; some who died gave
reason to hope they had found mercy, "even at
the eleventh hour;" while others who proceeded
to Botany Bay, it is believed, proved that they had
not heard the Truth in vain.

On the arrival of the Missionaries at Cape Town,
they were kindly received by General Dundas, Lieu-
tenant-Governor of the colony. It had been originally
intended that all the brethren should labour together,
but it was afterwards decided that Messrs. Kicherer
and Edwards should settle among the Bushmen,
while Vanderkemp and Edmonds should proceed to
Kaffraria. Accordingly, having received recom-
mendatory letters from the English Government to
the farmers and others, Dr. Vanderkemp left Cape
Town, and arrived, in July, 1799, at Graaff-Reinet,
the most distant colonial town, and the nearest to
the Kafirs. From thence he proceeded to the
interior. It was a daring undertaking, for the state
of things in that part of the country through which
he had to pass was, at that period, very critical.
The colonists in the interior were much dissatisfied,
and many of the cruelly persecuted Hottentots had
combined with the Kafirs to attack the settlers.
All was in a state of disturbance; and through
this agitated district his route lay. Dauntless of

soul, he proceeded, and pitched his tent amid a
people fierce, superstitious, and inured to war,
exposed to the nightly visits of hungry hyenas,

ROUGH TRAVELLING.

journeying through rough and trackless ravines and
plains. Nothing could cool his zeal. After under-
going a series of hardships and perils, he reached

13 *

the territory of Gaika, the Kafir chief acknowledged by the English Government, from whom he requested permission to remain in his country.

Here is his own account of their first interview. "September 20th, 1800. After we had cut a way through the wood, we went on, and arrived at Gaika's cattle-kraals, then the place of his residence. About one hundred Kafirs flocked together, and after we had remained in suspense about ten minutes, the king approached, advancing slowly, attended on each side by one of his chief men. He was clad with a long robe of panthers' skins, and wore a diadem of copper, and another of beads around his head. He had in his hand an iron kiri, and his cheeks and lips were painted red. He stopped about twenty paces from us; we then stepped towards him, and he, at the same time, marched forward, and reached us his right hand, but spoke not a word. I then handed him his tobacco-box, which we had filled with buttons. He accepted it, and gave it to one of his attendants. At a distance behind him stood his captains and women, in the form of a half-moon, and at a greater distance the rest of the people. I called aloud to know if there were any one who could interpret, but none answered, only some smiled. After about a quarter of an hour a white man arrived, who proved to be a Dutchman named Buys. The king then sat down upon an ants' hill, Buys placed himself at his left hand, and Gaika then inquired, through Buys, if this box were intended for him. I replied in the affirmative, he thanked us, and said he was much pleased to see us, and desired to know our purpose and what we wanted of him. I answered, our object was to instruct him and his people in matters which would make them happy in this life and after death; that we only asked his leave to settle in his land, expecting his friendship and protection. Gaika said that we were come at a very unfavourable time, when the country was all in confusion, and he therefore advised us to relinquish the desire to live with him. 'I cannot protect myself,' he said, 'being in perpetual danger on account of my enemies; I am unable, therefore, to entertain you as you ought to be entertained.'"

It was some time before the cautious and crafty king would give his consent that the Missionaries should remain in his domains, and when this was granted, and a suitable spot of ground selected, the Doctor, in his pure Christian simplicity says: "Brother Edmonds and I cut down long grass and rushes for thatching, and felled trees in the wood. I kneeled down on the grass, thanking the Lord Jesus that He had provided us a resting-place before our enemies and Satan, and praying that from under this roof the seed of the Gospel might spread northward through all Africa."

Here, for some eighteen months, the devoted evangelist laboured; producing, apparently, little impression on the minds of the Kafirs, but eagerly improving every opportunity to recommend the Gospel, and rejoicing in any ray of hope and light. Constantly exposed, as he was, to danger from the disaffected colonists and the Kafirs, the only comfort he enjoyed during this period was in seeing a favourable influence produced on the minds of several Hottentots, then living in the country. This man of genius and learning, who had been the companion of courtiers and students, when told by a poor Hottentot woman that she constantly prayed to Jesus to reveal Himself to her, felt his heart overflowing with joy, to which he gave expression in the following entry in his diary :—" I prayed the Lord that it would please Him to accompany the unworthy efforts of His humble servant with the influences of His Spirit; and, oh! how did my heart rejoice that the Lord had given me in this wilderness, among tigers and wolves, and at such a distance from Christians, a poor heathen woman with whom I could converse confidently of the mysteries of the hidden communion with Christ. Oh! that I may not be deceived! Lo, my winter is past—the voice of the turtle is already heard in the land." At one time, being exposed to the suspicion and jealousy of some of the people, he thus writes :— " Satan roared like a lion. It would not be prudent to mention particulars; but it was resolved that I should be killed, as a conspirator against the king."

A time of severe drought prevailed at another period. The native magicians failed in their attempts to make rain, and Gaika, who was impressed with the demeanour and conduct of the Missionary, applied to him. In a letter to the Society, dated Quakobi, in Kaffraria, December 28th, 1800, Dr. Vanderkemp

says: " The season has been uncommonly dry; men,
beasts, and vegetables have perished for want of food.
Many persons applied to me to give rain, and on the
30th October, being upon the road and having slept in
a field, I met a deputation sent by the king, with a
present of two cows and their calves, to request in a
more solemn manner for rain. I answered as usual,
that I could not give rain, but that I could and would
pray for it. Taking a walk afterwards through the
desert, I reflected that God certainly would give rain,
if I could pray for it in the name of Christ; and at
the same time I found some desire that God might be
glorified. That night I came to Quakobi, where
Gaika's men had been waiting for me. We then
prayed for rain, in subordination to the Divine will.
The next morning the Lord gave plentiful rain, last-
ing three days. This made an impression upon the
minds of the Kafirs, who said, 'Tinkhauna * has
talked to the King on high, and He has given us
rain.' They are, however, as superstitious as ever
with respect to the power of their magicians. The
very moment I write this, the king lets me know that
he wishes I should pray God for him: but he has
also ordered a woman, pointed out by his magicians
as the cause of his distemper, to be burnt alive by
red-hot stones, and will probably kill more of his
people, who will fall victims of his superstition."

The sojourn of our evangelist in Kafirland was
not prolonged, but, though unattended with visible
fruits at the time, it was not without good results;

* The name which the Kafirs always gave to Dr. Vanderkemp.

and it impressed them with a high respect for his character. "There was something," says Dr. Philip,
"in the appearance of Dr. Vanderkemp which made
a favourable impression on the minds of those who
conversed with him. Such as saw him once never
forgot him, and they always afterwards spoke of him
with great respect. To the favourable impression
made on the Kafirs by his exertions, we are indebted
for the openings we now enjoy for the propagation
of the Gospel among that interesting people." *

CHAPTER II.

THE FRIEND APPROVED.

At Graaff-Reinet — Persecution of the Hottentots — Government
proposal for an Institution for their relief — Committed to Dr.
Vanderkemp — Removal of the Institution to Bethelsdorp — A
glimpse of a true hero — Description of the Mission settlement
—Andries Stofiles, the Kafir chief — Virulent animosity of the
Boers — Vanderkemp's devotion to his charge — His efforts to
abolish slavery — Personal sacrifices for the cause — Failing
health—Cited to appear at Cape Town—His evidence before the
Government commission—Protection granted to the natives—
Final illness—" Light! "—The past and the present.

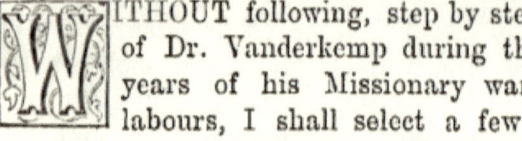ITHOUT following, step by step, the course
of Dr. Vanderkemp during the succeeding
years of his Missionary wanderings and
labours, I shall select a few incidents of
special interest, which will enable the reader to per-

* It deserves record, that during the brief period he remained in
Kafirland, Dr. Vanderkemp drew up a rough sketch of a grammar of
the language, and formed a vocabulary of about eight hundred words.

ceive more of the excellence and devotedness of his character.

After moving about from place to place, he arrived at Graaff-Reinet, where he found two other Missionaries, Messrs. Read and Vanderlingen, and there he continued for a time, instructing the Hottentots, who flocked thither in numbers to seek a refuge from the enmity of the Boers. But the opposition of the settlers again broke out, and they appeared in arms, surrounded the villages, and took possession of some of the houses, firing on the inhabitants and the soldiers. Many balls were actually aimed at Dr. Vanderkemp's person, but he escaped unhurt. At this critical juncture he received a communication from the Governor, General Dundas, in which he intimated a desire that the Doctor should form a Missionary Institution for the benefit of the Hottentots then scattered on the borders of the colony; and in compliance with this proposal, the brethren quitted Graaff-Reinet with 109 Hottentots, which number was soon augmented to 221, and proceeded to Botha's Place, in the neighbourhood of Algoa Bay, where the Governor had assigned them a location, engaging to supply them with provisions for the first year.

During the period they were in this place the unsettled state of the country, and the neutrality they observed between the contending parties, exposed them to many hardships, and frequently placed their lives in imminent danger; yet they continued there for some months, and a pleasing glimpse is given of their proceedings in the Directors' Report, ex-

tending from May to September, 1802. They say:
"Considerable progress has been made at the settlement; a number of houses have been erected by the
Hottentots, on a plan superior to those they have been
accustomed to build. . . At present they have sufficient means of subsistence, and already have begun
to raise both wheat and rice. The good effects of the
establishment are already seen in the improved morals

HANKEY, SOUTH AFRICA.

of the natives; their order and cleanliness, as well as
in their sobriety and industry. About 200 of them
constantly attend Divine worship, which is for the
present conducted in a barn, and their behaviour is
serious, and their singing remarkably harmonious.
But they worship also out of doors; and the simple
and venerable appearance of the good Doctor, in the

midst of his family, leading their devotions, upon a
lawn surrounded with shrubs, and enlightened by the
beams of the moon, is a pleasant scene to look upon.
Mr. Read, who has conciliated the particular affection
and high esteem of Dr. Vanderkemp, passes a great
part of his time at Algoa Bay, preaching there to
the English soldiers stationed at that place, besides
attending to the instruction of children, whose progress in reading and writing is satisfactory."

After a time the colony of the Cape was again ceded
to the Dutch, and the new Governor, General Janssens,
arrived at Algoa Bay on the 2nd of May, 1803. He
had been intimate, in his younger years, with Dr.
Vanderkemp, and although by no means sympathising
with his religious opinions, he showed himself very
friendly, dispensing with the state of governor and
general, and waiving all ceremony, renewed the friendship of former days, and conversed with his old
comrade on terms of cordiality. Although prejudiced by the false representations of the enemies
of the Missionaries, he was, in a measure, convinced
by the reasonings of the Doctor, and disposed to
favour his views. Finding the colonists implacably
hostile, he proposed that the Institution should be
removed to a new station, and a tract of land about
ten miles in circumference, some distance to the
northward of their former location, was assigned them
in permanence. The situation was most unsuitable,
and the soil unproductive, but the Missionaries had
no alternative but to accept the grant. After the site
had been fixed upon, the Governor requested Dr.

Vanderkemp to give it a name, observing at the same time that he disliked Scriptural names, and that he hoped he would not give it one from the Bible. Pausing a moment, and recollecting that he had preached on the preceding Sunday from Genesis xxxv. 2, 3, the Missionary named it *Bethelsdorp*. The Governor's knowledge of the Scripture did not enable him to detect the irony conveyed in this proceeding, and next day, when he came to know it, and found the laugh turned against him, he acknowledged that it was perfectly fair.

This transaction is related in a letter, dated May 30th, 1803, and the writer says they were then about to enter immediately on the possession of the new place. Some nine months subsequently the Institution was visited by the Commissary-general, De Mist. He was accompanied by Dr. Lichtenstein, who published an account of his travels, in which is given the following interesting record of his interview with Dr. Vanderkemp :—

" On the day of our arrival at Algoa Bay," he says, " the commissary-general received a visit from Vanderkemp. In the very hottest part of the morning we saw a waggon such as is used in husbandry, drawn by four meagre oxen, coming slowly along the sandy downs. Vanderkemp sat upon a plank laid across it, without a hat, his venerable bald head exposed to the burning rays of the sun. He was dressed in a threadbare black coat, waistcoat, and breeches, without shirt, neckcloth, or stockings, and leather sandals bound upon his feet, the same as are worn by the Hottentots.

"The commissary-general hastened to meet and receive him with the utmost kindness. He descended from his car, and approached with slow and measured steps, presenting to our view a tall, spare, yet venerable figure. In his serene countenance might be traced remains of former beauty, and in his eye, still full of fire, might plainly be discerned the powers of mind which had distinguished his early years. Instead of the usual salutations, he uttered a short prayer, in which he begged a blessing upon our chief and his company, and the protection of Heaven during the remainder of our journey. He then accompanied us into the house, where he entered into conversation freely upon many subjects, without any superciliousness or affected solemnity.

"The commissary-general reminded him that they had known each other thirty-six years before, at Leyden. He was then himself studying the law, and Vanderkemp was in garrison, as a lieutenant of dragoons. He named to him the coffee-house where they had often met, and talked over many occurrences that had happened jointly to them. The Missionary remembered these things very distinctly, observing that he was then leading a very dissolute life, and referring to his subsequent conversion and present course. He related many things worthy of remark during the time he lived among the Kafirs, and elucidated several circumstances that happened in the late unhappy war with them."

Many and grievous were the trials to which the Missionaries and their charge were subjected in the

new settlement of Bethelsdorp. The sterility and
want of water of the tract of land assigned them
were the source of constant distress, and compelled
them to lead a hungry, self-denying life; insomuch
that they were, for a length of time, without bread,
nor could they grow a sufficiency of vegetables. But
the heaviest troubles came from the enmity of the
wicked, and the cruelties and oppressions practised
upon the poor natives. Yet, notwithstanding all these
discouraging circumstances, many cheering marks of
the Divine blessing were given them. The journals
of Dr. Vanderkemp contain records of the good
effected. The following extract from one of them will
interest the reader. It was written after some years
of faithful labour :—

" The external state of Bethelsdorp puts on gradually a more pleasing appearance. The people become
more industrious, and the knitting-school flourishes
under the care of Brother Read's wife. Formerly we
had no corn of our own; but this year the Lord has
shown us it is in His power literally to change a
desert into a fertile field, by sending such abundance
of rain that we have the promise of a copious harvest.
The number of the inhabitants also increases, so that
we have been obliged to surround the square which
composes the village with a second, and that with a
third square, which will, in all probability, soon be
filled up. Our fields are covered with cattle,
amounting to about twelve hundred head, not including the sheep and the goats. There is an abundance of milk and butter, and other necessary articles,

as clothing, corn, and flour are brought by the boers in waggons, as to a market.

"As to the state of religion, we have great reason to praise and glorify the holy name of God. The Word of Life is by no means lifeless among us, and though we cannot well estimate the number of those whom we have cause to suppose are true Christians, yet we believe it to be considerable. There are not a few in whom the work of grace is plainly evident. Among these we number two slaves and a Hottentot, who frequently come over on the Sunday to hear the word of God; and three Kafir women, one of whom, called Leentje, was remarkable for integrity of life, and not less for assiduity and fervour in prayer. She was taken ill at a farm in our neighbourhood, and desired to see Brother Vanderkemp, who fetched her home in a waggon, and took her to his house. There she spent almost night and day in prayer and close communion with heaven. One morning she sent for him, requesting him to give her love to all the people of God, and desired to be carried into the open air; which being done, she said, 'Now I will go to my God;' and turning on her side, reclined her head upon her arm, as if asleep; but, looking more attentively at her, it was found she was dead. 'She walked with God and was not, for God took her.'"

It was a great source of satisfaction to the brethren that frequent visits were paid to the settlement by parties of Kafirs. "We are happy," they say, "to be placed in a situation where numbers of these people are daily passing and repassing. Sometimes they

attend at our seasons of worship, nor do our Hottentot brethren omit any opportunity of speaking concerning Christ to them, and many of them at times
have expressed a wish for persons to come among
them and instruct them."

Bethelsdorp was visited, in 1804, by Congo, a powerful Kafir chief, who brought with him his two sons
for education ; and Tzatzoe, another chief, with his
family, resided for some time there, and also left
his son with the Missionaries. This youth—young
Tzatzoe, became a decided Christian and a useful
Missionary to his countrymen, and in 1836 accompanied Dr. Philip to England.

It was at Bethelsdorp that Andries Stoffles first
heard the Gospel. He was by birth a Hottentot, but
having been taken prisoner by the Kafirs, was carried
from his native country, on the borders of the Great
Fish River, into Kafirland. There he continued for
some time, learned the Kafir language, and was employed as an interpreter. In that capacity he accompanied a Kafir chief to Bethelsdorp about the year
1810. Stoffles was then in a savage state and ar-
rayed in Kafir fashion,—his only clothing a dressed
cow-skin thrown loosely over his shoulders, and his
body smeared with grease and red ochre. He was
by no means deficient, however, in natural ability ;
from his boyhood he had been an acute observer,
and was gifted with an excellent memory and sound
judgment, to which were added an active mind and a
sanguine temperament.

When first he attended Divine worship at Bethelsdorp, he was so ignorant of its purpose and meaning as to suppose that the people had assembled to receive rations of provisions or presents of beads and buttons. His second attendance at the house of prayer was thus described by himself: " The preacher spoke of everything which I had done from my childhood. I said to myself, ' This is very strange! Surely my cousin must have gone to the Missionary and told him all about me.' But he said, ' No, he had not mentioned me to the Missionary;' adding, ' It is the Bible which tells you about your own heart.' "

The conviction of sin smote immediately the conscience of the man, and he was no longer the same. Yet he returned to the Kafirs, and tried to be happy in his former ways,—in dancing and merriment, and idle pleasures, but conscience still pursued him, and he was ill at ease. Continuing thus oppressed in mind, he returned to Bethelsdorp, and again listened to the preaching of the Gospel, whereby his convictions were strengthened and the agitation of his mind increased. Overcome by these mental conflicts, it is said he often hastened from the chapel to the bush, weeping aloud. There he would spend hours and even days apart from human intercourse, praying for pardon and help, and seeking rest to his heavy-laden spirit. Thus he continued for two or three years,—bowed down under a sense of guilt, beset by the terrors of self-condemnation, and unable to apply to himself the consolations of the Gospel of peace. At length his prayers were answered, a clearer light was shed abroad in his soul, and he saw,

14

by faith, the Lamb slain for the remission of our sins, and peace was imparted to his spirit at the foot of the Saviour's cross.

In company with Dr. Philip and Tzatzoe, Stoffles came to England in 1836. He wished, he said, to exert himself in this country on behalf of his nation —to see the people by whom the Gospel was sent to his native land—and to express his gratitude to them for this inestimable boon. To a certain extent he effected his purpose. Before the Aborigines' Committee of the House of Commons he stated the grievances of his afflicted countrymen, making a strong impression in their favour and his own. His fervent, unaffected piety, and the animated addresses he gave to the friends of Missions in various parts of the kingdom, won for him the sympathy and Christian regard of all.

Not many months elapsed, however, before his health began rapidly to decline, and the influence of this climate being evidently injurious to him, he left England, and for a time seemed to rally, but after reaching the Cape he suffered a relapse, and his death followed on the 18th of March, 1837. In his dying hours his mind was calm and composed. He had never, he said, enjoyed more of the presence of God his Saviour than during the voyage. When he felt that he should not recover he expressed regret that he was unable to tell his people what he had seen and heard in England, but was cheered in the joyful assurance that he was about to depart and be with Jesus.

Alas, for the wickedness of selfish and ungodly

Dr. Philip, Mr. Read, Andries Stoffles, and the chief Tzatzoe, before the Committee of the House of Commons

men! Far from receiving the assistance and friendly sympathy which they so much needed in their labours of love, the Missionaries were abused and maligned; and so fierce was the hatred entertained by the colonists and farmers against Dr. Vanderkemp, that one of the latter went to Cape Town, and without ceremony asked leave of the Governor to shoot him! General Janssens replied by asking significantly whether "he had seen the gallows on his entrance to the town?" On another occasion Vanderkemp was advised, for safety, to leave the Hottentots for a season. His reply was, "If I knew that I should save my own life by quitting them, I should not fear to offer that life for the smallest child among them." "So great love" may well fill our hearts with admiration and thankfulness. Vanderkemp was in truth the first public defender of the Hottentots, the pioneer in that great struggle which terminated, through the persevering exertions of Dr. Philip, on the 17th of July, 1828, in the effectual emancipation of that people. In truth, the Missionaries were the only protectors these poor people had. "At the Missionary Stations the Hottentots are treated like rational beings," says Dr. Philip, in his "Researches," "and there they are taught the value of their labour; and these things are crimes, as unpardonable in the eyes of their oppressors as opposition to the continuance of slavery is in the eyes of the West Indian planters and their abettors."

On the 19th of April, 1805, Dr. Vanderkemp, in reply to a letter from Governor Janssens, thus wrote:

"You acknowledge the great wrong which the colonists, *perhaps here and there,* do to your Hottentots. This expression, Governor, shows that you are still uninformed of the true situation of things in this country, or at least in the Uitenhage district. Not '*perhaps,*' and '*here and there,*' but very certainly, and pretty nearly in all parts, does this oppression prevail; nor is it only particular inhabitants, but the landdrosts themselves, from whom the oppressed ought to find protection, who make themselves guilty in this respect."

At length the reiterated clamours against the Missionaries so far prevailed with the Governor, that during the year 1825 Vanderkemp and Read received orders to repair to Cape Town without delay, in order to answer the accusations made by the boers against them. Before leaving the village (Bethelsdorp) the Doctor, in an address to his people, referred to the words of David when driven, by the rebellion of his son, from his capital: "If I shall find favour in the eyes of the Lord, He will bring me again, and show me both it and His holy habitation; but, if He say, I have no delight in thee, behold, here am I, let Him do to me as seemeth good unto Him."

They were detained several months at the Cape, and had no apparent prospect but that of being soon sent out of the country. In the beginning of the following year, however, the British became masters of the colony, and Sir David Baird, the commander of the victorious army, restored the brethren to their station, after treating them with the greatest politeness.

Not long after their return, the Doctor twice nar-
rowly escaped with his life, first, from the fall of a
heavy frame of wood, and next from the attack of an
infuriated ox. Some time after these events Dr. Vanderkemp, writing to the Directors, intimated his
opinion that the Institution at Bethelsdorp might now
be committed to the direction of another Missionary,
"which will make me free," he says, " to devote the
subsequent days of my far-advanced age to His service
among some of the nations hitherto unacquainted
with the way to everlasting happiness." Under the
same date, the Doctor's colleague, Mr. Read, wrote,
giving a favourable report of their charge, and he
concludes with the account of a day of rejoicing
recently held to celebrate the approaching abolition
of the slave trade. He says: "We held a day of
public thanksgiving; assembled all our people, young
and old, and impressed on their minds the horrid
iniquity of trading in human flesh, that our youth
might remember it to their latest years. Brother
Ullbrecht conducted the worship. A hymn was sung,
composed by Dr. Vanderkemp, and very applicable to
the occasion. The sympathetic feelings of our brother
for the poor people have induced him to redeem seven
of them from slavery, which has cost him between
£800 and £900. Being eye-witnesses of the horrid
usage of the poor slaves in this colony, we agreed to
be urgent at the throne of grace, in public and private,
that the Lord may be pleased wholly to do away with
this great evil. . . . Whilst I am writing, there comes
in an old grey-headed slave, who had heard of my

being here, and with difficulty got permission to come and hear the word of God. He listened to what I said of Christ with tears of joy."

The benevolence of Dr. Vanderkemp led him, as we see in the above passage, to sacrifice property, as well as time and effort, on behalf of the wretched outcasts of Africa; but this feeling carried him to extremes, and from a mistaken idea that he should succeed in elevating them, he married one of the women he had thus ransomed. In this matter he greatly erred, and, says Dr. Philip, "he lived to see and regret his mistake."

There is a deeply interesting passage in Mr. Moffat's "Missionary Labours," which will help us to see in what manner this great and good man was occasionally misled by the ardour of his feelings, and also that, grievously as he was maligned by the enemies of the cause, there were souls of kindred nature who admired and sympathised with him. After dwelling with enthusiasm on the character and work of Dr. Vanderkemp, Mr. Moffat says:—"But it may be said this is a partial view of his character; and it is only just to admit that the Doctor was eccentric, and many, very many, of his personal hardships were self-inflicted. Though his mission to the Kafirs was a bold, and in Africa an unprecedented undertaking, he was always within reach of civilised men; and, except when Gaika detained him a short time in the country, had always an asylum open to receive him. In a colonial village where there were many who admired and were ready to serve him, the Doctor would go out to the water, washing his own linen, and frequently, at home and abroad, he would dispense with hat, shirt, and shoes, while the patron and advocate of civilisation. These were anomalies and shades of character which of course added nothing to his usefulness; while his ultra notions on the subject of predestination left a leaven in some of the African churches which it required the labour of many years to remove."

It is also but justice to add that Dr. Vanderkemp was not without sympathy. There were many noble-minded colonists who took a deep interest in his sufferings and labours, who felt strong compassion for the spiritual destitution of the Hottentot race and the slave population, and who were liberal in supporting the cause. These were noble minds, who wept over the country's wrongs; and it is scarcely possible to conceive the Doctor's feelings when, on his journey to Graaff-Reinet, beyond the Gamka River, he came to the house of Mr. de Beer, who, on hearing the object of the party, "received them with uncommon joy, and calling his family and slaves together, fell upon his knees and uttered this remarkable prayer: ' O Lord, Thou hast afflicted me with inexpressible grief in taking my child from me, whom I buried this day; but now Thou rejoicest my soul with joy greater than all my grief, in showing me that Thou hast heard my prayers for the conversion of the Kafirs, and giving me thus to see the fulfilment of Thy promises.' He then addressed them, and sang several psalms and hymns relative to the calling of the heathen."

It has been mentioned on a former page that Dr.

Vanderkemp was desirous to change the scene of his labours, and he had fixed on the island of Madagascar as a desirable post. His health, however, had been for some time declining, and he had suffered a slight attack of apoplexy, which he considered an intimation that his end was not far distant. In one of his latest letters to the Directors he concludes with the following expressions of resignation and thankfulness : " The path by which God is pleased to lead me is not smooth and uniform ; but I have the more reason to bless His holy name for healing the wounds which I now and then receive in my flesh from its thorns. He continues to support me in the troubles to which I am, by the nature of my work, exposed ; and I have more than once experienced that He who slept in a storm can give rest to my soul, though all around me is agitation and alarm."

The close of the weary struggle was not long delayed. A few months before his decease, the Missionary and his colleague were summoned to appear before the Governor at Cape Town. Thither they immediately repaired, and produced such evidence of intolerable oppressions, as satisfied the authorities that a strict investigation was requisite. A special commission was appointed by the Earl of Caledon for the purpose, but before it could take effect the Doctor had been released from his sorrows, and was called up to the joy of his Lord. On the morning of the 7th December, 1811, he was taken ill. His exhortation, and especially his prayer on the preceding evening, were solemnly impressive, and in the morning he expounded a chapter very strikingly. Afterwards, feeling indisposed, he said to Mrs. Smith, a devoted friend and fellow-labourer, who was with him, " Oh ! my friend, I find myself extremely weak, and should be glad to have an opportunity to settle my own affairs." Alas ! no such opportunity was afforded. The same evening he was seized with a cold shivering, a fever ensued, and he retired to bed, never to rise again. His disorder rapidly progressed, notwithstanding the use of suitable treatment, and it soon appeared he was sinking. So oppressive was the nature of his disorder that he was unable to speak without difficulty, — a lethargic heaviness indisposed him to make any effort, and clouded his mind. About two days before his decease a friend asked him what was the state of his mind. His short but emphatic answer was, " All is well." As he spoke he smiled, and presently after- wards uttered the word " Light." He continued sen- sible to the last, but in extreme weakness, and on the Sabbath morning, December 15th, he gently breathed his last, in the sixty-fourth year of his age, and the thirteenth of his Missionary labours.

To attempt a panegyric of Dr. Vanderkemp would be alike vain and impertinent. His career speaks for itself. Such a consecration of talents, literature, and science, as is exhibited in his example, fills us with admiration. His was an heroic virtue springing from pure Christian love, and, as Dr. Philip has said, "When we consider how much, at that time, the aborigines of Africa wanted a protector, and reflect upon the courage, zeal, incorruptible integrity and weight of character attached to the Doctor, we must admire the wisdom of Providence in directing his attention to this sphere of action." He adds, in conclusion : " His history in Africa furnishes sufficient proofs of his devotedness to the great objects of his Mission ; but it is to his exertions in the cause of the oppressed aborigines that we are to look for the grandeur of his character and the most efficient part of his service."

I do not think I can more appropriately close this chapter than by a quotation from the last Report of the London Missionary Society on the present state of the Mission in South Africa. " Time would fail us to tell," says the writer, " of the great progress made in the Cape Colony among both coloured people and settlers during the last fifty years. The fiftieth ordinance, full emancipation, civil rights effectually secured, law and justice duly administered, a constitutional government, free election and a free parliament, have been accompanied by the gathering of numerous churches, the increase of family religion, the spread of education, and the evangelisation of large numbers of the native population.

" If we ask what effect this Christian work has produced among the colonial settlements, we may look at the town of Uitenhage. It stands in a valley, nearly surrounded by hills, but open on the south to the refreshing breezes from the sea, which is distant eighteen miles. The broad streets, laid out at right angles, are shaded with oak and willows and Australian gum-trees ; a stream of water from a perennial fountain runs through the whole, which feeds abundance of fruit and forest trees, brightens the settlement with flowers, and secures to it the pleasant name of the Garden of the Eastern Province. Three thousand people living in spacious houses, painted a sober yellow, and duly shaded from the heat by great blinds and shutters, manage the stores and shops, which are well supplied with necessaries and luxuries, while a keen competition stimulates an active, bustling life. For the English and Dutch populations have been erected numerous churches and schools, and the coloured population are also well provided for."

As to the feelings of the European families towards the native races, whose freedom was secured by so many struggles, one of our Missionaries—the son of the honoured Dr. Philip—says : " I have lived to see a very great abatement of their prejudices, both against Missions and against colour, and I have very strong hopes of an amalgamation of the population in all Christian ordinances."

Well may we say, with thankful voices, What has God wrought ! Could the venerable evangelist, whose history we have been recording, arise to gaze upon the scene now presented by the people whose ignorance and degradation called forth all the energies of his enlightened soul, how great would be his rejoicing ! Happy are they who walk in the steps of his faith, and, animated by the same love, carry on the blessed work of Missionary labour in Africa !

NEGRO CUTTING SUGAR-CANE.

JOHN SMITH:

THE MISSIONARY MARTYR OF DEMERARA.

CHAPTER I.

BRITISH GUIANA.

The memory of a noble life worthy of reverent treasuring — Early
career of Mr. Smith—Solemn dedication to the work of God—
Missionary operations — Appointed to the London Mission at
Demerara — Sketch of previous Missions in the Colony —
Oppressed condition of the negroes—Mr. Post, founder of the
Guiana Mission—Violent opposition of the planters—Tokens of
the Divine blessing.

ANY years ago I chanced to find myself in
a Roman Catholic chapel at Bristol. The
officiating priest, after completing the pre-
liminary services, ascended the pulpit and
preached a lively and impressive discourse. One
thing he said I have never forgotten. In proof of
some doctrine he advanced, he quoted a passage from
"Holy Writ." The text was not canonical, and my
lips immediately moved with girlish eagerness as I
asked myself, "Where does he find that?" Scarcely
had I done so when the preacher said, "Some one pre-

sent may possibly ask for chapter and verse.　I refer you, my hearers, to one of the books of the Apocrypha, for our Holy Church does not scatter her sacred leaves to the winds, as did the Sybil of old. Nay, she collects them reverently, and carefully treasures them, and suffers them not to fall into oblivion. Like a tender mother, she cares for all her offspring, and holds them ever dear and precious."

Now, this careful and loving spirit I want my young readers to call into exercise as they read this chapter.　I wish to endear to them the memory of one of our early Missionaries, who died the death of a martyr for his Saviour's cause, and whom the Church of Rome, had he belonged to her communion, might probably have canonized.　Would that all the saints in her calendar were equally worthy of remembrance with him whose history you are now to read!

John Smith was born on the 27th June, 1790, in a village of Northamptonshire.　His father was a soldier, and lost his life while fighting in one of the battles between the English and French on the plains of Egypt.　The boy was left to the care of a widowed mother, whose straitened circumstances were insufficient to afford him regular education.　The little instruction he received in his early days was that which he picked up at a Sunday-school, to which he was occasionally sent.　At the age of fourteen he was apprenticed to a tradesman in London, whose favour and confidence he secured by the steadiness of his behaviour.　His master, finding how much he had been neglected, kindly offered to teach the lad, and under his fostering care he soon made satisfactory progress in knowledge.

Little is known concerning his early manhood. It appears, from private papers, written many years afterwards, that he was without any serious regard to spiritual things. He says: " It pleased God, in the course of His providence, to remove me to London, where the charms of the metropolis, the allurements of my new associates, and the wicked propensities of my depraved heart, soon almost entirely effaced the good impressions made at the Sunday-school." While thus careless and ungodly, he was led in some way to go to Silver-street Chapel, where he heard a sermon preached by the Rev. E. J. Jones. He was then about nineteen years old, and he relates the impression made upon his heart by the venerable appearance of the preacher, who, standing up, opened the Bible, " for which," he says, " I had a kind of superstitious veneration; and when the fourth commandment was read, my conscience smote me, and I was at once convinced of sin. Blessed be God, that conviction never left me." From this time he began regularly to attend the means of grace ; but for several months was greatly distressed in spirit under a sense of his guilt in the sight of God, and having no clear understanding of the way of salvation made known in the Gospel, was full of trouble. Speaking of this period, he writes : " I roamed from place to place, seeking rest but finding none. At length I went, in 1810, to Tonbridge Chapel, which was just opened, when the Rev. J. Leifchild preached from Isa. lv. 6, 7,

15

'Seek the Lord while He may be found,' &c. As he commented on the words, 'He will abundantly pardon,' it was like life from the dead; it dispelled my fears, eased my conscience, and gave me confidence in the mercy of God."

Not long after this, the youth was seized with a severe illness, from which it was thought he could not recover. He then solemnly dedicated himself to God, and determined, should he be spared, that his life should be spent in the service of the Most High. To this resolution he was enabled by Divine help steadily to adhere, and the remainder of his days proved the ardour of his love, and the sacredness of the vows he had taken. He found his earliest sphere of usefulness in labouring as a Sunday-school teacher, conducting himself in all his engagements with so much diligence, prudence, and consistency, that he by degrees obtained much influence with his companions. They looked to him for counsel in difficulty, and learned to rely upon his kindliness and judgment. In short, the desire to be useful in his Master's service became more and more the ruling principle with the young ardent spirit. His exhortations to the pupils in his class were so serious and impressive, that his companions perceived he was making rapid progress in the Divine life, and his superiors were of opinion that he showed capabilities of a more than ordinary kind, and that he ought to seek some sphere of more extensive usefulness.

After a time the mind of the youth was directed to the subject of Christian Missions, and as he pondered it in secret, his soul was fired with ardent zeal for the sacred cause. He longed to be sent to the heathen, that he might make known among them the Gospel which had given him a new and blessed life; and at length he took courage and wrote, expressing his feelings, to the Rev. G. Burder, one of the Secretaries of the London Missionary Society. His zeal and firmness of purpose were put to the test by a delay of two years, when, by the advice of Mr. Burder, he offered himself to the Directors in the usual manner; and, after due deliberation, his services were accepted, and he was placed under the care of Mr. Newton, of Witham, in Essex, assisted by whose judicious instruction, he pursued with diligence the requisite training for his arduous task, and conducted himself in such a manner as to secure the affection and confidence of his tutor, who said of him: "We esteemed him as a son, and never did we part with a young man who had so strongly engaged our affections. I was fully persuaded he would, by the grace of God, prove a blessing wherever he went."

When the period of his studies was completed, the Directors determined to appoint Smith as a Missionary to Demerara, from which colony they had recently received a request that a Minister of the Gospel should be sent to instruct the slaves on a certain plantation named Le Resouvenir.

Before proceeding further, it may be interesting to give here a short account of British Guiana, and the early proceedings of the London Missionary Society

there.   Demerara, Essequibo, and Berbice, now
composing that province, were originally three
distinct Dutch colonies, but were finally ceded to the
British crown about 1814.   It is a maritime tract
of coast land, extending for a space of some three
hundred miles, between the River Coventen, the
western limit of Surinam, and the frontier of
Spanish Guiana, at Cape Nassau.   The whole coast
is so flat that it is scarcely visible till the shore
has been reached, tops of the trees only being seen,
which appear as if growing out of the sea.   When
the territory first came into the possession of
Britain, it was covered with dense and almost im-
penetrable forests, but great improvements were in
time effected.   British industry felled the woods,
and availing itself of the natural fertility of the
soil, has rendered this one of the most productive
regions in the New World.   Demerara ranks, as
to West India produce, second only to Jamaica, and
the coffee of Berbice is superior to that of any of
the islands.

At the time of the occupation of this country by
the British, there were 150,000 slaves in the colony,
for whose instruction nothing was done, their minds
being wrapped in heathen darkness, and their
bodies held in unrighteous and cruelly oppressive
bondage.   In the year 1805, a Wesleyan Missionary
from Dominica visited Demerara, hoping to establish
a Mission there.   He was summarily dismissed in
a few days, being ordered by the Governor to return
in the mail boat which had brought him.   Not

EBENEZER CHAPEL, DEREHAM.

long after this, Mr. Post, the proprietor of plantation Le Resouvenir, feeling his mind concerned about the religious instruction of his slaves, wrote to the Directors of the London Missionary Society, requesting their aid; and, in the year 1807, the first Christian Minister to that country was sent by the Society, and on the 6th of February, 1808, Mr. Post's long cherished and earnest desire was accomplished, and he welcomed the Rev. John Wray to his house, receiving him with the utmost cordiality, and erecting for his use a new building, called Bethel Chapel, and also a residence for the Missionary.

The preaching of the Gospel was vehemently opposed by the planters, most of whom looked upon Mr. Post as a fool or a madman, and accused him of introducing anarchy, disorder, and discontent among the negroes. These attacks did not however change the good man's purpose, and after a short time he desired a second instructor for his people in George Town, situate in the Charlestown district, whither Mr. Davies, another of the London Missionary Society's Missionaries, was sent, and speedily entered on the work, crowds of negroes coming, on the Sabbath-days, from distant parts of the country to listen to the glad tidings of salvation.

In the mean time, the Missionary at Bethel chapel continued steadily pursuing his labours with good success, as we learn by the following extract of a letter from Mr. Post, dated January 12th, 1809 :—" It would be ingratitude to our God and

Saviour not to praise His name for what He has done. He has built His temple in this wilderness, and I trust has given us reason to call it *Bethel*, because many of the ignorant negroes have experienced the presence of the Lord. It is not possible that such a change could otherwise have been effected in their conduct, both on mine and other estates, especially on the estate next to mine. They were formerly a nuisance to the estate, from their drumming and dancing two or three nights in the week, and were looked on with a jealous eye on account of their dangerous communications; but they are now become the most zealous attendants on public worship, catechizing, and private instruction. No drums are heard in the neighbourhood, except where the owners have prohibited the attendance of their slaves. Drunkards and fighters are changed into sober and peaceable people, and endeavour to please those who are set over them."

After Mr. Post's death, in 1809, Mr. Wray continued to labour at plantation Le Resouvenir, now and then visiting other parts of the coast. Subsequently, labourers from various other Societies followed in the track of these solitary pioneers, and "the Word of the Lord grew and multiplied," so that, by the beginning of the year 1817, nine years after the arrival of Mr. Wray, "many old men and women," we are .told, "as well as young ones, with books and catechisms in their hands and pockets," were to be found among the slaves in Demerara and Berbice.

CHAPTER II.

AT WORK IN DEMERARA.

Arrival in Demerara — Harsh reception by the Governor — Forbidden
to teach the negroes — Nothing daunted — Progress of the Gospel
— Revolting cruelties of the planters — "141 lashes!" — Disheartening influences — Steadfast under difficulties — British
legislation on behalf of the slaves — Withholding of the news
by the planters — Spirit of disaffection among the negroes —
Suspicions against Mr. Smith — His endeavours to quiet the
slave population — The eve of the storm.

MR. WRAY having removed to Berbice, as
related in the foregoing pages, the choice
of the Directors fell on John Smith, as a
suitable person to succeed to the post thus
vacated at Le Resouvenir; and after having been
ordained to the ministry, he left his native land,
accompanied by his wife, in the ship *William Neilson,*
bound for Demerara, where he landed on the 23rd
of February, 1817. A few days after his arrival our
Missionary was introduced to Governor Murray, who
received him in a most ungracious manner. His
account of the interview is as follows :— " His Excel-
lency frowned upon me; he asked what I had come
to do, and how I proposed to instruct the negroes. I
answered, by teaching them to read, by making them
learn Dr. Watts's Catechisms, and by preaching
the Gospel in a plain manner. To this he replied
sharply, ' If ever you teach a negro to read, and I

hear of it, I will banish you from the colony immediately.'" Such a threat might have daunted a man of feeble spirit, but he persevered, and entreated that a second interview should be granted him, when he so well pleaded his cause, that he obtained permission to preach, and the promise of protection. Thus authorised, he commenced his work by preaching his first sermon in Bethel Chapel, on the 9th March, and wrote thus to his beloved tutor, Mr. Newton: —
"Although it was a wet day, the chapel was nearly full. I was much pleased with the negroes, who were more attentive than many congregations in England. Many, very many, are hungry for the bread of life; there is a great prospect for success; many hundreds of negroes attend my preaching, besides white people."

. It was a sad restriction laid on the Missionaries that they were forbidden to teach any of the slaves to read. Yet notwithstanding this prohibition, several of the adults and of the children who could not read a letter, knew the catechism by heart; and what they had learned they were most anxious to teach their companions, and in this way the good seed was scattered, and a blessing attended it.

Towards the close of the first year, Mr. Smith wrote to the Directors, giving a short account of his progress. "Since my last," he says, "I have been constant in preaching to the negroes, and catechizing them; the number of hearers has been and is increasing, and more come than can gain admittance. It would rejoice your hearts could you see the poor blacks sitting around the outside of the chapel under the cabbage trees; but it is painful to see them excluded for want of room, after walking, as some do, many miles. It is a most pleasant sight to behold these people coming to church on the Lord's Day morning. We have a practical comment on Psalm lxxxiv. 6, 7. The negroes come from the different plantations in companies, and when they draw near to the house of prayer, they stop and drink at a pool which Mr. Post had made to provide the people with fresh water." After detailing some particulars concerning his daily work, he adds : " But while the sacred cause prospers, we are violently assailed by a multitude of enemies. Our character, as a body of Missionaries, is represented in the local newspapers in the blackest colours; but amidst all, it is a great support to my mind to reflect that we are not used so ill as our Master was. The same things were said of the Lord Jesus, and we, as His servants, must not murmur if we meet with the like treatment."

Disheartening as it was thus to be unjustly accused and maligned, the distress experienced by the sight of the miseries endured by the unhappy slaves was far more afflicting to the heart of this good man. Very affecting allusions are constantly made in the diaries of Mr. Smith, from which a few extracts will suffice to show at once the unfeigned humility and simple piety of the man, and the terrible nature of the trials he had to undergo.

" Wednesday, 3rd Sept. — Saw some negroes working in irons, and one whose skin was entirely cut off his back by the whip. Never was I more oppressed by the degradation of the human species, or my feelings more keenly touched. . . Last night, or rather early this morning, I was awoke out of a sound sleep by a heavy peal of thunder. Several most tremendous claps followed, which made the house tremble and the glasses clatter. Hark! I pause in the midst of this to count the lashes on a naked slave. When the flogging was over, my wife, who was in the next room, called out, 'Did you count those lashes?' I said, 'Yes; 141.' She replied, 'I counted 140.' Ah! the men who spend the Sabbath evening over the bottle and glass, diverting themselves with cards and backgammon, are haunted by hideous dreams and fearful forebodings during the hours of sleep, and then rise to wreak their vengeance on the unhappy—it may be the innocent—slave.

"Sunday, July 19th.—I felt my spirit moved within me at the prayer-meeting, by hearing one of the negroes pray most affectionately that God would overrule the opposition made by the planters to religion, for His own glory. In such an unaffected strain he breathed out his pious complaint, and mentioned so many particulars as to the means used to keep them from the house of God, and to punish them for firmness in their religion, that I could not help thinking the time is not far distant when the Lord will make it manifest by some signal judgment that He has heard the cry of the oppressed (Exodus iii. 7, 8)."

It was only in seeing the fruit of his earnest endeavours to promote the spiritual well-being of the

poor blacks, that hope and consolation were found.
"If there be anything on this side heaven," he
writes, "which can gladden our hearts, it is to behold
whole families of heathens embracing the Gospel, and
living so as to glorify God. This joy many of your
Missionaries realise, and it is mine. The success with
which it pleases God to bless my feeble labours far
exceeds my most sanguine hopes. . . . It is
delightful to me to see the people coming to chapel
on a fine moonlight evening, and from their constant
attendance, I am sure it is no less so to them. From
their prayers I often learn they prize the privilege of
evening worship. After a day's labour (as field slaves
labour), amid the harsh sound and perhaps harsher
feel of the bloody and busy whip, surely the sound of
the Gospel of Peace, promising rest to the weary,
must exhilarate their spirits and comfort their hearts."

Sad and revolting are the pictures constantly
recurring of the barbarous usage inflicted by the
overseers. Three successive entries of the Missionary's diary tell but the record of a short period of
perpetual grief and annoyance : — "Monday, April
3rd.—I cannot resist noting here that a few minutes ago (about six a.m.), hearing the whip crack,
I listened to count the lashes, and reckoned a hundred
and five stripes on one individual. The person flogged
was Phillis, a woman, punished for running away.
May 1st.—The flogging of the negroes so much
annoys and affects me, that I can think of little else.
On inquiring who it was that had such a flogging
yesterday morning, one of the negroes told me it was

Phillis. I observed I was sorry she had done anything so bad as to deserve such punishment. The negro replied, 'Mr. Hamilton has not done yet.' On hearing eighty-six lashes this morning on one person, I resolved to note them down. In the evening I preached from Matthew xxi. 1–6. July 24th. Saturday.—The days of this week have passed away, and I have done almost nothing. The negroes are worked so hard that they have no time to come to me for instruction, and for me to go to them is impossible. Besides the smallness of the congregation, which is very discouraging, we are much annoyed during the evening services by the noise of the cattle mill grinding the coffee, and often by the flogging of the negroes, the crack of the whip, and the cries of the people. In addition to this, the noise of the crapeaus, the frogs, and the clouds of flying beetles driving against one's face, and getting down one's neck and bosom, beside the host of mosquitoes, render the evening services at this season extremely irksome. I scarcely know what I pray for or what I preach; but were I to give them up, it might be accounted indolence on my part, and might serve as an excuse for the absence of people on other occasions."

Thus, almost heart-broken by the sight of misery he was unable to alleviate, himself despised and calumniated, and his efforts to do good thwarted by the opposition and hatred of the slave-masters, no wonder the heart of the Missionary was greatly "discouraged, by reason of the way." In addition to these outward trials, Mr. Smith suffered from natural feebleness of constitution, and he appears to have felt that, in all probability, his span of life would be short. In his private notes reference is frequently made to this debility of constitution. Writing on New Year's Day, 1821, he says: " Having obtained help of God, I continue to this day. Whether I shall live to see the end of the year, God alone knows. ' Man that is born of a woman is of *few* days.' Perhaps mine are nearly spent. During the past year my conduct has not been what it ought to have been ; far from it. I feel and lament it. O God, pardon my sins ! That gracious text, Psalm ciii. 13, 14, comforts me. Last week I read part of ' Shower's Reflections on Time and Eternity,' a valuable little book. . . . This morning we were awoke, about five o'clock, by the singing of the negroes. They had an early prayer-meeting, to seek the blessing of God at the commencement of the year, and to consecrate themselves anew to His service. Several of them came from the prayer-meeting to wish us a happy new year. ' We mean,' they said, ' to serve God better this year ; hope God shall help us.' "

In the course of the year 1822 Mr. Smith was cheered by a visit from Mr. Wray, the former minister at Le Resounvenir. He spent two days among the people, and expressed his great satisfaction in seeing many of those who had been the first-fruits of the Gospel there walking in the truth, conducting themselves with consistency, and rejoicing in hope. Others had been removed to a better world, having died in the faith, while many more were zealous in the good ways of the Lord, and eager for the enjoyment of their religious privileges. The number of negroes under regular instruction was about two thousand, and all along the coast, for a distance of some seventy miles, the people were anxious to be taught.

We are now approaching the disastrous period of the revolt of the negroes on the east coast of Deme-rara. This unhappy event occurred in August, 1823, and was seized on by the colonial authorities as a fitting occasion for destroying the reputation and suspending the labours of the devoted Missionary. During the whole of his career he had been watched with the most suspicious vigilance, but even his in-veterate enemies were unable to fix a stain upon his character. Little did he anticipate the storm which was at hand. The eventful year, the year of his arrest, trial, and condemnation, dawned upon him without the least warning. The first entry in his journal is as follows: "January 2nd, 1823.—God's providence smiles upon me at the commencement of a new year. I bless Thee, O my God, that I can look back to the events of the past twelve months with unmixed gratitude, and that I can look forward with lively hope. I could wish here to note some of the mercies received, but shall have occasion to refer to them in my next letter to the Directors." A few days later, he writes: " On the road to-day I was overtaken by a boy, whom I found to be one of Dr. M'Turk's slaves. I inquired why he did not come to chapel, to which he replied that his master would not allow him ; and he added, in a serious tone, ' Massa, the Doctor

don't like us to know God.   Once he heard me say,
" God knows," and he was angered, and made me eat
the soap he was washing with, and gave another boy
a horse-spur, and made him spur me, because he said
I knew God.'   And this doctor is a member of the
Legislative Assembly !"

Who can be surprised that Governor Murray should
refer, after the insurrection, to great irritation and
susceptibility on the part of the negroes, when such
atrocious acts as these were perpetrated by members
of the colonial legislature ?   No wonder that men
treated as the negroes were should at length have
been goaded into an attempt to recover their rights as
human beings.   Mr. Smith frequently describes the
slaves as perplexed and excited by the needless re-
strictions enforced on them as to their attendance on
Divine worship, yet he never for a moment dreamed
of their rising in open rebellion against their masters.

At this period the great body of the English nation,
roused to a righteous indignation by the fearful
sufferings of the negro population, resolved upon
the abolition of slavery throughout the British West
Indies; and as an expression of this feeling, Mr.,
afterwards Sir T. Fowell Buxton, moved the following
resolution in the House of Commons:—" That the
state of slavery is repugnant to the principles of the
British constitution and of the Christian religion, and
that it ought to be abolished gradually throughout
the British colonies, with as much expedition as may
be found consistent with a due regard to the well-
being of the parties concerned."

16

To this resolution Mr. Canning moved an amendment, to the effect that it was expedient to adopt effectual measures for ameliorating the condition of the slave population in his Majesty's dominions.

This amendment was carried, and in conformity with it certain resolutions were agreed upon and transmitted to all the West India colonies, and the regulations founded upon them were sent in the shape of an Order in Council to Demerara and the other crown colonies. These important documents were received by General Murray, the Governor, on the 7th of July, 1823. Among other salutary enactments, it was ordered that the hours of daily labour should be limited to *nine*, and that the flogging of women was at once and for ever to be abolished. The planters looked upon these measures of the home Government as an unwarrantable interference with what they regarded as their vested rights, and thought proper to withhold from the public the instructions they had received. They met and discussed the subject, and imprudently let drop some casual remarks, which were eagerly caught up by the negro slaves who attended upon them. *Something* had been done at home for the benefit of the people, it was soon said, and the good news was eagerly spread and believed, and frequently exaggerated. Before long the slaves had got hold of the notion that the King and Parliament of England had made them free. Surprised and grieved that no official information was given them about the "New Law," as it was termed, they believed that the colonists had determined to withhold the boon of freedom from them, and to retain them in slavery. No wonder that discontent, deep and universal, prevailed. The more so, as no relief was given them, their burdens were rather increased than diminished, and the flogging and excessive labour went on as before.

Alluding to this state of things, Mr. Smith mentions in his diary that Quamina, one of the deacons at Bethel Chapel, came to him to inquire if the report were true that the King had sent orders to the Governor to free the slaves. On being assured this was not the case, he said he knew something was in agitation, for that his son Jack had been told it by the Governor's own servant, who heard his master talking about it with some gentlemen. Others of the congregation at the chapel applied to him for information, and he did his best to quiet them, saying that if they waited patiently matters would be made plain. Still the irritation among the slaves increased, and their deep dissatisfaction was no secret to the planters.

On Sunday, August 17th, Mr. Smith conducted the services at his chapel as usual. He overheard Quamina, the deacon, and another negro talking together afterwards about the "New Law," and remonstrated with them, telling them to be patient, and do nothing to provoke the Governor. The next morning, feeling very unwell, he went to George Town for medical advice, and on his return wrote in his diary : —
" Monday, August 18th.—Early this morning I went to town to consult Dr. R—— as to my health. It is ten months since I had his first advice, and the pain

16 *

and weakness have increased, so that I have found it
difficult to keep about, and more difficult to preach.
He says that a thorough change of air, such as a
voyage to Bermuda or England, would be desirable."

This was the last entry he ever made, and deeply
affecting it is to reflect that one so gentle and holy
was hurried to the grave by the cruel usage of wicked
men, who persecuted him to the death, and cast a
dark stain of obloquy upon his memory.

CHAPTER III.

THE INSURRECTION.

Open rebellion of the negroes—Success of Mr. Smith in moderating
their violence—His arrest by Government as a participator in the
rebellion—In the hands of enemies—Cruel treatment of the
Missionary and his wife—The Court of Inquiry—Perjury of insurgent slaves with regard to Mr. Smith's character—Their unavailing recantation—Sentence of death passed on the Missionary
—The felon's dungeon—Sinking through disease—"God will
not leave me!"—Death—Burial—Sensation in England on
receipt of the intelligence—The martyr's death not in vain—
Abolition of slavery throughout the British empire.

THE negroes were now all in open rebellion.
On the evening of Monday, the 18th August,
the day when Mr. Smith went to George
Town, the insurrection broke out. About
half-past six, when returning from a short walk, the

SMITH CHAPEL, DEMERARA.

Missionary and his wife heard a loud and unusual noise. The manager of the estate, Mr. Hamilton, called out in a hurried voice to them as they were passing. They went up to his house, and found it besieged by forty or fifty men, all naked, and brandishing their cutlasses, shouting and gesticulating fiercely. They forced the outer doors and filled the lower part of the house. Going in amongst them, Mr. Smith inquired what they wanted? "We want the guns and our rights," was the reply. In vain he entreated them to desist and to depart peaceably. They were furious, and quite beyond his control. He persuaded them, however, before he left, to refrain from injuring the manager, whom they were about to put into the stocks. "How all this will end," said the Missionary to his friend Mr. Mercer of Trinidad, "I know not. I feel perfectly safe, not because we have so many soldiers patrolling about, but because I am conscious we have never wronged any one." The day following, Quamina, the deacon who has been mentioned before, came, at Mrs. Smith's request, to the Mission house, as she hoped through him to obtain some information as to what was going on. This man had a son named Jack Gladstone, who, though more intelligent than the generality of the slaves, was a gay, dissolute youth, very irregular in his attendance at chapel. He and one Paris, a man of some intelligence and great bodily strength, were the principal authors of the scheme formed on the east coast, the design of which was to seize and put into the stocks all the white people on the estates, and then to proceed to

town in a body, to claim the "Freedom" which the
vague current rumours had led them to suppose was
granted by the King.   How far Quamina was cogni-
zant of his son's proceedings was never known; but
the fact that he had been sent for by Mrs. Smith, and
seen in conversation with the Missionary after the
insurrection had broken out, told much against the
latter.   It was affirmed, and probably believed by the
authorities, that this man was himself a rebel, and
they charged it as a crime against Mr. Smith, that he
had not secured him and immediately given information to the Governor.

We have the assurance of Mr. Smith that he was
entirely ignorant that Quamina was even a reputed
rebel; and so, all unconscious of coming events, the
missionary family remained quietly at home until
the next day, Thursday, the 21st August, when, as
he was writing a letter to the Secretary of the
London Missionary Society, giving an account of
what had transpired, he was suddenly interrupted
by the forcible entry of a company of infantry, who
carried him and his wife, under a military escort, to
town.   The specific charge upon which Mr. Smith
was arrested was that he had refused to enrol himself in the militia, in compliance with the Governor's
proclamation which placed the colony under martial
law.   The serious charge afterwards brought against
him, that he was a ringleader or encourager of the
rebels, was an afterthought.

The good man had indeed fallen into the hands of
cruel enemies, ungodly men, who hated the very idea

of instructing the unhappy slaves, and regarded the
Missionaries as incendiaries of the most mischievous
character. They were also alarmed, and with good
reason, for the very thought of insurrection is one
of dread, and these slave-drivers lived always on a
volcano, threatening at any moment to burst forth
and destroy them. Hatred and fear thus combined,
and the terrific power of martial law was called into
action. In vain did the few pious and benevolent
men who wished to act as mediators for the negroes
urge the desirableness of openly declaring to the
people what the New Regulations actually were.
This plan was adopted at Berbice, by permission
of the Governor there, and *all remained quiet.* Mr.
Smith and Mr. Austin, the excellent chaplain of the
garrison, were anxious to obtain the same permission
from Governor Murray, but he refused, and confusion
and bloodshed ensued. Those who knew most of
the character of the people, and of what actually
transpired, believed that this course of conduct was
the most fatal in its consequences. Mr. Austin, who,
to his undying honour, stood by our Missionary as
his firm friend and advocate throughout all his trial,
subsequently declared this, and said: "I am persuaded,
from the intimate knowledge which my most anxious
inquiries have obtained, that, in the late scourge
which the hand of the Almighty has inflicted on this
ill-fated country, nothing but those religious impressions which, under Providence, Mr. Smith had been
instrumental in producing—nothing but those principles of the Gospel of Peace which he had been

proclaiming, could have prevented a dreadful effusion of blood here."

It is a sad tale we have now to tell, of suffering and injustice, and our hearts must ache when we remember that the same evil passions are still working in the hearts of the disobedient and ungodly, and the fruit thereof is Death.

The place of confinement to which the Missionary and his wife were conveyed was a small room or rather garret, near the roof of the Colony House, exposed to the burning rays of the sun, when the thermometer in the shade at their own house in the country stood at an average of eighty-five degrees. Their condition, thus suffering from heat, was rendered still more distressing by their having been hurried away without even a necessary change of raiment.

All the letters, diaries, and other papers belonging to Mr. Smith, were retained under seal, and he was not allowed the use of pen and ink, nor permitted to write even to the Directors of the London Missionary Society. Thus inhumanly treated, he was kept closely confined from August to October, with two sentries, one at the bottom of the stairs and the other at the door of his room, which was ordered to be kept open day and night.

The most strenuous endeavours were now made to fasten upon him the charge of having instigated the slaves to revolt, and it was hoped that a plea might thus be afforded to expel all Missionaries from the colony. A Court of Inquiry was convened, before which, for several weeks, a great number of persons were examined touching the circumstances of the insurrection. Amongst them were some of the insurgent slaves connected with the congregation at Bethel Chapel, who, fear-stricken and in terror of their lives, basely brought false accusations against the man who had been the messenger of peace and love to them. Some of these perjured slaves, who had thus belied the truth, when, contrary to their expectation, they were afterwards tried and condemned, recanted in the most abject manner, confessed they had spoken falsely, and asserted with their latest breath the innocence of the persecuted Missionary.

Untrustworthy and contradictory as were the statements thus elicited from the terrified slaves examined before the Court of Inquiry, Smith was gravely charged with being the cause of the revolt, and at length was put upon his trial to answer this fearful charge. Although the insurrection had been entirely suppressed, and there was no longer a just cause for the continuance of martial law, it was still in force, and was so during five months, from the 19th of August, 1823, until the 19th of January, 1824; and it was under this fundamentally illegal and unconstitutional jurisdiction that proceedings were carried on. The four counts in the indictment preferred against the prisoner contained in substance an accusation of conspiracy and rebellion. Throughout the trial every effort was made by his unconstitutional judges to place him at a disadvantage; and had there not been in their minds an inveterate prejudice against the prisoner, it seems hardly possible they should have come to the decision delivered by the court. The substance of the sentence given went to declare that Smith had promoted discontent in the minds of the negroes; had guilty knowledge of the revolt, which he concealed; and did aid and abet it by consulting with and advising Quamina, one of the insurgents, whom he permitted to go at large, well knowing his guilt. His precise offence was termed misprision of treason, and the court having convicted him thereof, sentenced him *to be hanged by the neck till dead*, but begged to recommend him to mercy. This judgment was pronounced on the 24th of November, and the feelings of the prisoner may be better imagined than described when, from the room in which he was confined, above that in which the court sat, he heard the loud shouts of rejoicing when the verdict was returned. Immediately after the sentence had been pronounced he was removed to the common jail, where he was placed in a room on the ground-floor, with stagnant water beneath, the pernicious miasma from which, passing through the boards of the room, some of which were a quarter of an inch apart, acted as deadly poison upon him in his weakly condition. Notwithstanding the remonstrances of the doctor who attended him, he was kept in this unwholesome cell for seven weeks. Previous to his trial, Mr. Smith was not suffered to communicate with the Directors, but after his sentence this restriction was removed, and he wrote an affecting letter, giving a detailed account of all that had occurred. "Of my personal sufferings," he says, "I will only say that the painful nature of my confinement, with the disease under which I have for some months laboured, have pressed very heavily upon me. I have, however, much consolation from the consideration of my innocence of the crimes laid to my charge. That I *am* innocent I have not only the testimony of my own conscience, but the attestation of all my friends who have made strict inquiries into my conduct relative to this affair. I am bold to affirm that I never gave utterance to anything that could make the slaves dissatisfied, and I trust the Directors will seriously consider the hardship of my case, and make every effort on my behalf."

Four days later he wrote to his old friend and employer, Mr. Davies, of London, closing his letter as follows :—" I feel pretty happy in my mind. · I know not what awaits me : sometimes I think my decaying frame will presently sink, but I am in the Lord's hand, and am willing He should do with me what He pleases. Indeed, I often feel anxious for the time to arrive when I shall inhabit ' a house not made with hands.' Pray for me." It was not long before the malady which oppressed him, greatly aggravated by the miseries he had endured during his incarceration, assumed a fatal character, and it became evident his days were numbered. The last effort of his pen was a farewell letter to the Directors, dated January 12th, 1824. In it, after acknowledging the kind and sympathising answer he had received to his former communication, he says : " I have endeavoured from the beginning to discharge my duties faithfully. In doing so I have met with unceasing opposition and reproach, until at length the adversary found occasion to triumph over me. The Lord's hand is heavy upon me, still I can praise His name, that though my outward afflictions abound, yet the consolations of the Gospel also abound towards me, and I believe He will do all things well. In much affliction, your useless, but devoted servant, J. SMITH."

Three days later he became exceedingly ill, and his strength quite exhausted. He expressed his confidence in God, saying that his mind was kept in perfect peace, and that he looked to heaven as his home where he should soon be. " I try," he said, " to forget the past and to look to the future. God will not leave me at last in my trouble ; no, I find Him a God near at hand, and not afar off."

Thus did he " in patience possess his soul," and trusted in God that He would deliver him. He died on the morning of the 8th of February, continuing perfectly sensible to the last moment.

The authorities, after making the necessary examination into the circumstances of the decease, ordered that the body should be buried before daylight next morning. They also forbad the widow, and a friend who attended her, to follow, notwithstanding their earnest remonstrances. Mrs. Smith could not refrain from being present, although not permitted to accompany the funeral party. She and her friend accordingly left the jail at half-past three in the morning, dark as it was, accompanied only by a free black man carrying a lantern, and proceeded to the burial-place, where they witnessed the mournful spectacle. One true friend was there whose love proved strong as death. The funeral service was read by the Rev. W. S. Austin, who thus ventured to incur the general odium of the colonists, and to vindicate the character of the man whom he believed perfectly innocent of the crime laid to his charge.

When the body of the persecuted Missionary had been thus stealthily consigned to the grave, two negro workmen, a carpenter and a bricklayer, who had been members of his congregation, wishing to protect and mark the spot where their benefactor lay, began to rail in and brick over the grave; but as soon as this came to the knowledge of the First Fiscal he forbad the work, and ordered the bricks to be taken up, the railing removed, and the whole frail memorial of humble affection demolished!

There remains yet one touching little incident to mention in reference to the personal history of our Missionary. At the time that he lay sick in his prison he was compelled by his prosecutors to draw a bill upon the funds of the London Missionary Society, to defray the expenses of his (so-called) trial. Many years after, the Secretary of the Society, when arranging some old papers, met with this bill. In looking at it his attention was drawn to one corner of the sheet, and, on examining it more carefully, he found written in a minute hand the reference, 2 Cor. iv. 8, 9, on turning to which he found the text, "We are troubled on every side, yet not distressed; we are perplexed, but not in despair; persecuted, but not forsaken; cast down, but not destroyed."

"Here is the patience and faith of the saints:" and who but must recall to mind the words of St. Paul when, encouraging the Thessalonians amid the persecutions and tribulations they endured, he said, "It is a righteous thing with God to recompense tribulation to them that trouble you, and to you who are troubled, rest with us, when the Lord Jesus shall be revealed from heaven with His mighty angels."

The immediate consequences of this flagrant case of colonial oppression were highly important, and seldom has any event excited so lively an interest in this country. When intelligence of the Missionary's death reached England, it produced a general feeling of indignation against the injustice of the courts, and of pity for the victim. The sympathies of the people were vehemently stirred, and they finally concentrated in a deep, universal, and determined feeling against the execrable system of slavery. Men of the noblest character and highest genius came forward to plead the cause of truth and freedom, and the celebrated debate upon Smith's trial ensued. On that never-to-be-forgotten occasion the beloved Wilberforce for the last time appeared in public, and in a strain of impressive eloquence vindicated the character of the Missionary, and thus concluded his life-long devotion to the cause of the unhappy victims of West Indian bondage.

During three nights the great discussion was carried on in the House of Commons, and it is not too much to say that it ultimately led to the abolition of slavery in the British dominions. The measures of the abolitionists all over the country became from thenceforward more bold and decided, as their principles commanded a more general and ardent concurrence; and thus the cause of negro emancipation owed more to the sufferings and death of the humble Missionary, John Smith, than to all the other enormities which have been perpetrated under that accursed system.

I do not think this narrative can be more fitly concluded than by giving the reader a short extract from Lord Brougham's speech on Emancipation, as reported in the "Morning Chronicle" of the 20th of February, 1838. The eloquent speaker thus refers to the eventful day: "The 1st of August arrived; that day so confidently and joyously anticipated by the poor slaves, so sorely dreaded by their hard taskmasters; and if ever there was a passage in the history of a people redounding to their eternal honour, it is to be found in the conduct of the emancipated negroes throughout the whole of the West India islands. Instead of the fires of rebellion, lit by feelings of lawless revenge and resistance to oppression, the whole region was illuminated by the sunshine of contentment, joy, thankfulness, and good-will to all men. No civilised people, after gaining an unexpected victory, could have shown more delicacy and forbearance than was exhibited by the slaves at the great moral consummation which they had attained. There was not a word nor an action which could

17

gall the feelings of their masters, or wound the ears of the most feverish planter in the islands. All was rejoicing, mutual congratulation, and hope. . . . They kept as a sacred Sabbath the day of their liberation. Having enjoyed the advantages of religious instruction in a great degree, they enjoy its consolations to a great extent. They have received these, not from the ministrations of the Established Church (not that such ministrations have been withheld), but other instructors are found more conversant with their feelings, and therefore more acceptable to them. The patient and zealous Missionary, the meek and humble pastor, has been the one to lead the poor negroes into the path of life. The Missionaries have not set themselves above those whom they teach; they are not too refined or too delicate to be useful; they pass their time among their humble flocks, and are their friends and companions in the common affairs of life, as they are their guides in religious concerns; and I cannot pass over this subject without offering my humble tribute of heartfelt admiration for the labours and zeal of these disinterested men."

RICHARD KNILL:

MISSIONARY TO INDIA AND RUSSIA.

CHAPTER I.

HOME SERVICE.

Personal recollections of Mr. Knill—Early years—"A praying mother"
—Start in life—Enlists into the militia—Obtains his discharge—
Change of heart—Joins the church at Bideford—First thoughts
about the heathen—Sabbath breaking—Penitence, and renewal
of life—Tract distribution—The swearing grenadier—The Word
not returning void—An unexpected meeting—Hoxton Academy.

HOPE this chapter will prove a great favourite
with my juvenile readers, for it contains
the history of the early days of a good and
devoted Missionary; and many a lesson of
wisdom may be learned from his experience. I had
the pleasure to know Mr. Knill, and have often heard
him address large and deeply interested assemblies
on Missionary occasions. He was tall and striking
looking, with an earnest intensity of manner which
convinced the hearers of his sincerity and zeal.
His whole soul seemed to be in his words, and you

felt that out of the abundance of his heart he was speaking.

It was not till long after, when his useful life had

HINDOO TEMPLE.

closed and his memoirs were published, that I learned the particulars contained in the following pages, many of which are taken from his own early reminiscences.

He was born at Braunton, a township or village in the county of Devon, which lies embosomed in orchards amidst a picturesque and fertile valley. His father, whose ancestors had been known for many generations in the parish, was a thrifty, sagacious man, who could turn his hand to a great variety of occupations, and make himself generally useful. His original trade was that of a carpenter, but, by the help of a small patrimony, he gradually relinquished that business for more congenial pursuits. Occasionally he would plan and work at the construction of a house, and at another time he would be equally at home in valuing the timber of an estate, selling a farming stock, making the draft of a lease, or drawing up "the last will and testament" of a dying neighbour. These useful services, united with a tall person, a benevolent countenance, and a goodly wig, procured for him the familiar but honourable soubriquet of "the counsellor."

His wife was a woman of fair education and excellent judgment, the daughter of a substantial neighbouring farmer, distinguished for kindness to the poor and for a generous hospitality. Richard, named after his father, was the youngest of their four children, and was born in the spring of the year 1787. The only event related of his boyhood was one which nearly cost him his life. On his way to school the little fellow had to cross a stream, spanned by a bridge of two flat stones. As he was trying one day how far he could push a stick under this rustic contrivance, he over-balanced himself, and fell in. The splash reached the ear of a poor widow, carding wool beside her cottage door. Looking out she spied a child's hat floating on the stream, and darting to the spot, succeeded in drawing the little owner, by his flaxen locks, from under the bridge. Mr. Knill never forgot Molly Robins; he used to say, in after years, "Ay! she could not read, but she saved my life. Feeble powers, if well employed, will do wonders."

The parents of Richard Knill were not, at the time of his birth, experimentally acquainted with the great truths of religion. The parish in which they lived was not blessed with a Gospel ministry, and the inhabitants generally were in a condition of deplorable darkness as to spiritual things. But a happier time was at hand.

"God," said Mr. Knill, in an early MS. of "Reminiscences," "remembered them in their low estate. A young man, named Joseph Evans, the son of a farmer who had been for some years in Barnstaple, came home, and opened a shop. He gave notice to a few of his friends that he should have a religious service at his house on Sunday evenings. It was much ridiculed by the people generally, but my beloved mother, who had known Mr. Evans from a child, attended his meeting. There the Holy Ghost applied the word with such power to her soul, that she could not stay away. The Lord Jesus Christ became very precious. She rejoiced with joy unspeakable. My father was highly displeased at this; and I never recollect his speaking unkindly to my mother, except about this change in her religion. But she sought comfort in prayer, and would often take me with her into her chamber, and say, ' Kneel down with me, my dear, and I will pray with you. Your father and your brothers will not join me.' "

The lad wondered why his darling mother wept so much, and where she got such remarkable prayers for his father and brothers.

" I understand it now," he afterwards said; " and I have good reason to believe that her prayers for those she loved were answered, and that she has met them all in heaven, except myself; and I trust, through rich grace, she will meet me there also. Blessed be God for a praying mother !"

In his thirteenth year Richard was apprenticed to business, and at the close of his apprenticeship he went abroad into the wide world to make his fortune. He took short journeys to the neighbouring towns, and succeeded in procuring work. But he afterwards looked back with sorrow and regret on this portion of his youth. He found, as many a youth similarly circumstanced has found, temptation too strong for his young, untried virtue. In the midst of wicked companions he forgot the prayers of his pious mother, and became fond of singing foolish songs and breaking the Sabbath, thus stifling the voice of conscience, and fighting against God. And all this while he was still in his teens.

At length the fancy took him to enlist into the militia, where he hoped soon to get into the Band, and then it would be, he fondly believed, "music and songs all the year round." His passion for music was, at this time, a great snare to him, for it led him into society he might otherwise have avoided, and by whom he was presently induced to take the fatal step. "I enlisted," he says; "and this nearly broke my mother's heart. 'Now,' she said, 'body and soul are lost; oh! what can be done?'" In this emergency Mr. Evans—that excellent man whose teaching had been the means of his mother's religious convictions—proved himself a true friend. He called on the afflicted parents, and offered to try and procure the youth's discharge. Their hearts were filled with joy at this proposal, and Mr. Evans immediately applied to Colonel Bevis, who had such great influence with the lord-lieutenant of the county, that he succeeded in obtaining the desired boon. "I will do it," said the colonel; "but you must get a substitute, and keep Knill out of the way until the matter is settled." It was, indeed, no easy task; for Richard, being upwards of six feet high, had been placed among the Grenadiers, but the substitute, being shorter, could not occupy his place. Great dissatisfaction was felt by the major of the regiment, who was, however, obliged to yield to the will of his brother officer. The poor youth who took the place of young Knill soon volunteered into "the regulars," and was killed in the heat of battle. This incident was keenly felt by our young prodigal. He saw what an escape had been his, and acknowledged the good hand of God's providence on his behalf.

A passage in his "Reminiscences" gives us a striking account of what next befell him :—

" During the proceedings in this matter," he writes, " I was shut up. Mr. Evans gave me a room, and I came down night and morning to family prayer. This was a new and strange scene to me. I had never been present at family prayer in my life. The first night that I was in this good man's house, about nine o'clock, he rang the bell, and his shopmen and servants all came into the parlour and sat down. I looked with surprise, and wondered what was coming next. When all were seated, he opened the Bible, and read a portion to his household. They then arose and fell upon their knees. The sight overpowered me. I trembled; I almost fainted. At last I kneeled down too. I thought of my past life; I thought of my present position; I thought, ' Can such a guilty creature be saved?' I heard but little of my kind friend's prayer. All my soul turned in upon myself. My conscience said, ' This is how true Christians live; but how have I lived? God has not been in all my thoughts; but now I will begin to seek mercy.' "

The solemn resolve then made he was enabled, by God's grace, to keep. That very night, on entering his bed-chamber, he looked around for a Bible. Not finding one, he took a hymn-book that lay on the table, some verses from which he read as he knelt beside his bed, and then poured out his heart in broken prayers, before lying down to rest. " Behold, he prayeth! " said the holy angels, who rejoice over one sinner that repenteth. Poor wanderer! there is joy on thy behalf in the blessed world above. " Never have I gone to Barnstaple, of late years," says his note-book, " without going to weep over the hallowed spot where God fastened the arrows of conviction in my heart."

From that time there was a marked change in his conduct. He could no longer sin without feeling the pangs of an awakened conscience. Yet there were many steps to be taken before his feet could steadily and peacefully walk in the way of God's commandments. Providence again appeared on his behalf. A good woman, by name Mrs. Isaac, of Bideford, wanted a young man to conduct her business, and to instruct her only son; and Richard, being recommended by his friends, was taken into her service. Shortly after this removal he made acquaintance with a Mr. Thomas Spencer, a young man about his own age, who lived next door to his employer, and who chanced to hear the stranger youth singing very sweetly, while walking in the garden. The idea occurred to him that so fine a voice would be a great acquisition in the choir of the chapel which he attended; and, after a time, he succeeded in inducing Richard to accompany him, and to attend the ministry of the Rev. S. Rooker.

"And now," he tells us, "the songs of the world were exchanged for those of Zion, and every week the teaching of Mr. Rooker brought some fresh meaning to my strains. He was a holy man of God, and a sound theologian, deeply read in the old divines. A hungry soul could feed and thrive on his ministry, and an inquiring spirit find rest. It was just what I needed to nurse my incipient piety, expand my religious views, and fit me for active service."

After a short time, the two friends, Knill and Spencer, sought admission as members, and were gladly welcomed by the excellent pastor, who found in them a valuable addition to the community, full as they were of youthful zeal and energy. Frequent prayer-meetings were held among the junior members, and it was noticed by those who attended them that the prayers of Richard Knill were full of an earnestness, a devotion, and a breathing after piety, which went to the hearts of others. The Sunday-schools, which had hitherto been under the old system of paid teaching, were now taken on the principle of voluntary instruction, and throve with new life and spirit.

It is deeply interesting to trace the first kindling of the flame which soon burnt with holy ardour in the breast of the future Missionary. It was on occasion of an anniversary sermon at the chapel that Mr. Rooker, discoursing on the advantages of Christian education, read some passages from Buchanan's "Christian Researches in the East," a book which was then attracting much attention in the country. As he read the thrilling picture of the wretched pilgrims toiling to reach the idol Juggernaut, and flinging themselves beneath the bloody wheels, one of the teachers, sitting in the aisle at the head of his class, was observed with large tearful eyes fixed upon the preacher, and his fine open countenance beaming with mingled wonder and compassion.

"It was," he said, long after, "like a spark on tinder. It set me on fire to go to the heathen. I did not know of Missionary societies; but my thoughts were set to work, and I borrowed books and informed my mind upon the subject. I was afraid to mention my impressions to my pastor, but they smouldered until the Lord's time came."

About this period in his history there occurred an incident which he himself thought proper to record as a warning and a beacon to any youth setting out on a Christian course, and tempted to sin against his conscience. It seems difficult to realise that one so earnest and good should have yielded to the temptation of Sabbath-breaking, but so it was. If there be any youthful reader who is in danger of backsliding from the narrow road on which he has entered, may this passage in the experience of Richard Knill serve at once for a warning and an encouragement! Let him beware of bringing sorrow and remorse home to his heart, and of clouding the fair morning of his newly-begun day of grace!

It chanced one Sunday morning, as he was on his way to the school, he met three of his former companions, who said they were bound on an excursion up the river, on whose shining surface the early sun was brightly gleaming, giving promise of a lovely summer's day. Partly by jokes and partly by persuasion, they induced him to join their party. Presently the boat was gliding gently up the stream, and the houses of the town disappeared behind the richly-wooded banks. Just then the sound of the church bell came softly over the water, signifying that it was nine o'clock, and that in due time divine service would commence. Sweet were the vibrating notes, calculated to soothe and tranquillise the spirit of those who heard them with joy, as a welcome summons to a glad and grateful service; but, oh! the anguish they inflicted on the mind of Knill! It was, he said, perfect agony, and he could imagine like emotion only in the breast of the poor criminal who heard the prison clock striking the hour of his fate on the morning of his execution. That well-known sound had been to him for months past the signal for commencing the Sunday-school, and at this very moment he was expected to take his post at the head of his class. Imagination brought to his mind's eye the whole scene; and how he longed for the wings of a dove, that he might fly to his place, and escape from what he felt to be a snare of the enemy of souls. Could he have got to shore, he would gladly have done so; but he was compelled to remain the livelong day with his comrades, who vainly endeavoured to cheer him by their laughter and raillery. One thing he did, and it was worth doing. He solemnly resolved never to break the Sabbath again, and never more to associate with the ungodly, but to come out from among them and be separate. And God, in His mercy, enabled him to keep his vow.

From this time his deepened convictions of duty led him to endeavour, by all the means within his power, to do good. One of these efforts at usefulness was long after brought to his remembrance in a most satisfactory manner. The North Devon Local Militia was about to be disbanded at Barnstaple. The regiment consisted of one thousand men, who were soon to return to their families in almost every parish of the northern division of the county. It was suggested to him by one of his friends that here was a noble opportunity for distributing religious tracts in the dark villages around. A thousand distributors would in this manner be secured for the work, if the tracts could but be given into the hands of the men. Knill asked how it could be done? His friend replied, "I have not nerve enough to give the tracts to the soldiers; but I will furnish you with them, provided you will circulate them." To this he readily agreed, and lost no time in going to work. The men were assembled in the barrack-yard, waiting for the signal to deliver up their arms. Making his way to the Pioneers, who stood at the right, he said, "Friends, will you carry home a beautiful little book to your families?" They gladly received them. Next he came to the Band. He selected the tract, "Christ is the Only Refuge from the Wrath to Come," and offered it to the sergeant. Looking at the ardent youth, the man said, "I am told you go about converting people; can you convert me?" He replied, "It is not in my power to convert people; but were it so, the first person I would convert, sir, should be Sergeant Reynolds." "Well," replied he, "that is plain enough." "Yes, and sincere, too. Now, the tract may convert you, sergeant; it was written by that great man, Mr. Hervey, who wrote 'Meditations among the Tombs.'" "Ah!" said he, "I have read that book, and I will take your tract and read it too." This was very encouraging, for immediately all the

musicians took tracts. The next in array were the
Grenadiers, who were all pleased, until he came to
one rough sort of fellow, who took the tract and held
it up; then asked, with an oath, "Are you going to
convert me?" "Don't swear at the tract; you cannot hurt it; but swearing will harm your own soul."
"Who are you?" he cried, in a rage; then, turning
to his comrades, "Form a circle round him, and I
will swear at him." The men did as they were bid,
and the wretched man swore fearfully. Knill's only
answer was tears; they flowed copiously, and the
sight touched the feelings of the other men, who said,
"Let him go; he means to do us good."

At length the thousand tracts were distributed, and
committed in humble trust to Him who hath promised, "My word shall not return unto me void."

Many long years passed away; Knill had been for
some years in India, and on revisiting his native
land, he went to Ilfracombe, where he was invited to
preach in the open air. Preparations were made for
his coming, and his intention was announced, so that
a goodly assemblage congregated. During the time
he was preaching, he observed a tall, grey-haired man
in the crowd weeping, and by his side stood a tall
youth, apparently his son, who also was weeping. At
the conclusion of the service, both advanced towards
the preacher, and the father said, "Do you recollect
giving tracts to the local militia at Barnstaple some
years ago?" "Yes." "Do you remember anything
particular occurring at the time?" "Yes; I recollect
one of the Grenadiers swore at me until he made me

weep." "Stop!" he said; "oh! sir, I am the man.
I never forgave myself for that wicked act; but I
hope it has led me to repentance, and that God has
forgiven me. And now, let me ask, Will you forgive
me?" As may be imagined, this unexpected and
affecting interview quite overcame the feelings of Mr.
Knill. He would not part with the reclaimed swearer
until they united in prayer together that they might
meet in heaven. "Is not this encouragement?" he
asks. "May we not well say, One tract may save a
soul?"

The piety, tact, and courage he thus early displayed, encouraged the friends of Richard Knill to
hope that he might be fitted for usefulness as a
minister in the Church of Christ. After serious consideration, and consulting those who seemed most
capable of judging as to his powers, he was induced
to seek admission as a student at the Western
Academy, a theological college of the Independents.
His account of the reception he met there is pleasing
and suggestive. He says:—

"Into this school of the prophets I was cordially
welcomed in the autumn of 1812. It was a fine,
retired, happy place, for those who wished to be
happy in it. Many and great were its advantages.
One of these was that the students formed part of
the family, took their meals at the family table, and
kneeled around the family altar. The presence of .
ladies always has a refining effect on young men,
who, in general, need refining. This privilege we
had. Mr. Small, the superintendent, made a point of

calling the students by name between five and six every morning, and a fine was levied on those who were not downstairs before six o'clock. It gives me pleasure to recollect that I was never fined. I learned habits of punctuality which have been of use to me through all my life. In looking back on this step, I feel that it is a very solemn matter for a young man to leave the business in which he has been brought up, and enter upon a life of study for the ministry; if he fail as a preacher, he is ruined. His student's life has unfitted him for returning again to business; and in this way many a grievous mistake has been made. Ministers cannot be too cautious in recommending young men to our colleges."

THE CAR OF JUGGERNAUT.

18

CHAPTER II.

MISSION WORK.

The Master's call—A solemn hour—Dedicated to the work—Gosport
Missionary Academy — Ordination at Leeds -- Impressive
services—Partings—Arrival in India—Labours at Madras—
A religious horse—Failure of health—Return to England—
Appointed to St. Petersburg—Establishment of an Evangelical
Christian Church—Inundation of the Capital—Death of the
Emperor Alexander—Imperial ukase against the circulation of
the Scriptures—Labouring under difficulties—Family trials—
Recalled to England—Pastoral Settlement—Death.

AR from forgetting his early friends, and
the scenes of his youth, he cherished their
memory with tender affection, and lost no
opportunity of renewing his intercourse
with them. Writing to the son of his former
employer, Mr. T. Isaac, he says :—

"This season reminds me forcibly of my first
acquaintance with you, — an acquaintance which,
I trust, will be strengthened and matured even to
eternity. It is now six years since that memorable
hour when I began to seek the Lord—when I
began to live. I am astonished when I consider
the innumerable mercies the Lord has conferred
upon me since that period. Oh! that I could
feel grateful, as I ought. At times I can very
clearly trace the Lord's hand in leading me to live
with you, in drawing me to hear that good man,

Mr. Rooker, preach the glorious Gospel, in sweetly constraining me to attend the prayer-meeting, and, at last, in bringing me to this place. And cannot you behold in it the Lord's doing? Then lift up a song of praise for me."

Of his student days we have not much to record, but what little is related suffices to show that, from his first attempts at preaching, he gave evidence of that peculiar power he subsequently showed in touching and carrying with him the feelings of his listeners. When he preached his first sermon to his fellow-pupils, he spoke with so much force and pathos upon the love of Christ, and His claims to the gratitude of redeemed men, that they forgot to criticise, and melted into tears. What more speaking eulogy could they have given?

In the month of April, 1814, a Missionary meeting was held at Bridport, Dorset, a town twelve miles from Axminster. It was one of the first which had been held in that part of the country. Missionary meetings were then great novelties. Richard Knill had never been present at one, nor had any of his fellow-students. The Rev. Mr. Saltern wrote on the occasion to the tutor of the Academy, inviting him to attend and to bring his students, " for," said he, " it may do them good. The Rev. Dr. Waugh, of London, is to preach, and I should like them to hear him." Accordingly, the youths all went to Bridport, and the venerable and beloved Dr. Waugh preached. He spoke of the perishing heathen, and of the Gospel which could alone give them salvation from

18 *

death. After a most impressive appeal, he concluded with these words: "Brethren, the trumpet of the Gospel cannot blow itself, it must be sounded by men—redeemed, converted men—those who themselves have tasted the joys of pardoned sin, and who can tell from their own happy experience what a Saviour Jesus is. We want such men, and we must have them." Then casting his eyes around, he fixed a piercing glance on some object, and in melting tones, said, "Is there in this congregation one young disciple of the Lord Jesus Christ who has love enough to his Master to say, 'Lord, here am I, send me?'"

The appeal went to the heart of our young student, who silently uttered the words, "Lord, I will go." It was a solemn hour with him, one for which he afterwards blessed God, and rejoiced in the assurance that he should for ever bless God in its remembrance. When the service was ended, the party was invited to dine with the ministers; but he had no appetite for food, his heart was too full. He quietly retired, and procured from a friend the loan of a little chamber, where he spent some hours in solitary prayer and fasting. On that little room he often thought in subsequent days, for there he spent some of the most blessed hours he ever knew in self-consecration, and in solemn renewing of his vow, "Lord, I will go." The next day he opened his mind to his tutor, who, when he had fully conversed upon the matter, and revealed the feelings that were flowing in his heart, wrote to the Secretary of the London Missionary Society to make inquiries. In the meantime, Knill went home to consult his honoured parents, and to obtain their sanction. He had occasioned them sufficient anxiety and trouble about enlisting, and he dreaded again wounding their feelings. His father listened to him with calmness, and said, "I will oppose no obstacle in your way; but what will your mother say?" The youth thought himself secure on that point, for he knew that her heart was full of love to the Saviour. But he was mistaken. The mother's feelings were too strong. She exclaimed, "How can you think of leaving me? I am now advancing in age, and have always comforted myself with the thought that you would be at hand to pray with me, and to cheer me when I pass through the valley of the shadow of death. I cannot give my consent. You should first lay me beneath the clods of the valley." As he listened to her impassioned appeal, he felt utterly at a loss, for he knew that no blessing can accompany the son who disobeys his mother, and breaks her heart. He waited, and took no further step until he should see the way open to him. And it was not long before his desire was accomplished. His excellent mother betook herself to prayer; she prayed for many days and nights, too, and at length she came one morning to meet her son with a smiling countenance and tranquil mien. Catching him to her heart in a fond embrace, she said, "Now, my dear boy, it is all settled; God has given me grace to say to you, Go! and I bless

Him for putting it into your heart to go; and I adore Him that He has given me an Isaac to offer upon His altar. Go, my son, go!" And from that hour until the day she died, she did nothing but encourage and cheer him in all his way.

This great obstacle being so happily removed, he gladly signified his decision to those friends who promoted his object, and soon received an intimation that he should repair immediately to London, there to take the further steps needful. From thence he addressed a letter full of intense feeling to his revered friend, Mr. Rooker, at the close of which he exclaims:—

"Oh! my dear sir, how full of joy is the hope of spending an eternity with a multitude out of all nations, kindreds, and people, and tongues, who shall speak the same pure language, all join in the same harmonious song, and all unite in adoring our blessed Redeemer!"

The Committee who examined the qualifications of the youth were favourably impressed with the way in which he passed his examination, and he was accordingly admitted to the Institution at Gosport, where students preparing for the ministry in heathen lands were trained and instructed. Here he passed about a year and a half. It was a time of hard work and much excitement. In his "Reminiscences," he says:

"For those who, like myself, were to remain but for a short time, it was 'life in earnest.' I have often wondered how any of us survived. We

had to write from the Doctor's various lecture books
as much as would moderately fill up a man's time.
In addition to this, we had to prepare for the various
classes, and to preach almost every Sunday. The
tutor's great soul was set on the conversion of
sinners abroad, but he could not bear the thought
that any should perish for lack of knowledge at
home. Hence his zeal for breaking up every inch
of fallow ground in Hampshire."

We cannot follow him through the particular
details of this laborious season, but will quote from
one passage in his "Reminiscences," written when
he had been just a year at Gosport. After the
other students had been dismissed, the tutor requested Knill to remain, and told him he had
received a letter from the Secretary of the London
Missionary Society at Leeds, earnestly begging that he
would send a Missionary to address the annual meeting which was just about to be held, and adding,
"If you have a Missionary about to leave, we wish
him to be ordained in Leeds." "Now," said the
Doctor, "you are one of the first who will leave,
and I wish you to go. What say you to it?"
Mr. Knill felt sorely disappointed, for his heart was
set on having his ordination service at Bideford,
among all his old friends and companions. He
intimated as much. "It is natural you should
wish this," was the reply, "but you are public
property now. *You must live for the whole world.
We must sacrifice personal feeling if we wish to
be useful.* Remember, there are eighty thousand

people at Leeds. Take two days to consider it."
At the end of the appointed time his answer was
given in the affirmative, and he went to Leeds.
The narrative of his journey is given in a letter
to one of his friends :

" On Friday evening I reached the destined spot,
after travelling nearly three hundred miles without
the least injury. Surely journeying mercies are
not among our smallest blessings ; for though there
is no fiery cloudy pillar to direct, yet a providential
Hand is visible in protecting amidst so many
dangers and accidents. . . . On the Sabbath I
preached three times, and on Monday gave the
address to the united congregations. On Thursday,
the branch Missionary society meeting commenced.
I preached one of the sermons, and in the evening
the meeting for business was held at Salem, which
is by far the largest. If you had been there, I
am certain your heart would have leaped for joy.
The next day was appointed for my ordination.
Ah, sir ! this is important work ; never did I feel
more forcibly that remarkable saying of the Apostle,
'Who is sufficient for these things ?' I was
almost overwhelmed : my departure, my work, my
death, and judgment were all presented to my view,
and scarcely any one present did not deeply feel
it ; scarcely an eye was seen but in it stood a tear.
. . . On Wednesday last I preached my farewell,
from the text, 'Who am I, O Lord God ?' &c.
I believe there never was such a scene witnessed in
Leeds before ; it is not in my power to describe it."

The intense interest attending these services did not arise exclusively from the comparative novelty of the Missionary enterprise, and the prepossessing character and aspect of the youthful Missionary. It was a time of blessing, and it appears that permanent and happy results followed. One of the ministers who took part in the services, writing twenty years afterwards, said that great effects were produced in many congregations, and that many persons were added to the churches, who continued to adorn their profession, while a general impulse was given to the zeal of Christians. One result of the visit came to the knowledge of Mr. Knill himself, thirty-three years afterwards, in a singular manner. He was attending a public meeting, at which one of the speakers, a minister among the Wesleyans, gave an account of his conversion. He said a feeling of great interest had been produced in his native town by the ordination of a Missionary there. At that time he was a stout, growing lad, and a bold blasphemer. One of his relations, a pious man, said to him, " Samuel, there is a young man in the town who is going abroad to preach to the black people, and he is to take leave this evening, by preaching to the young. Thou must go, lad." He accordingly went. The chapel was much crowded, but being a strong fellow, he pushed his way, and got where he thought he should have a full view of the preacher. All were in expectation. Presently he made his way through the press to the pulpit stairs, and ascended into the pulpit. He was a tall, thin, pale young man; and the sturdy lad, as he looked with curiosity on the stranger, said to himself, "Is *he* going to the heathen ? Then I shall never see him more. I will listen." He read and prayed, and then gave out his text, "There is a lad here." It pleased God to bless the words spoken, and the youth was pricked to the heart. Next Sunday he went and joined himself to the Sunday-school; then he began family prayer in his father's house, and was made the means of his father's and brother's conversion. The speaker concluded his address at the meeting with these words: "I have now been a regular preacher in our society for thirty years, and God has smiled on my labours. I owe it all to that sermon. I have never seen the preacher since, and perhaps I shall never see him; but I shall have a glorious tale to tell him when we meet in heaven." The scene that ensued when Mr. Knill came forward and introduced himself to the speaker, may be more easily imagined than described.

From Leeds the newly-ordained Missionary returned to Gosport, where he remained some short time longer, and, in the month of February, 1816, the time of his embarkation for India being at hand, he went to Devonshire, to take leave of those nearest and dearest to him. It was a sore trial to one so warm-hearted and quick in feeling. " Services such as those I then engaged in, surrounded by weeping friends and early associations, were very trying to my spirits," he says. "I used to think sometimes that I could weep no more, that the fountain of tears must be exhausted." But the most tender and afflictive of these parting scenes was when he came to take leave of his beloved parents, especially his admirable mother. She gave him, as a farewell token, her wedding ring, saying, "This is the dearest thing I possess. Your father gave it me as a pledge of his love; in his presence I give it to you as a proof of our united love to you." In another month he was on the mighty ocean, hasting on his errand of mercy.

A short account of Mr. Knill's Missionary work must conclude this chapter. He was first sent to India, and stationed at Madras, where he went diligently to work—preaching, visiting the schools, and studying the native language. The congregations on the Sabbath were large, several officers of the army stationed at Madras being in the habit of attending. The young ardent Missionary was a favourite with them; his sincere, open, and direct manner being quite to their taste. His influence was a good one; and in the case of a young civilian who had adopted infidel principles, his preaching was made "the savour of life unto life." Convinced of the error of his ways and a sincere penitent, the youth left his infidel associates, burnt his infidel MSS., and made a public recantation.

Mr. Knill took much interest in the native schools; he visited them daily, and was constantly going his rounds. He tells an amusing story on this subject. He says: "My horse at last knew as well where to stop as I did. This nearly cost a Bengal officer his life. Captain Page—a good man, who was staying with us—requested me one morning to lend him my

horse and gig to take him to the city. The captain
was driving, officer-like, when the horse stopped suddenly, and nearly threw him out.   He asked, ' What

PREACHING IN INDIA.

place is this ?' The answer was, ' It is the Sailors'
Hospital.' They started again, and soon the horse
stopped suddenly, and the captain was nearly out

as before. 'What is this?' 'A school, sir.' At length he finished his business, and determined to return another way. By doing this he came near my schools, and again and again the horse stopped. When he reached home, he said : 'I am glad that I have returned without broken bones, but never will I drive a religious horse again.' "

Unhappily, the burning climate of India proved injurious to the health of the young Missionary, and he was laid aside with severe illnesses. Death seemed at hand, and it was only after repeated attacks that he at length relinquished all idea of continuing in the country which he had fondly hoped would be his home for life. One morning in February, 1819, after a residence of about three years in India, he set sail for Colombo, where he secured a passage on board an English-bound ship, and in due time safely reached England.

After a short sojourn in his native land, Mr. Knill was sent to St. Petersburg to minister to a congregation of pious English residents in that capital, who had applied to the London Missionary Society, stating their circumstances and wishes. It was a somewhat delicate position, requiring prudence and circumspection, as the Russian Government was known to be exceedingly jealous of foreign teaching, and prohibited all proselytism. The number of persons composing the congregation was small, but it included several individuals of great intelligence and fervent piety, whose counsel and influence were of the utmost value to the youthful pastor. In a short time his simplicity of purpose and ardent zeal secured the affection and cordial co-operation of his new friends, and a course of usefulness was opened to him, upon which he entered in a spirit of humility and prayerfulness, his diaries giving evidence that his whole heart was engaged in the service of his Saviour.

Among those who formed the little church at St. Petersburg were the two brothers, Messrs. Walter and John Venning, both men of extraordinary zeal and piety, holy and devoted followers of Christ; the former of them well known as a philanthropist, whose deeds of benevolence secured him the title of a second Howard. This excellent man, on his dying bed, thus exhorted Mr. Knill: "I wish to say to you, labour for Jesus Christ as long as you have breath in your body." This parting counsel was never forgotten, and found a response in the heart of him to whom it was given.

One of the first schemes for Christian usefulness which engaged the attention of Mr. Knill was the establishment of a school for poor foreigners, which, from small and difficult beginnings, gradually progressed, and soon numbered three hundred children, who were taken from the lower orders, and rescued from ignorance and misery. "If you have never been out of England," said Mr. Knill, "it is impossible you can form an idea of the depraved state of a large city with little religion in it. Books cannot convey a thousandth part of the real state of things."

Not a few were the trials and anxieties attendant

upon life in the Russian capital. One of the most overwhelming calamities that occurred during the period of which we speak was the inundation which occurred in the middle of November, 1824. Mr. Knill writes : " On the 23rd of the month the wind was high, and the waters rose very much. About 10 a.m. next day, some of the streets near the Neva were beginning to be covered ; but the people would not believe the waters could rise much higher, forty-seven years having elapsed since the city was inundated." Alas ! they were soon undeceived. " By 2 p.m. the city presented a scene the most awful that can be conceived. Every place was deserted. There was nothing visible that had life, and the streets were filled with ships, boats, watch-houses, and floating trees, and even coffins from the cemeteries, with property of various kinds. Several entire villages were carried away, with scarcely a cottage left." So great was the loss of life that it surpassed anything of modern times. Many thousands were hurried into eternity in a moment. " May I never lose," says Mr. Knill, " the impression which I now have of the value of the soul and the importance of preaching the Gospel while it is day."

Great was the misery consequent on this awful flood, and the opulent Russians were not wanting in their endeavours to aid the suffering multitudes who had lost their all.

The death of the Emperor Alexander, who had been the steady friend of the Missionaries, was a grievous affliction and loss to the good people of Mr.

Knill's charge. They soon felt the heavy hand of oppression, and the new Emperor, yielding to the advice of the "Holy Synod," issued an ukase, which had the effect of stopping the distribution of the Scriptures, and closing the operations of the Russian Bible Society. Domestic trials also fell heavily upon the good man, who had to mourn the loss of a lovely little daughter and his beloved parents.

Year succeeded year, and still, amid increasing difficulties, he held on his way, taking for his motto the apostolic injunction, "In season and out of season." That he was "in labours more abundant," the following extract, written when he had been nearly ten years in Russia, will show: "We distributed about six thousand Bibles last year; we support six native teachers in India, and one in Georgia; we have more than two hundred children in our schools, as large a congregation as could be expected; many pious people diligent in good works, and the poor, the ignorant, and the wretched are relieved. For all these mercies and favours what can I render?"

But the time approached when this career of usefulness was to be cut short. A terrible messenger visited St. Petersburg in the year 1831, and the deep shadow of death was cast over the Missionary's household. In the course of ten days the happy, healthy family was shattered to pieces. Both parents and the children and servants were attacked. Two of the little ones were quickly numbered with the dead. Both Mr. and Mrs. Knill were brought very

KNILL'S CHAPEL, NEY NOR, INDIA.

low, and several of their friends were carried off by the pestilence. "These trials came upon us so rapidly, that I was struck dumb," said the afflicted man of God; "I was overwhelmed. My flesh trembled for fear of God's judgments, yet my heart cleaved to Him as my God, my Father, and my Friend."

The sorrows and trials of their faithful and honoured agent awakened the sympathy of friends at home, and after mature consideration, the Directors of the London Missionary Society proposed to him in the spring of the following year (1832) to visit England, and devote some time to the work of representing the Society, and stirring up a Missionary spirit through the country. To this Mr. Knill readily acceded, with the expectation of returning, after a short season, to his charge at St. Petersburg. But this was not to be the case. His services at home proved so acceptable, that, being from time to time induced to prolong his stay, he ended by settling for the remainder of his days in his native country.

Honoured, beloved, and useful, he died at the age of seventy, testifying with his dying breath to the truth and excellence of the gospel he loved. "It has been a blessed world to me, and a blessed Church to me. Not one good thing has failed of all that the Lord has promised," said the expiring saint. Who would not cry in response, "Let me die the death of the righteous, and let my last end be like his"!

19 *

"My album is the savage breast,
    Where darkness broods and tempests rest
        Without one ray of light;
To write the name of Jesus there,
And point to worlds both bright and fair,
And see the savage bend in prayer,
        Is my supreme delight."

Moffat

ROBERT MOFFAT:

APOSTLE TO THE BECHUANA TRIBES.

CHAPTER I.

A PERSONAL REMINISCENCE.

Thirty years ago—Time and its changes—The departed ones—Lines
for my Album—Causes of Mr. Moffat's first visit to England—
Charm of his Missionary addresses—A well-remembered story
—The surly Dutch farmer—The first sermon to the heathen—
Namaqualand.

 HAVE now brought my pleasant task to a
conclusion, but before laying aside my pen
I add a few pages, which may perhaps be
called a reminiscence of the beloved ROBERT
MOFFAT, the honoured and venerable Missionary, who
has recently returned from the scene of his long life's
labour, to tell of all the past, and to cheer our hearts
by spending his remaining days in our midst.

Well do I remember him when, thirty years ago, he came on a visit to my native city, and spent a few days under our roof. Then he was in the meridian of life, full of spirit, animation, and hope. His bright eye sparkled with joy as he told the stirring adventures, with the recital of which he thrilled all young hearts. His figure, tall and lithe, his countenance olive-coloured and sun-burnt, his movements agile, and his whole frame indicative of health and vigour. Oh! what a contrast to the appearance he presented when, some four or five months ago, he came to call on me. Both were changed past recognition had we met at a distance. " Is it indeed you ?" and, " Can it be your very self?" we mutually exclaimed. Ah! what changes does time work. He would go up to his " prophet's chamber," and see the room which he had formerly occupied during his short stay. Afterwards, as we talked together, he cast a wistful glance at the vacant chair, and thence to the portrait over the mantel-piece — the likeness of my beloved father. He could readily sympathise with my feelings, for he had a short time before lost his wife, who, after a life's faithful fellowship of his joys and sorrows, expired, praying with her last breath for the welfare of the poor heathen tribes whom she had loved so well.

The lines placed opposite the beginning of this chapter were written in my album by Mr. Moffat, when he visited Norwich in 1842. At that time he had been more than twenty years in Africa; and his object, in returning to his native land, was to superintend and complete the printing of his translation of the New Testament into the native language of the Bechuana tribes.

This translation had been the grand object of his desire, and for many years he had devoted every spare moment to that work, every interval of time which he could snatch between teaching, preaching, ploughing, or labouring at the forge or the press, being given to it. When completed, the operation of printing so large a book was found an insuperable difficulty. The Gospel of Luke had, indeed, been carried through the press by the Missionary translator and his colleague, but now it was judged expedient that he should come home with his treasure, that he might have the necessary aids and appliances in the work. And hence it came to pass that he found his way through the length and breadth of the land, pleading the Missionary cause, and everywhere exciting a lively interest on behalf of poor, unhappy, and oppressed Africa.

In his addresses on these occasions there was an irresistible charm, in part owing to the simplicity of his manner and the vivacity of his descriptive power. One could not forget his tales, they were so life-like and picturesque. For example, though so many years have passed since I heard him, I still can remember a tale he told at one of the meetings here. It had reference to the beginning of his Missionary life. He had left England in 1816, being at that time barely of age, and found himself landed at Cape Town, eager to commence work. But—not so quick: he must

pause awhile, and wait till he should have the permission of the British Governor to go on his errand
to the heathen beyond the boundaries of the Cape
Colony. Leave was for some time refused, and he
had to wait day after day. But the interval of suspense was not misimproved: he took up his abode
with a kind and pious Dutchman, who taught him his
own language, so that, when he departed on his way
into the interior, he was able to preach to the Boers,
and to as many of their native servants as had gained
a partial acquaintance with the language of their
employers. This proved no small advantage, as
he showed in the tale spoken of.

It happened, one evening, soon after he began his
journey up the country, that he found his way to the
homestead of a Dutch boer, of whom he modestly
begged a night's lodging, which was, however, refused
by the burly farmer, who harshly bade him begone.
Happily, there was "a gude wife" at hand, who overheard the appeal of the young Scotch stranger-lad,
and looked at him with friendly glance. "I'll e'en
try her," was the thought of the moment; and he
pleaded not in vain. The "mither's heart" yearned
toward the fair-favoured, pleasant-spoken "chield,"
and she bade him welcome to both bed and board.
But, whither was he bound, and what his errand?
Well, he was going to Orange River, to Namaqualand, to preach to the rude native tribes there. What
a strange, mad idea! "Going to Namaqualand—
that hot, inhospitable desert region; and will the
people, do you suppose, care to hear your words, or

understand them, if they would listen?" Such was
the disheartening view they took of his project. However, it was night-fall, and the family must go to rest.
But first would the stranger address a few words of
Christian counsel to them, and let them hear what he
had to say?

To this he gladly acceded, and soon the barn was
resorted to, and Moffat, looking for his congregation, saw his host and hostess, with their family of
three boys and two girls. There were hosts of black
forms hovering near at hand; for it seemed the surly
boer had some hundred Hottentots in his service, but
never a one was there in the barn. He waited, hoping
they might be coming; but no, not one came; still
he waited, as expecting something. "What ails you,
that you do not commence?" "May not your servants
come too?" said the brave youth. "Servants!"
shouted the master; "do ye mean the Hottentots,
man? Are you mad, to think of preaching to Hottentots? Go to the mountains and preach to the
baboons, or, if you will, I'll fetch my dogs, and you
may preach to them!" This was too much for the
tender feelings of the youth, and the tears began to
trickle down his cheeks, for his heart was too full
to hold. After a while he opened his Testament, and
read for his text the words, "Truth, Lord; yet the
dogs eat of the crumbs that fall from their master's
table." A second time the words were read, and then
the host, vanquished by the arrow so skilfully aimed,
cried out, "Hold! you must have your own way.
I'll get you all the Hottentots, and they shall hear

you." And he was as good as his word. The barn was soon filled with rows of dark forms, while with eager looks the swarthy crowd gazed at the stranger, who then preached *his first sermon to the Heathen.* We may readily conceive that he spoke with words of power, and that he never forgot that night.

The next day he proceeded upon his journey to Namaqualand, his path leading over rocky mountains, and parched and arid plains—a country on which "the curse of Gilboa" seemed to rest, where the fountains were few and precarious, and of human beings no trace was visible. At one period of the journey they had to pass three days on a burning plain, with scarcely a breath of wind stirring, and what there was feeling as though it came from the mouth of an oven. It seemed as if they must perish with thirst and fatigue, and terrible were the sufferings of their poor oxen. Water could only be procured near a neighbouring mountain, where they had to dig an immense hole in the sand, in order to get a scanty supply, "exactly resembling the old bilge-water of a ship," but which was drunk with eager avidity.

It was truly "a barren and a miserable country" on which he gazed. He inquired of one who knew it well, and who had spent some years in the land, "What is its character and appearance?" "You will find," was the reply, "plenty of sand and stones, a thinly-scattered population, always suffering from want of water, and plains and hills roasted like a

TRAVELLING IN AFRICA—HAULING UP THE WAGGON.

burnt loaf, under the scorching rays of a cloudless sun."

Of the truth of this description Mr. Moffat had soon ample demonstration. "Sometimes," he says, "for years together, the rivers are not known to run; after the last stagnant pools are dried up, the natives dig holes or wells in their beds, sometimes to the depth of twenty feet, from which they procure water, but of very inferior quality. Branches of trees are placed in these excavations, and with great labour, under a hot sun, the water is handed up in wooden vessels and poured into artificial troughs, from which the panting herds partially satiate their thirst. Thunderstorms are eagerly anticipated, for during these only does rain fall; but frequently these storms pass over with tremendous violence, striking the inhabitants with awe, yet without a single drop of rain descending to cool and fructify the parched and barren waste."

CHAPTER II.

Toiling under difficulties—The solace of music—Smoothing a shirt—
Africaner, the savage and the Christian—Visit to Cape Town—
Marriage—The Bechuana Mission—A wife's wisdom—Standing
to the post—Saved from the invaders—Kuruman Mission Station
—The first Native Christian Church—Visit of the Rev. J. J.
Freeman.

RRIVED at the place of his destination, our
Missionary had but a sorry reception, and in
his journal thus described his circumstances :
—" I had no friend or brother with whom I
could participate in the communion of saints—none
to whom I could look for counsel or advice; a barren
and a miserable country; a small salary of £25 per
annum ; no grain, and consequently no bread—and
no prospect of getting any, from the want of water to
cultivate the ground—and destitute of all means of
sending to the colony."

So forlorn a situation called for unusual powers of
self-denial and heartfelt devotion, and as hardships
and difficulties increased, his zeal waxed warmer and
his faith grew stronger. He set to work holding
services, opened a school, and itinerated amongst the
neighbouring "werfs," or villages. His food was milk
and meat, on which he lived for weeks together, but
was not unfrequently obliged to have recourse to the

" fasting-girdle." After a busy day's occupation, he
was wont to retire, in the stillness of the evening, to
some rocky granite-boulders in the neighbourhood of
his station, there to commune, in joy and sorrow,
with his heavenly Father ; and sometimes he took his
violin (once belonging to Christian Albrecht), "upon
which, as he lay stretched on his mat, he played and
sang that well-known hymn—a favourite with his
mother—

> " Awake my soul, in joyful lays
> To sing thy great Redeemer's praise."

This mention of his mother recalls to my memory
one of his tales, which I must record for the benefit
of my youthful readers. "My dear old mother," he
says, "to keep me out of mischief in the long winter
evenings, taught me how to knit and to sew. When
I told her I meant to be a man, she would say, 'Lad,
ye dinna ken where your lot will be cast ;' and she
was right, for I have often had occasion to use the
needle since. Once, I remember, she showed me how
a shirt might be smoothed by folding it properly and
then hammering it with a piece of wood. Resolving
one day to have a nice shirt for the Sabbath, I folded
up one, and, having prepared a suitable block, I laid
it, not on a smooth hearthstone, but on fine granite,
and hammered away in good earnest. Africaner came
by and said, 'What are you doing?' 'Smoothing
my shirt,' I answered. 'That is one way,' he replied. And so it was, for, on holding it up to view, I
found it was riddled with holes, some of them as large
as the point of a finger ! "

The Africaner cursorily mentioned in this tale was no other than the renowned Kafir Chief, so long the terror and scourge of all the regions around the Cape district,—a man whose atrocious deeds were held in such abhorrence that a thousand dollars were offered to any one who would shoot him; and when Mr. Campbell crossed Africa in his first journey, he was more alarmed with the idea of meeting this human tiger than with all the other dangers to which he was exposed. Great, indeed, was the change effected by Divine grace. Dr. Philip said of him, when he visited the Cape in company with Mr. Moffat, in 1819, " He is a judicious and excellent Christian. How would you have been filled with admiration of the power and grace of God had you seen and heard the man who some years ago burnt our settlement at Warm Bath, conversing about the love of Christ, while the tears ran down his cheeks!" Africaner showed the most constant and warm affection and consideration for his friend and teacher, Mr. Moffat; tended him in sickness, supplied his wants, and when it became necessary that he should visit Cape Town, expressed his readiness to accompany him there, although it was a very hazardous step, as he well knew the inhabitants of the Colony held him in dread, and that the reward mentioned above was offered to any one who would kill him.

That visit to the Cape was the turning-point in Mr. Moffat's history. There he was married to the faithful partner of his life, who lived with him through all his sojourn in the wilds of Africa, and returned

with him when he came home at the close of life.
She expired a few months after reaching England.
The testimony to herself which her own lips, in all
simplicity, gave, was perhaps the highest that could
be given of a Missionary's wife. Some one was con-
gratulating her on having been a great helper to her
husband. "Yes," she replied ; " I always studied my
husband's comfort, never hindered him in his work,
but always did what I could to keep him up to it."

Shortly after their marriage, the young couple
were appointed to the Bechuana Mission, a new and
untried field, one of the foremost posts in heathen
soil, and beyond which were regions thickly populated
by races who had never seen the face of a white man.
For a long time they had to struggle with the most
disheartening difficulties. During more than five years
the people continued callous and indifferent to all
instruction, unless accompanied by some temporal
benefit. At length, Mr. Moffat said one day to his
wife, " Mary, this is hard work." She replied, " It
is hard work ; but take courage, our lives shall be
given us for a prey." " But think," said he, " how long
we have been with these people, and no fruit appears."
Her answer was full of wisdom : " As yet the Gospel
has not been preached to them in their own tongue
wherein they were born. They have heard it only
through interpreters, who themselves have no just
understanding, and no real love of the truth. We
must not expect the blessing until you be able, from
your own lips, and in their own language, to convey
the glad tidings to their hearts." " From that hour,"

20

said Mr. Moffat, in relating the conversation, "I gave myself with untiring diligence to the acquisition of the language."

Great, indeed, were the difficulties of mastering the Sechuana, and much increased by the variety of its dialects and their difference from the language of the nation generally. The Bechuanas, who speak the Sechuana, are of numerous tribes; and while in the towns the purity and harmony of the language are better preserved, in the isolated villages of the desert they seem to have a variety of patois which alter the whole character of the tongue. Despite, however, all obstacles and innumerable discouragements, the Missionaries perseveringly continued at their work. But at length there came a crisis, when the superstitious natives, terrified by a prolonged drought, which they attributed to the machinations of the strangers, informed them that they must leave the country, and that, in case of refusal, violent measures would be resorted to. The chief who conveyed the message stood at their cottage door, spear in hand, with his twelve attendants. But Moffat proved himself in courage and nerve a match for them all. He stood undaunted before them, and plainly said, "We will not go. You may shed my blood if you will, but not till you have slain me will you be rid of us." "These men," said the bewildered chief to his followers, "must have ten lives. Since they are so fearless of death, there must be something in what they say of a hereafter."

Not long after this time, events occurred which

A SOUTH AFRICAN VILLAGE.

greatly changed the feelings of the people, and produced results most favourable to the Mission. Rumours came from various quarters of the advance, from the interior of the country, of an invading army, numerous and most formidable. These reports proved true; and Mr. Moffat having learned that a fierce section of the Basuto race were advancing in the direction of the Bechuanas, seeing the impending danger and the utter incapacity of the people to withstand the enemy, hastened to Griqua Town to obtain assistance from friends there. By this prompt and sagacious step, he saved the chief and people, who had shortly before been intent on driving away their friend and deliverer.

After the invaders had been successfully driven back, the people, grateful for the deliverance obtained, readily granted a new site for the Mission—the place which they had occupied being unsuitable—and the village of Kuruman—a name familiar to all our ears—was selected for the purpose. Here the Missionaries established themselves, and were soon fully employed in laying out the new station, itinerating among the natives, and translating the catechism, hymns, and simple lessons into the Sechuana language.

It was not until the year 1828 that they saw the fruit of all their toil. Then they were at length rewarded for their enduring perseverance. Aid in the erection of a chapel and school-house was voluntarily and cheerfully given. Improvements in the social habits of the people very soon followed; they became familiarised with several of the arts of civilised life. Their greasy skins were covered with decent raiment, and those who attended public worship behaved with great decorum. Altogether the position of the Mission was such as to excite most pleasurable emotions in the hearts of those who now realised in some degree that their strength had not been spent in vain.

The formation of the first native Church in Kuruman was an epoch in the history of the beloved Moffat. In the presence of native strangers from all parts, he conducted the whole of the first service in the language of the country. Hymns and prayers, lessons and sermon, were all in Sechuana, as was (as a matter of course) the preparatory examination of the candidates for membership. The number of the Church members just equalled that of the College of the Apostles; and in the evening of the day they sat down together at the communion service.

In 1849 Mr. Freeman visited Africa, and on arriving at the Kuruman, was cordially welcomed by Mr. Moffat and his family. He gave the following pleasing account of the village as it then appeared: "The Mission premises, with the walled gardens opposite, form a street wide and long. The chapel is a substantial and well-looking building of stone. Beside it stands Mr. Moffat's house, which called forth the wish that every Missionary had one like it—simple, yet commodious. The gardens were well-stocked with fruit and vegetables, requiring much water,

which was easily got from the 'fountain.' On
Sunday morning the bell rang for early service.
Breakfasting at seven, all were ready for the schools
at half-past eight. The infants were taught by Miss
Moffat in their school-house; more advanced classes
being grouped in the open air or collected in the
adjacent buildings. A spacious and lofty sanctuary,
and airy withal, was comfortably filled with men,
women, and children, for the most part decently
dressed."

CHAPTER III.

THE VETERAN'S RETURN.

The gradual process of civilisation—Leaving the sphere of labour—
Distress of the Natives — Review of the past — Civilizing in-
fluences of Christianity — A written language and a translated
Bible—The song of Simeon—A ray of light in a dark place.

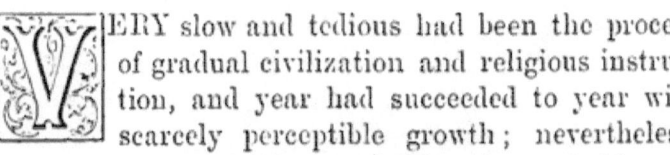ERY slow and tedious had been the process
of gradual civilization and religious instruc-
tion, and year had succeeded to year with
scarcely perceptible growth; nevertheless,
the new habits of life were taking firmer hold upon
the people, and the examples set by their teachers
were leading them to the high point of civilization of
building for themselves substantial dwellings, and
arranging them with neatness and order within.

But this is not the place to give the subsequent

history of the Bechuana Mission. I pass on to the close of Mr. Moffat's history. Early in the spring of 1870, accompanied by Mrs. M., he left the scene of his life-long toil — sorely unwilling indeed as he was to quit the land of his adoption. "Oh! that parting!" he exclaimed; "it was hard to witness it without deep emotion. It would have been pleasant just to remain with the people among whom I lived so long, by whom I am beloved, and whom I love. Not only from Christian converts, but from heathen chiefs, did I receive tokens of goodwill. They sent letters deploring my departure, and presents to induce me not to quit the country, but to remain, promising to give me so much more if I would do so. It was gratifying to see these tokens, especially from the heathen, and those able to appreciate one's labours among them. One sent an ox, another a kaross, and so on: a lady of quality sent me four feathers. Some of them asked how they were to live, how they were to exist, if I went out of the country; that is the form of expression among them."

Recurring at large to the difficulties met with at the first outset, Mr. Moffat has mentioned many gratifying proofs that not a few of them have been overcome. "For many years," he says, "they saw no conversions; but, by the blessing of God on persevering exertion, they now would meet, almost wherever they went, with companies of natives who professed to be members of the Church of Christ. Not very long since it was considered dangerous to travel in the interior—in fact, half a dozen miles from the station. Now, the natives could be depended upon, and it was quite common for traders to travel through their midst, without the least fear of plunder or interruption. In former times traders were often basely murdered, or, at best, not suffered to return. Now all fears had been dispelled. Once the natives would not buy anything, not even a handkerchief. They might now and then be induced to buy a few trinkets or some beads, but nothing of a useful or substantial kind. It was not so now. British manufactures to the amount of £60,000 now passed yearly into the hands of the native tribes round about Kuruman. Travellers could now go to any of those parts, and be sure that none of the native tribes would harm them, and murders, formerly quite common, were now rarely heard of. Companies of natives could be passed through without fear, and they showed special respect to the Missionaries."

He has further said that many natives at the Kuruman are well able to discuss and argue upon the doctrines of the Gospel. "He did not mean they could enter into any lengthy or out-of-the-way points; but this he would say, that they could talk sensibly upon any general question. They might not always stick to a text, but they would rarely depart from the meaning of the Bible. And these were a people who, forty years ago, were nothing better than savages, but who, by the blessing of God upon the labours of those who devoted their lives to the work, had been brought to be intelligent disciples of the Gospel of Christ."

Thus, on a review of fifty-two years' labour, the venerable Missionary finds, instead of a solitary station, a number of central stations, extending more than three hundred miles beyond the Kuruman (not to speak of what his son-in-law, Livingstone, has effected on behalf of Africa); and, instead of a race of illiterate and fierce savages, a people to some extent capable of appreciating and cultivating the arts and habits of civilised life, with a written language of their own, in which they can read the Holy Scriptures. There was a time when he was wont to say, " If I could but see the Word of God in Sechuana, I should sing the song of Simeon;" and now he has seen the desire of his heart, thanks be to the God of his salvation who has thus honoured and blessed His servant.

I cannot do better than close this notice with a quotation from one of his own addresses, in which he dwells upon the vast importance of having the Bible in the language of the people. " This will be seen," he says, " when we look on the scattered towns and hamlets which stud the interior, over which one language, with slight variations, is spoken as far as the equator. When taught to read, they have in their hands the means not only of recovering them from their natural darkness, but of keeping the lamp of life burning even amidst comparatively desert gloom. In one of my early journeys with some of my companions, we came to a heathen village on the banks of the Orange River, between Namaqualand and the Griqua country. We had travelled far, and were

MOFFAT CONVERSING WITH THE FAMILY OF A CHIEF.

hungry, thirsty, and fatigued. From the fear of being exposed to lions, we preferred remaining in the village, to proceeding during the night. The people at the village rather roughly directed us to halt at a distance. We asked for water, but they would not supply it. I offered the three or four buttons which still remained on my jacket for a little milk. This also was refused. We had the prospect of another hungry night at a distance from water, though within sight of the river. We found it difficult to reconcile ourselves to our lot, for, in addition to repeated rebuffs, the manner of the villagers excited suspicion. When twilight drew on, a woman approached from the height beyond which the village lay. She bore on her head a bundle of wood, and had a vessel of milk in her hand. The latter, without opening her lips, she handed to us, laid down the wood, and returned to the village. A second time she approached with a cooking-vessel on her head, and a leg-of-mutton in one hand and water in the other. She sat down, and without saying a word, prepared the fire and put on the meat. We asked her again and again who she was. She remained silent, till affectionately entreated to give us a reason for such unlooked-for kindness to strangers. The solitary tear stole down her sable cheek as she replied, ‘I love Him whose servants ye are, and surely it is my duty to give you a cup of cold water in His name. My heart is full therefore. I cannot speak the joy I feel to see you in this out-of-the-world place.’

"On learning a little of her history, and that she

was a solitary light burning in a dark place, I asked her how she kept up the life of God in her soul in the entire absence of the communion of saints. She drew from her bosom a copy of the Dutch New Testament which she had received from Mr. Helm, when in his school some years previous, before she had been compelled by her connections to retire to her present seclusion. 'This,' she said, 'is the fountain whence I drink : this is the oil which makes my lamp to burn.' I looked on the precious relic, printed by the British and Foreign Bible Society, and the reader may conceive how I felt, and my companions with me, when we met with this disciple, and mingled our sympathies and prayers together at the throne of our heavenly Father. 'Glory to God in the highest, and on earth peace, goodwill to men!'"

UNWIN BROTHERS, THE GRESHAM PRESS, CHILWORTH AND LONDON.

www.ingramcontent.com/pod-product-compliance
Lightning Source LLC
Chambersburg PA
CBHW021032030726
47496CB00006B/1497